FAST TRACK

Also by Fern Michaels . . .

FERN MICHAELS

FAST TRACK

KENSINGTON BOOKS
http:/www.kensingtonbooks.com

KENSINGTON BOOKS are published by

Kensington Publishing Corp.
850 Third Avenue
New York, NY 10022

Copyright © 2008 by Fern Michaels

All Kensington titles, imprints and distributed lines are available at special quantity discounts for bulk purchases for sales promotion, premiums, fund-raising, educational or institutional use.

Special book excerpts or customized printings can also be created to fit specific needs. For details, write or phone the office of the Kensington Special Sales Manager: Kensington Publishing Corp., 850 Third Avenue, New York, NY 10022. Attn. Special Sales Department. Phone: 1-800-221-2647.

Kensington and the K logo Reg. U.S. Pat. & TM Off.

Library of Congress Card Catalogue Number: 2007933518

ISBN-13: 978-0-7582-2714-0
ISBN-10: 0-7582-2714-0

First Printing: March 2008
10 9 8 7 6 5 4 3 2 1

Printed in the United States of America

FAST
TRACK

Chapter 1

Big Pine Mountain
North Carolina

It was a fortresslike compound. A training ground. Of sorts. State-of-the-art. First-class accommodations. In the spook world of covert operations and espionage, it was beyond anything the CIA or the FBI could think of. The only facility that came remotely close was NORAD on Cheyenne Mountain in Colorado and was maintained by the government of the United States. Thanks to the taxpayers of the good old US of A. In the interests of security, the only accesses to the site on Big Pine Mountain were by helicopter and cable car.

The women, also known as the vigilantes, clustered together in the dark, their eyes on the helicopter pad and the platform that housed the cable car that had gone missing an hour ago. Off in the distance they could hear the *whump-whump* of helicopter blades. Company was coming, and the women knew it wasn't a social visit. Then they heard the screeching sound of the cable car coming up the mountain. They jostled one another for a better look in the rain-filled, pitch-black darkness.

Isabelle Flanders craned her neck. "A perfect evening

for late-night visitors of the clandestine kind. Who do you think they are?"

"Probably the kind of people Charles doesn't want us to see or meet before he sets things up. This is just a guess on my part, but I think they're our next employers," Nikki Quinn said.

"We *could* go outside instead of hiding indoors and see for ourselves. I for one like to know what's going on, especially if it involves me. Or us as a whole. Charles is big on need-to-know where we're concerned. I think I need to know," the ever-verbal Kathryn Lucas said.

Alexis Thorne weighed in, "It would be nice if just once we bested Sir Charles, now, wouldn't it? By one-upping him, I think we could take the visitors down with one eye closed and our hands tied behind our backs. A preemptive strike, so to speak. Or if you don't like that, we can strut our stuff to let them see who they're dealing with. Whatcha think, girls?"

Yoko Akia looked around. "Two of our posse are missing. Myra's in the main house, and I haven't seen Annie since around ten o'clock, when she said she was going to bed early. Don't we need to confer with them? Personally, I love the idea."

The women as one shrugged. Nikki took the high road, lawyer that she was, and said, "They're going to be really pissed if we act without them. I say we call them on their cell phones and tell them to meet up with us right here. But be quick, the helicopter is about to land. The cable car is almost here."

Kathryn was already speaking on her cell. She nodded to the others, meaning the two older women were on the way.

"What about Charles?" Alexis asked. "I'm sure he's going to be doing the meet and greet."

"I say we take him out first. It's the last thing he'll be expecting. If we're to believe our own PR, we're the best of the best. Let's prove it," Kathryn said.

The door to the women's quarters opened silently. The dogs, Murphy and Grady, growled softly but didn't move.

"It's raining," Annie de Silva said.

"We're taking Charles out first. You in or out?" Nikki asked coolly.

"In," Myra said in a shaky voice.

Annie's whoop of pleasure was her "in" vote.

"Then let's do it, ladies," Kathryn said.

The women held a quick whispered conversation, then moved out into the dark night, the dogs leading the way. The steady *whump-whump* of the helicopter was so close it was deafening. It also masked the sound of the cable car sliding into its nest on the platform's well-greased tracks.

The pungent scent of pine and the smell of the warm summer rain were aphrodisiacs on the women as they spread out and circled their quarry: one Sir Charles Martin. Murphy streaked forward to meet Charles head-on, while Grady barreled in from the side as Yoko, the rain beating down on her, kicked Charles from behind with one tiny foot and brought him to his knees. Alexis and Isabelle snapped on a set of flexi-cuffs, then yanked their host to his feet and dragged him to the bushes just as the cable car came to a stop. Nikki had pulled off one of her socks and stuffed it in Charles's mouth.

The wind from the rotors of the Bell JetRanger was so strong it almost knocked over Myra and Annie, who were fiercely holding on to each other. The rain slapping at them from the force of the winds felt like a tidal wave.

Two men and a woman stepped out from the helicopter. The woman foolishly tried to open an umbrella. It blew away in the wind. Kathryn yanked a small penlight out of her pocket and flashed it twice. There was no point in trying to speak or shout. The pinpoint of light moved off just as Nikki led two fine-looking gentlemen, dressed in Savile Row suits, out of the cable car and into the pouring rain.

Mercifully, the helicopter was shut down and put to bed. The high-pitched whine was silent. A bolt of thunder roared overhead as a vicious streak of lightning danced across the sky, lighting the mountaintop from one end to the other.

Their thumbs up in the air in a sign of victory, Yoko and Alexis led Charles toward the newly arrived guests.

As a group, they ran toward the main building, Charles and Myra's lair. The others called it the Big House. Inside the brightly lit kitchen, the women stared down at the delectable spread of food and drink laid out on the counters and on the table.

"Well done, girls," Charles beamed when the sock was taken out of his mouth and the flexi-cuffs removed. "Don't for one minute think you 'captured' me. I knew what you were going to do before you made the decision to take me on. In other words, I allowed it. I wanted your new employers to see you in action. Ladies, meet your new employers. Names at this juncture are not important. I don't expect they will be important later on, either. I'll show each of our guests to a room where they can change into dry clothes. I suggest you all do the same. Twenty minutes, ladies, not one minute longer. Are we clear on this?"

"Crystal," Kathryn said with a bite to her tone. "My ass, you allowed us to take you. You didn't know what hit you. I'm not going anywhere until you admit it, *Sir* Charles," she hissed.

Charles turned slightly so that he was in profile to his guests. He winked at Kathryn.

Nikki nudged Kathryn and whispered, "We'll make an issue of it later. We need to get changed. You know how pissy he gets when we're late."

"Ask me if I care," Kathryn said as she trailed behind the others, Murphy at her side.

Inside their own quarters, as they grappled with whatever they could find in the way of clean or dry clothes, the women kept up a running commentary concerning Charles and what had happened. In the end, a show of hands agreed that they had indeed caught Sir Charles flat-footed. And that he was trying to save face with his guests by his roguish wink. But they also agreed they could be wrong.

"A crapshoot," Annie said.

Adorned in yellow slickers with matching Wellington boots, the little group made it back to the Big House in the allotted time. They peeled off their rain gear before they trooped out to the kitchen where Charles was handing out drinks.

Charles's guests waited until the women were seated before they took their own seats for what their host referred to as a midnight feast: Lobster and shrimp and a foot-long cracked-pepper tenderloin. Emerald green peas from the garden behind the main house that were sugar balls of sweetness. Mountain tomatoes, lush and pulpy in the crisp garden salad. And finishing off the meal, tiny potatoes no bigger than a nickel drizzled with butter and fresh herbs. Everyone ate heartily including Charles.

The table conversation dealt with the different species of pine trees on the mountain, the virtually impossible access, satellite television, and the new iPhone, which was just hitting the market.

No one seemed to mind when Charles said he hadn't had time to prepare a dessert, and coffee and brandy would be served in the conference room down the hall.

Five minutes later, the members of the Sisterhood, in their casual clothes and slicked-back wet hair, sat down at the long pine table and looked at the five strangers sitting across from them.

Charles stood up and immediately got to the point.

"Our guests this evening have come a very long way to talk with us, and this meeting must be kept absolutely secret. Our guests are a special task force appointed by the World Bank. Three of our guests are also board members. They want to hire you to help them out before a current situation gets out of hand and has worldwide repercussions. They came with a check in hand that bears only a signature. What that means is you can name your own price and fill in the blanks. This piece of paper is a mere token. If you accept this mission, the money will be wired into a special offshore account expeditiously. These monies will *not* come out of the World Bank funds. Concerned wealthy individuals have donated funds for this mission, people who care about fighting global poverty. People who wish to remain anonymous."

"What is it you want us to do?" Myra asked a gray-haired man sitting directly across from her. "Is it a single person or a group of people who pose a problem for you?"

The woman sitting next to him spoke in a soft, cultured accent. She looked around at her colleagues, who simply gave curt nods to indicate she should speak. "The current president of the World Bank appears to have his own agenda where funds are concerned. We've done a discreet audit, and a rather large sum of money appears to be missing. The funds in question, which were to go to several poor countries, were suspended, then a small amount was supposedly used to set up ragtag offices in other war-torn countries, without concern for security in those countries. That amount was a mere drop in the bucket, so to speak. We can't seem to find the balance of the money."

"How much money are you talking about?" Annie asked as she leaned closer to the table, her eyes locked with those of the woman who was speaking.

"Close to two billion dollars."

"Billion with a *b?*" Kathryn asked.

"I believe billion is spelled with a *b*. Yes," the woman said curtly.

"And you can't find two billion dollars?" Nikki asked, disbelief ringing in her voice. "Do you mind if I ask who minds the store?"

"Oh, we could find it if we want a world crisis on our hands. We prefer to let sleeping dogs lie and to exercise other . . . options. I believe that's an expression Americans use to mean leave things as they are, is this not so?"

"If you're concerned about keeping this under wraps, aren't you concerned that the poor countries for whom those funds are earmarked might go public?" Alexis asked.

"Of course we're concerned. That's why we're here. The situation is contained for the moment. Time, however, is of the essence."

"How much time?" Nikki asked bluntly.

A stoop-shouldered man with a gray beard raised his head and spoke quietly. "No more than two weeks, and that's extending the time beyond what we're really comfortable with."

"Where does the current president reside?" Yoko asked.

"He owns an apartment in the Watergate. A very lavish apartment, I might add," a rotund little man with jet-black hair said. He had a heavy beard and glassy dark eyes. "He also has several mistresses. He's a divorced man whose ex-wife hates him. He has two children. They aren't particularly fond of him, either. He leads a very expensive life."

The woman spoke again with apparent distaste. "Maxwell Zenowicz held a very high post in your current government's administration prior to taking on the job of president at the World Bank, but he was not qualified for the job. He is an appointee. I believe it was a political favor that secured the job for him. He has surrounded himself with people with the same moral compass he has."

A tall, stately gentleman with chiseled features looked around the table and focused on Charles Martin. "We want him out. And the people surrounding him. We want no repercussions of any kind. Nothing must lead back to any of us or to any member of the World Bank. It goes without saying we want the funds returned as quickly as possible. We," the man said, motioning to his colleagues, "have it on good authority that the current president of the World Bank is a close personal friend of many people in the current administration, not just the president of the United States. We have been told that if anyone can do this, it's your little band of women."

"Little band of women!" Kathryn exploded. Her eyes narrowed as she looked around at the others to see how they were reacting to this sudden blasphemous statement.

Before things got out of hand, Charles hastened to step into what he knew could well turn into a battle royal. To his eye the volatile Kathryn looked like she was single-handedly going to wipe up the floor with the current speaker. The speaker looked like he was wondering how he would fare.

The man realized that his poor choice of words had created a situation. "I apologize, madam, but I do not know how to refer to you and the others. I only know what I have read in the papers and seen on television. My sincere apologies. Do you prefer the term 'vigilante'?"

"No harm, no foul," Kathryn said grudgingly. She wondered if the *stiff* talking to her knew what the phrase meant. She leaned back in her chair, her hand dropping to stroke Murphy's head. The bad moment was over.

With the preliminaries ended, Annie said, "It's time to talk turkey, ladies and gentlemen."

And they got down to business.

Chapter 2

Breakfast on Big Pine Mountain was served in the main dining hall. When they first came, it had taken a while to get used to the walk because the women had to trek from their individual living quarters across the compound. They liked to complain about the rain and the snow and having to get dressed three times a day just to eat. These days they didn't think twice about sprinting outdoors as they raced one another to the dining room.

Living as fugitives on Big Pine Mountain had its pluses and minuses. The main plus was that they were back in the United States. The main minus was that they were still fugitives. Although they hadn't actually lived on the premises of Pinewood in Virginia, Myra's palatial estate, they had had access to all the amenities, and they hadn't been wanted fugitives. When the law caught up to them, and they moved to Barcelona, Spain, atop a mountain owned by Countess Anna de Silva, they'd lived as fugitive recluses unless their help was needed on special projects brought to them by Charles Martin.

Here, back in the States, as Isabelle had said, they were merely trading their lavish style of mountain living for a more rustic one. Or, as Yoko had put it, "We're on our home turf here."

The women seated themselves in the dining room. It was a pleasant room with a huge fieldstone fireplace that rose from the floor to the ceiling. Beautiful flowers from one of the many gardens were on all the tables. Greenery hung from the beams overhead. All the tables, chairs, and end tables were solid oak, all polished to a high sheen. The floors were also solid oak, buffed and polished so that you could see your reflection in the old wood. In the days of Kollar (Pappy) Havapopulas's reign on the mountain, this very dining room had hosted all the covert agents under his tutelage who came there for training. Nothing had been changed because, as Charles had put it, "We don't know how long we'll be in residence." The women were all right with that simple explanation because they knew nothing lasted forever.

They all had chores. Yoko saw to the plants and flowers, Alexis tended the vegetable gardens, Isabelle did kitchen duty, Kathryn maintained the pool, while Nikki helped Charles in what they called the command center. Myra and Annie supervised to make sure everything ran smoothly. Unlike their command centers back in Virginia and Spain, this particular computer center was Kollar's and occupied a separate room in the Big House. It worked for all of them.

Breakfast this morning was simple and hearty—bacon, eggs, ham, toast, fresh fruit, coffee, and juice. It was all set out in chafing dishes on a sideboard that ran the entire length of one wall. At each end of the sideboard were two glorious arrangements of yellow roses, thanks to Yoko. The smell was sweet and heady.

Myra, a stickler for the finer things in life, marveled that here on this mountain, the Havapopulas family, father and son, had exquisite crystal, china, and silver. There was no sign of a paper napkin or a plastic tablecloth. Everything was linen. Everything was as fine as her heirlooms back in Virginia. She did love a pretty table setting.

Charles's main rule—never discuss business until a meal is over—was strictly adhered to. They made small talk, Yoko talking about the gorgeous roses that were now in full bloom, Kathryn discussing the water temperature of the Olympic-size pool.

When they were finished eating, the women all carried their dishes to the kitchen, poured more coffee, and got down to business.

"What time did our guests leave?" Nikki asked.

"I heard the helicopter at first light," Alexis said. "Grady hates the sound and wanted out, but I waited till it took off. The cable car was already descending, so it left first."

"What do we think about last night?" Isabelle queried.

"I don't think those people told us the whole story. Something wasn't quite right about it all. Just a feeling," Kathryn said. "It goes without saying that everyone has an agenda. It could be something as simple as those people wanting to get rid of Zenowicz so they can get someone to take his place who will be more *friendly* to their specific cause, whatever that cause is. It's all politics no matter how you look at it."

"I felt it, too, and I think you're right," Yoko said.

The others for the most part agreed.

"I didn't go to bed after the meeting. I went online to see what I could find out about the World Bank," Annie said.

The women leaned forward. "And . . . ?" they chorused as one.

Annie loved being the center of attention. She preened for a moment. "Well, the president of the World Bank is an American, as we know. But do you all know that a European is the head of the sister bank, the International Monetary Fund? No one mentioned that last night, did they? If I had a crafty mind, which I do, I'd say this has something to do with Americans versus Europeans. The United States is the bank's biggest financial contributor. It's a decades-old tradition, and me thinks those people who were here last night might not want to keep it that way. In other words, politics."

"A turf war?" Nikki asked.

"Without a doubt," Annie responded. "The World Bank was created in 1945. The object was to rebuild Europe after World War II. You might not know this, and I didn't either, until I checked it out, but the bank provides twenty billion dollars a year for projects like building dams, roads, and, of course, fighting disease. The bank offers interest-free loans to the poorest countries. I, for one, would like to see their books."

"And our guy was in charge of twenty billion a year? I could see the temptation to pocket a little. I could also see some creative accounting where those interest-free loans are concerned," Alexis said. "Don't forget, I did hard time for people just like this, who framed me."

The women were silent for a moment as they digested Annie's information.

"So, I guess what we're saying is our guests last night have agendas of their own that they didn't fully disclose," Nikki said. "But in the end, that's not what our job is about. Of course, if we find a way to . . . uh . . . change things, we will."

"Yes, dear, it would appear so," Myra said.

"I wonder who those anonymous donors willing to give us a blank check are. We need to decide how much to charge now. It goes without saying that we aren't going to keep the money, right?" Nikki asked.

"As long as the money isn't coming out of the World Bank, I say we hit them where it hurts," Kathryn suggested. "Anonymous means *anonymous*, and we're never going to know. Let's go with ten million and set up a fund where we disperse the monies to our own needy, but let's keep a little in reserve for an emergency. First crack off the bat I say we funnel some monies to Pearl Barnes so that she has enough funding for her underground railroad. Lizzie Fox can take care of all that. The more money they have, the more people they can get to safety," she said, referring to their last mission in the States where they posed as the G-String Girls to fight AIDS in Africa and save the Chief Justice's career.

"I'd like to see some money go to battered women's shelters," Alexis said.

"We can ask Judge Easter to take care of that. I think it's a wonderful idea, Alexis," Myra said.

"Animal rights," Kathryn said.

"All things children," Annie said.

"Done," Myra said smartly. "The children go to the top of the list."

"All this means is we have to go back to Washington. Again," Nikki said breathlessly. Going back to Washington meant she'd see District Attorney Jack Emery, the man she loved, again.

Yoko clapped her tiny hands in happiness because it meant she would get to see her love, Harry Wong, a martial-arts expert, to whom she was engaged.

"And just how are we going to get in and out of Washington again? The FBI is so hot on our trail, they're smoking. And, let's not forget Ted Robinson. That guy wants to take a bath in our blood. I'm thinking this time around it's going to be even more dicey," Kathryn said. "Another thing, do we seriously believe, even for one minute, that there aren't rumors, leaks, *something,* that things aren't right at 1818 H Street, headquarters of the World Bank? If you all believe that, I'll sell you the Key Bridge."

"Kathryn has a point," Myra said thoughtfully.

Isabelle poured more coffee just to have something to do.

"We need a plan," Annie said, excitement ringing in her voice. "The thrill of danger is so intoxicating. I just know this . . . this . . . mission is going to be the one that puts us on the map!"

"We're already on the damn map, Annie. Any little thing that goes wrong is attributed to us. We're supposedly in every state in the union. There have been more sightings of us than you can shake a stick at. We get credit or blame, take your pick, for everything that goes wrong," Kathryn grumbled.

"Yes, yes, but don't you see, that's what makes it so exciting. They're out there chasing their tails on all those false sightings, but when it comes down to the crunch, we move in and *strike!* It's all so perfect it boggles the mind!" Annie said.

Myra's tone was grudging when she looked at her old friend, and said, "She's right up to a point, and it does make some sense, but none of us should ever think of the FBI as stupid or lax. Ted Robinson, possibly, but sooner or later someone with some chutzpah is going to pay attention to him. He's gotten way too close to us too many times. He's not going to give up, and he's not going to go away. That's a given we have to deal with."

"So, we work around him. We'll get Jack or Harry to put a tail on him. This way we'll know what he's doing in real time and be prepared," Nikki said. Her expression darkened. "If it doesn't work, or if he invades our space, we'll simply take care of him."

"Ooh, ooh, that sounds . . . *lethal,*" Annie said, her eyes bigger than saucers as she anticipated going a few rounds with the *Post*'s intrepid reporter.

The women left the dining hall and walked out into the bright summer sunshine. Murphy and Grady waited patiently in the hopes someone would throw a stick so they could play. Kathryn obliged, and the dogs ran off.

The pine scent was heady after the night's heavy rain. Everything looked scrubbed to perfection. Overhead, the sky was cerulean, with huge cotton candy clouds. The birds in the trees were singing their morning song. In a word, peaceful.

"It seems so perfect, doesn't it? Almost mystical," Isabelle whispered to Yoko, who was walking alongside her.

"If you don't look deep enough as to why we're here in the first place," Yoko whispered in return. "Like Annie says, we have to pretend we're on vacation."

Murphy bounded up with the stick in his mouth; a moment later, Grady emerged from the thick pine forest with his own stick. Kathryn threw them again before the women climbed the six steps that led into the Big House.

Charles was waiting for them in the small foyer. He escorted them into the same conference room they'd occupied the evening before. The moment they were seated, the women bombarded him with questions and comments about their new employers.

"Ten million dollars, Charles. That's our fee," Nikki said. "We don't plan to keep a penny of it for ourselves. I hesitate to ask this, but: What happens if something goes wrong? What happens if we fail? I'm not saying that's going to happen, but I want to know, since we're the ones taking all the risks here. Just chalk it up to the lawyer in me."

"The money is yours, win or lose. I made that clear to our guests even before they arrived. They were in agreement with everything with one exception. Should things go awry, there is to be no mention of the World Bank or their visit here. I assured them of confidentiality. I knew you'd want to be philanthropic about it, so accounts have been set up offshore, in the Caymans and Switzerland. This was also done before our guests arrived. At the moment, dear ladies, that is the least of our worries."

"We want to know what they didn't tell us, Charles," Kathryn said, fixing him with a steely gaze.

"I'd wager quite a bit. People tend to be reticent when discussing matters such as ours. I just need a little time to figure out what it is. I will find it if it's there to be found. Right now, that is not the issue. As we all know, nothing is as it seems at first blush."

"Taking on the World Bank is about as serious as it can get," Kathryn said. "I can't even comprehend one billion dollars, much less twenty billion." Her voice turned ominous when she said, "People kill and get killed for money like that."

Myra looked at the women, and said, "Greed is the most powerful motivator in the world."

"Do we have any indication that Zenowicz suspects anyone is onto him?" Yoko asked.

"From what I was told, it appears not. He's carrying on his . . . uh . . . interesting lifestyle as though he doesn't have a care in the world. This is going to be a very big blow to the administration if it gets out," Charles said. "If you are successful, and there is no reason to think you won't be, when the administration gets wind of it, we won't be able to count on any . . . help from them. Just so you know."

"Who's next to succeed Zenowicz if he resigns? And all those White House people he surrounded himself with— they'll have to resign, too, won't they?" Yoko asked again.

Charles nodded. "It's a presidential appointment. I'm told there are several names on a short list. Ideally, the appointee should be an economist with experience in development. Someone who can work with the staff that Zenowicz has managed to alienate over the past few years. The institution has to be brought back together so it can function normally without any hint of scandal."

"And we're going to make this happen? How?" the ever-skeptical Kathryn asked.

Charles looked over the top of his glasses at the women seated at the table. "Correct me if I'm wrong here, but haven't you all said, on more than one occasion, that you're *women,* and you can do anything?"

Kathryn's feathers were ruffled. "Actually, Charles, what I said was we're women, we kick ass and take names later."

Charles tried not to smile. "That will work, too. Now, let me get back to work so I can map out a strategy to accomplish your objectives and keep you safe at the same time. I'm sure you're all going to want to bat this around, think of ways to . . . uh . . . punish the culprits."

"Guess that means we're dismissed," Alexis said, getting up from the table. "I'm going for a swim. Anyone want to join me?"

The others walked off, leaving Annie and Myra, the two oldest of the group, lagging behind. They opted for a walk through the pungent forest, Murphy and Grady at their heels.

When they were out of earshot of the others, Annie turned to Myra. "I find this a bit . . . frightening."

Myra looked at her old friend in stunned surprise. "Frightening? Is that what you said? And you didn't think getting up on a stage wearing a G-string and pasties frightening at our age?"

"That was *fun,* Myra. Well, it was until our latex started to melt. Taking on the World Bank is a Federal thing. That means a Federal prison if things get out of hand."

"Annie, Annie, Annie! The last issue of *Forbes* that I read had you listed as the richest woman in the world, richer than Bill Gates. That means you have more money than the World Bank. Which in turn means you could take over the World Bank if you wanted to," Myra said, her thoughts all over the map.

Annie's jaw dropped. "Do you think?"

"Absolutely."

"Will I be broke then? Destitute?"

"Except for maybe twenty billion or so."

"Oh, okay. I didn't know you kept such a sharp eye on my finances, Myra."

"Not me, *Forbes*. I just read about it. You know Charles, *Forbes* and the *Wall Street Journal* are required reading."

"Whatever would I do without you, Myra?"

"God only knows," Myra responded as she wondered if He would punish her for egging her old friend on but, as Charles always said, "if you don't take risks you'll never know."

Chapter 3

Liam Sullivan, editor in chief of the *Post* and Ted Robinson's boss, stood over his employee's cubicle watching the reporter sleep. He whistled sharply and was pleased to see Ted jump to attention.

"Since when do I pay you to sleep on the job, Robinson? You're on shaky ground as it is. You're back one week, and already you're taxing my patience. I can send you to the unemployment line in a heartbeat if that's what you want," Sullivan snarled.

"No, that's not what I want. Look, boss, I've been kicked to the curb, kidnapped because of those damn vigilantes; my girl bailed out on me; you give me the shit detail; my cats won't come near me; and I'm not sleeping at night. I know that's no excuse, but that's the way it is. Can't you cut me a little slack here?"

"Your problem is you're obsessed with those vigilantes. You need to forget about them. You're making this paper a laughingstock in the industry. If it's any consolation to you, I miss Maggie, too. Being as smart as you are, you should realize women are fickle. By the way, I want you to go over to the *Post*'s apartment and pack up her things. I owe her that much. One of these days she'll come back and want her belongings."

"I can't do that, boss."

"Ted, I wasn't *asking* you to do it, I was *telling* you to do it. In other words, it was an order. I am your boss. I make sure your paycheck gets signed every week."

Ted sighed. "What do you want me to do with her things?"

"Put them in storage. Take them home. Just clear out her things. We have a guest arriving tomorrow whom the *Post* needs to accommodate." His demeanor softened a little. "Didn't she send a note or say good-bye?"

Ted turned off his computer and rolled down his shirtsleeves. "No. She just fell off the face of the earth. Her cell phone just rings and rings. She had a second cell phone. I told you all about that. I never saw anything like it. Look, I know you don't believe me, but she hooked up with the vigilantes. I know it as sure as I'm standing here. She was last seen with Lizzie Fox, who, ironically, disappeared at exactly the same time Maggie did. High-dollar Lizzie, lawyer to the rich and famous, and she just packs it in. I-don't-think-so. Judge Easter is involved, too, and so are those cruds Jack Emery and Harry Wong. It's all one goddamn big conspiracy. Another thing, Chief, don't you find it a little strange that Chief Justice Barnes suddenly retired? And where's that live-in lover of hers? Everyone suddenly disappears. Even that dandy ex–son-in-law of hers resigned from the think tank where he worked. The guy was set for life, high bucks, and he blows it off just like Pearl Barnes. She was set for life, too. It smells."

Ted's voice turned desperate when he said, "Think about it, Chief, all of a sudden five people drop off the face of the earth. All five are connected in some way."

"All those people are of an age where they can do what they want. No missing person reports have been filed. That means the story is dead. D-e-a-d! Now, I want you out there pounding the pavement. I want some news. I want some credible stories. This is Washington, D.C., where things happen on an hourly basis. I know it's summer, and things slow down, but there's news out there. So go find it so I can print it, but first, get Maggie's stuff and store it away."

Ted almost exploded. "What? You want me to write gossip? That's crap, and you know it. Shirley is good at that. Tyson loves it," he said, referring to his colleagues. "Why me?"

"Because they're busy, and all you do is sleep on the job. I want my money's worth, Robinson, so get your ass out of here and get to work."

"Wait! Wait! How about I do a series on the disappearance of those five people? Whet people's appetites. I might come across something that leads to something else. C'mon, Chief, give me a break here. I can hire a few dicks, trail along, and write a short column, titled . . . something like, 'Where are they now?' You know how this town loves a good mystery. You're right, it's summer, it's slow. We might pick up some new readership."

Sullivan rocked back on his heels. He closed his eyes and tried to conjure up what Ted's column would look like. "Okay." He turned on his heel and marched back to his office. Ted let out a sigh so loud he startled himself.

He needed a plan. He definitely needed a plan. Not only did he need a plan, he needed a Plan B, a Plan C, and maybe even a Plan D. Hell, he might have to use up the whole damn alphabet. As he packed up his gear, his thoughts were all over the map. He needed to check out his bank balance. Maybe he could con his pal Espinosa, a sometime writing partner, into joining forces, and then he could tap Espinosa's bank account as well. Private dicks these days wanted retainers for sitting on their asses and hacking into shit no one else could get near. But first he needed to follow through on Sullivan's orders and pick up Maggie's things.

Ted's step was buoyant as he made his way to the lobby. Outside, he hailed a cab and directed the driver to the address where the *Post* kept an apartment for visiting flacks and people who were willing to sell a story for money. It always came down to money. Always.

Jack Emery stepped out of the shower, threw on a clean pair of sweats, and walked out to the main floor of Harry Wong's *dojo*. Harry was bowing low to show his class of police officers they were dismissed. He looked over at Jack and winced. He knew that look.

Jack sat down on a pile of mats and tied his sneakers. From time to time he looked over at Harry, who was staring at him. "What?"

"You know something, and you've been waiting for the right time to tell me. It's probably something I'm not going to like because from the expression on your face you don't like it, either. Tell me, or before your heart beats again, I'll break both your arms."

"Ooh, ooh, I'm scared. What the hell do you think I'll be doing while you're breaking my arms?"

"Howling in agony," Harry snarled.

"You excite me when you snarl. I go all atwitter. You know what, Harry, I keep worrying that this place is bugged. I know you said you sweep it every day, but those cruds at the FBI could plant something between sweeps. Soon as the class leaves, let's take it outside, where we can really talk. Better yet, I haven't had any dinner. Want to try that new watering hole on H Street?"

"The one where the World Bank is? The one where all the employees are women duded up in skintight attire? That one? The guy who set that up is making a mint. Give me five minutes to change. Check the doors in front, Jack. Make sure everyone is out. Some of those cop friends of yours are stragglers. I locked some guy in two weeks ago who was diddling around in the shower buffing his toe-nails or something. He was stuck in here all night. D.C.'s finest!" Harry snorted to show what he thought of his own comment.

"That's the one, but I forget what it's called. Do it, Harry. You buying?"

"Hell no. You invited me, remember?"

Ten minutes later the building was clear, and both men were outside. Harry slid onto his Ducati motorcycle, Jack behind him.

They made it to H Street in seven minutes, windblown but exhilarated.

Both men elbowed their way through the swarming crowds at the Fast Track. Harry was right, it was a gold mine for whoever owned the joint. The plus was that the food was supposedly wonderful, and everything was rea-sonably priced. At the moment it was standing room only. Jack left his name at the hostess desk. They walked back outside with a beeper that would buzz when it was their turn to be seated.

Jack fired up a cigarette, to Harry's dismay.

"You told me you were quitting. You lied."

"Yeah. I'm under lots of pressure. It's my pacifier. This is only my third one today, so stop nagging me."

"Are you going to tell me now, or do you want to be carted off to the hospital?"

Jack walked twenty feet to the curb, out of earshot of some of the other people smoking by the entrance. He turned so that his back was to the doorway.

"Charles called before I got to the *dojo*. I would have told you then, but you were holding a class. Something's up. Right here where we're standing."

Harry looked around, his Eastern eyes almost widening. "Here? At the Fast Track?"

"Not exactly," Jack said, blowing a perfect smoke ring. "Try widening your vision."

Harry turned completely around as he viewed the street and the buildings. His gaze went from left to right, then up and down. Jack almost laughed when he saw his friend swivel around to face him, dark questions in his eyes. "Are you saying . . . ?"

"Yep."

"Son of a bitch! So, that's why you wanted to come here."

"Yep."

"No. No. I mean no, Jack. My nerves are still twanging over that last mess with the G-String Girls. And that asshole Mitch Riley at the FBI before that. Are you crazy? We're at the top of the FBI's watch list. No. When are you going to get it through your head we're both too old for this shit? No."

"Looks like the girls will be here next week," Jack said as he fired up a second cigarette from the butt of his first one. "I guess you could call Yoko and tell her you don't want any part of it this time around. I'm going to ask Nikki to marry me. When it's over."

"I really hate you, Jack."

"Enough of this male bonding. We have to get things ready. At the moment, I don't know what those things are, but I have a few clues. I need you on this, Harry. I also have other news. Guess who else called me today?"

"The president?" Harry asked sourly. "You better not be telling me God called you."

"Not even close. Mark Lane, my old buddy from the FBI. As you know, he went private. But he has all these great contacts. He called me just as I was getting out of court. Ted Robinson hired Tick Fields, the private dick who advertises on TV. He plunked down a five-grand retainer at three o'clock this afternoon. A personal check.

Mark does work for Tick from time to time. And they're personal friends as well. Fields wouldn't disclose what he was hired to do, ethics and all that. All he would say was Robinson hired him."

"Don't tell me he's downwind of this," Harry said, jerking his head in the direction of the World Bank's headquarters. "If you just found out, how the hell could he scoop you? You must be slipping, Jack."

Jack blew another smoke ring, not as perfect as the first one. He tried still another, his gaze sweeping the street in front of him. "I don't think it has anything to do with *this*. I think he's trying to figure out where everyone went all of a sudden, including his old girlfriend, Maggie. He knew what went down a while back. He got slapped down at the *Post*. He's still smarting over that. Let's face it, Harry, we did rub the guy's nose in it. He's going to be on us like white on rice because he knows we're the key to it all. So that means we both keep a sharp eye out. Don't give him anything to feed off."

The beeper in Jack's hand went off just as he crushed out his cigarette on the curb.

"I knew I should have killed the son of a bitch," Harry said, trailing behind Jack.

"Sounds good, but we aren't in the business of blowing people away. You wouldn't do well in prison, Harry."

A sound that could have been mistaken for laughter escaped Harry's lips. "Who said anything about me going to prison? I would have framed you to take the rap."

"Oh," was all Jack could think of to say.

Harry emitted the funny sound again as he shouldered his way past the crowds to follow a leggy blonde hostess leading them to their table. She slapped down two menus, winked at them, and left. Neither man seemed to notice because they were too busy eyeing the three men at the next table: Ted Robinson, Joe Espinosa, and Tick Fields.

Chapter 4

The women looked at one another as they trooped into the Big House, where Charles was waiting for them. They chatted among themselves about how different it was here on Big Pine Mountain. In the beginning when they first formed the Sisterhood, meetings were held in the tunnels beneath Myra's farmhouse in McLean, Virginia, because it was essential that the meetings be kept secret. Then, when they moved to the old monastery in Barcelona, the meetings were conducted in the same manner, in the catacombs beneath the monastery.

Here on Big Pine Mountain, the meeting they were about to attend was held in Charles's computer room. The physical room looked different from the tunnels and the catacombs, but as usual, the equipment was so high-tech it would have been the envy of the CIA or the White House.

The windows afforded a clear view of the pine forest and the helicopter pad. The chairs were deep and comfortable, the plasma televisions huge, and the temperature on the cool side because of the special computers Charles worked on around the clock.

The women settled themselves in the chairs, their eyes on the bright red folders in Myra's hands.

Time for business.

The women slid their chairs closer to the table as they steeled themselves for what was to come. The rule was, Myra handed out the folders, but they were never opened until Charles gave the signal. First came an update, then the monster TVs were turned on so that Lady Justice could oversee the meeting.

It was always a sobering moment when Lady Justice appeared because the women knew what they were doing was illegal. When the legal system failed those in need, when there was nowhere else to turn, the Sisterhood stepped in and served up their own brand of justice.

They were about to break the law. Again. This time for money. It was a first for them. They'd carried out nine missions with funding from Myra and Annie's vast store of wealth. While they were accepting money to do this particular mission, they weren't keeping it. Or as Kathryn had said, "We're playing the role of modern-day Robin *Hood-ettes*."

It was Annie who'd said that simply taking the money meant they had crossed the line and become guns for hire. Then she went on to say, "And why not? We're the best at what we do, and if we can rectify a wrong with our expertise, why not take payment? Then, by giving the money away it makes it a win-win situation for the Sisterhood." Before she finally stepped off her soapbox, she'd said, "And screw anyone who doesn't understand."

The women offered up a standing ovation. Even Charles clapped his hands in approval.

The women now waited expectantly for Charles to end the call he'd just taken. They eyed the red folders now resting on the table in front of Myra. All of them noticed that they were thick folders.

Murphy and Grady got up and paced the room. The women frowned. The dogs were picking up on something.

Possibly the tension in Charles's shoulders. The dogs had been fine before Charles's special phone buzzed to life.

As one they knew it was a glitch. A problem of some kind. And the mission hadn't even started.

The moment Charles snapped the phone shut, the women sat up straighter. Myra picked up the folders. Nikki looked around, expecting a starter gun to pop announcing the beginning of a race. All she could think of was seeing Jack again. Within days. Just days. She closed her eyes, imagining how it would feel to be wrapped in Jack's arms and to kiss him with all her pent-up hunger. She almost swooned at the thought.

"Ladies!"

Nikki and the others snapped to attention as Myra slid the folders across the table. Charles pressed the remote control in his hand. Front and center on the plasma screen was a life-size picture of Maxwell Zenowicz, the president of the World Bank. He was tall, with a swarthy complexion and an impressive comb-over. He wore sunglasses that were too small for his hawklike face. Whoever had taken the picture had captured him in midstride. He was nattily dressed, his shoes buffed to a high shine. The Halliburton briefcase held tightly in his hand. It looked like he was about to enter the World Bank.

The next picture appeared to be of Zenowicz exiting the building. The sun had moved off to the west, so it was later in the day but still daylight. He still looked just as nattily dressed, but he wasn't wearing his sunglasses. He had small, hooded eyes.

The third picture was of Zenowicz entering the Fast Track watering hole.

Charles cleared his throat. "Mr. Zenowicz likes to socialize after work with the little people. Complete with his security force. He enjoys . . . uh . . . bellying up to the bar and buying rounds for all the lovely ladies who are gathered there. Prior to the opening of the Fast Track, Mr. Zenowicz walked several blocks to an establishment called the Capitol Grill. He orders a scotch on the rocks. Sips a little, never finishes his drink. He smokes but not in public.

"Mr. Zenowicz does not like to be called Max. His wrath is quick to be displayed if some friend or underling refers to him by any abbreviation of his name. It's a well-known fact that he likes to be called Mr. President. As you can see by the pictures, he dresses impeccably. He wears an impressive watch and his college ring. Married once. Ugly divorce. Wife will be more than cooperative if you feel the need to speak with her. Children, grown, lead their own lives. He is not included in their lives. He likes to socialize as long as he's the center of attention. He particularly likes young ladies. Early twenties. He showers them with gifts, flowers, trinkets. He drives a Bentley. He bought it brand-new last year for $300,000. He doesn't drive to work. He takes public transportation. The Bentley is kept in a heated garage, and he takes it out on the weekends. On occasion, if there is a VIP in town, he will pick them up personally at the airport in his Bentley. Any questions, ladies?"

"How old is he?" Alexis asked.

"Fifty-nine. He had a birthday two weeks ago. He threw himself a huge birthday party. The guest list was long and distinguished. Cost $50,000. It's a known fact that people in Washington don't like the man but they attended the soiree to get their names and pictures in the paper. I'm quoting now from the *Post*."

"Does he have any other residences aside from the Watergate?" Isabelle asked.

"Actually, he does. He has a condo in Jackson Hole, Wyoming. He also has an apartment in the Dakota in Manhattan, and there's a chalet-type getaway he visits from time to time in Hilton Head, South Carolina. His wife got the house in the Hamptons and the boat. Excuse me, the yacht. She also received an impressive settlement that ran into the high eight figures. Mr. Zenowicz did a bit of snapping and snarling, I'm told, when the judge awarded Mrs. Zenowicz a handsome alimony. He pays it on time but grudgingly. Mrs. Zenowicz is what we in England used to refer to as 'top drawer.' "

"Where did the money come from?" Myra asked. "I'm assuming all this happened before he took the office of president of the World Bank? If the man has that kind of money, why does he have to pilfer the money earmarked for poor, starving countries?"

Charles shrugged. "To some people a hundred dollars is a lot of money. To other people a million dollars is the end of the rainbow. Still others think a hundred million isn't enough. But to answer your question, he inherited a small fortune, which he turned into a very large fortune in the stock market. He was heavy into the dot-com area and got out in time but that's basically where he became a multi-millionaire. He also had the good fortune to be an only child.

"If there are no more questions concerning Mr. Zeno-wicz, then we'll move along to our next series of pictures. Open your folders and turn to page five."

The women opened their folders and flipped the pages.

"Whoa!" seemed to be the consensus when they looked down at the glossy photo staring up at them.

Annie pursed her mouth like she'd just bit into a lemon. Then she sniffed. "Obviously, the woman has been surgi-cally enhanced. None of what I'm seeing could possibly be real."

"From top to bottom," Yoko said.

"An easy seventy grand," Nikki said.

Myra gasped. "That much, dear?"

Nikki grinned. "Yes. She's too chiseled, too sculpted, too perfect. The boob job alone is about seven grand, maybe more, depending on the reputation of the plastic surgeon. Maybe some liposuction. *Full* face-lift. Eye job. The teeth are a dentist's dream. All caps. At least forty grand for that smile. Collagen in the lips. Nose job. Take a good look at the picture in the folder. This woman is *not* young. I put her in her midforties."

"Why would someone pay that much money to be sliced and diced?" Myra fretted.

"Earth to Myra," Annie said, waving her hand up and down in front of Myra's face. "To look like that is the reason. You're missing the point, she didn't look like *that* before she went under the knife. I think you're wrong, Nikki, I think she's closer to fifty, perhaps a little older."

"Is she Zenowicz's main squeeze? If so, I guess he paid for the . . . enhancements," Kathryn said.

Charles tried to hide his smile. "She's one of several . . . main squeezes, as you put it, Kathryn. But she's the only one he pays the bills for. This particular woman used to be a dancer in Las Vegas. She . . . uh . . . migrated to Washington after a meeting with Mr. Zenowicz last year. She now works as a liaison at the World Bank. The European Commission in Belgium, to be precise. She travels back and forth. She's well paid. Her hobby is shopping."

"What does that mean, 'well paid'?" Yoko asked.

Charles riffled his papers. "Her salary is $240,000 a year. She has a limousine at her disposal when she is in town. It's a perk she insisted upon. It's my understanding the lady has a very pleasing personality. She could very well be a nice person caught up in something she didn't anticipate. Be kind in your thoughts until you can prove otherwise."

"And what does she do to earn that astronomical salary?" Isabelle queried.

Kathryn uttered a very unladylike snort. "Well, it's obvious what she does. Kinky stuff. I'd like to see her résumé."

Charles had a hard time keeping a straight face. "Turn to page twelve."

The sound of the flipping pages was the only noise in the room.

"She speaks three languages besides English!" Kathryn said in awe.

Alexis burst out laughing. "Yeah, Brooklynese, Southern Belle, and kitchy coo. It says right here in her résumé she was born in Brooklyn. She moved to Atlanta for a while, then Vegas. No college degree. Where did she learn those three languages if it's for real? I stand by my assessment."

"Maybe she takes shorthand and types," Myra said.

Nikki looked at her adopted mother with disdain. "With those nails! They're like spikes."

Myra looked properly chastened. "So, dear, what you're saying is she earns that rather large salary being Mr. Zenowicz's . . . paramour, is that correct?"

"Oh, yeah," the women chorused.

"Ladies, ladies, enough of this jocularity. Miss Rena Gold is your access to Mr. Zenowicz. It would behoove you to make nice. Mr. Zenowicz has some top-notch security, which he pays for himself. Those rather large men who followed him into the Fast Track establishment are his daytime security. He has a total of eight guards, who rotate every other day. Pictures of each guard are in your folder along with what is known about each man. I want you to familiarize yourself with all of the guards. Each one of the men is licensed to carry a firearm. I can't as yet confirm this, but there is every possibility that, unbeknownst to Mr. Zenowicz, Miss Rena Gold has had several dalliances with one of the security guards. As yet that has not been proven. What is proven is she has no female friends. At least none that we've come across."

Kathryn snorted again. "Now, why doesn't that surprise me?"

Several more pictures of fresh-faced college girls appeared on the screen. Each one prettier than the next. In a word, wholesome, girl-next-door looks. "Two of the girls go to Georgetown University, two go to Catholic. At the moment, none of the four is of major importance."

Charles cleared the screen on the plasma TV and took a deep breath. "What I'm about to show you next is not pretty, so all of you, take a deep breath. What you are going to see are pictures of the two countries that never received the funds Zenowicz promised."

Picture after picture appeared on the huge screen, making it all the more horrendous. Starving babies, hollow-eyed mothers, emaciated fathers, dying grandparents. Naked toddlers eating dirt, their stomachs as huge as watermelons.

The women looked away, tears streaming down their cheeks. Charles wiped at his own eyes as he pressed his remote, and, blessedly, the screen turned black. "If you have even one qualm, one iota of distress that you're doing the wrong thing by taking on this mission, those pictures should allay all your fears. What say you all?"

Nikki was the first to speak. "I've always thought that we here in this great country should take care of our own first. I still believe that. Ten million dollars is a vast sum of money, so let's take a vote right now. Five million dollars stays here so we can do what we originally planned. The other five million goes to the World Food Bank with proper supervision. Or we could build schools. Any number of things. Five million dollars in countries like that will go a long way. If our mission is successful, then the monies earmarked for these two countries will get the people the help they need. Our contribution will be like icing on a cake. Do you all agree?"

A chorus of ayes resonated throughout the room. Not to be outdone, Murphy and Grady barked their approval.

"When do we start?" Annie asked.

"As soon as I get everything in place," Charles said. "Manpower is crucial in this mission. I need a full day, possibly a day and a half, before I'll be comfortable sending you into the lion's den."

"How are we going to get into D.C.?" Kathryn asked.

Charles smiled. "You're going to drive, but first I have to secure a base of operations. In order to do that, we need vehicles that are untraceable, and we need new identities that are foolproof. It all takes time, ladies."

The women muttered and murmured among themselves as they accepted their dismissal and left to go outdoors into the bright sunshine.

They headed toward the pool and the shaded patio, where they all sat down. Annie offered to fetch ice tea. Before starting to talk about the mission, they waited for her return by discussing the gerbera daisies that lined the pool area.

The moment Annie returned with the ice tea, they got down to it.

"The way I see it, we're outta here in around thirty-six hours," Kathryn said. "That cuts down our time. We all know we're going to hit a few snafus along the way, so I say let's get down to the dirty end and make some plans."

"And we have to come up with a suitable punishment. One that fits Zenowicz's crime. I'm really going to enjoy making that weasel squirm," Nikki said, the light of battle in her eyes.

They talked of other things then as they waited for

Annie to return with a second tray that held glasses and a plate of brownies.

"I wonder how Lizzie and Maggie are doing," Alexis said.

"What really surprises me, knowing Washington the way I do, is that there was no big ruckus in the media when Pearl Barnes resigned and her longtime lover disappeared," Isabelle said. "Perhaps 'disappeared' is the wrong word. I guess the politically correct verbiage would be to say they moved on with their lives. Lizzie's resignation, as well as Maggie's, should have stirred up some kind of controversy. And let's not forget that scummy ex-son-in-law of Pearl's."

"As individual cases it would mean nothing except to a few close friends," Myra said. "Taken as a whole, if anyone was astute enough to put it together, like, say, Ted Robinson, it could mean trouble for all of us. Nellie is in the clear and minding her own business."

"Jack and Harry say nothing is going on in town. Washington in the summer is pretty much deserted except for tourists. If there was trouble brewing, Jack would know," Nikki said.

The others watched as Annie poured ice tea generously into crystal glasses that matched the pitcher. "Did you all say anything exciting while I was gone?"

"Only that Ted Robinson is a pimple on our asses." Kathryn grinned.

"Why don't I buy the *Post?* Then we can fire him," Annie said.

The women stared at Annie until she flushed a bright pink. Her voice was defensive when she said, "I have enough money to buy the paper. The price is no object, if that's what it takes to get the man out of our hair."

"You're a fugitive, Annie. You can't go around buying up newspapers," Nikki said.

Annie sipped at her tea. "There are ways around every-thing," she responded airily. "Isn't that right, Myra?"

Myra's right eye started to twitch as she fingered the pearls around her neck. "Yes, there is a way around every-thing. At least that's what Charles has been saying since we formed the Sisterhood. Although Charles has been known to be wrong once or twice," she said vaguely.

"This tea is very good. Not because I made it, girls, but because I made it with simple syrup. My husband taught me how to make proper ice tea the way they do in the South. I really think my idea is a good one."

"You're brilliant, Annie," Kathryn said. "I need to think. What if we started a rumor that the *Post* was going to be bought up by . . . let's just say for now, an undis-closed buyer who wishes to remain anonymous. Wouldn't that be a hoot if in the end, when things got down to the wire, it gets out that somehow, some way, the vigilantes own the paper. Just think about *that!* That's providing Annie and Myra are right, and there's a way for Annie to buy the paper."

Myra's hands fluttered as she grappled with her pearls. "My goodness, imagine all that free press! Should we tell Charles about Annie's brilliant idea?"

The women as one jumped at her words. "Why?"

"As a courtesy," Myra said lamely.

A wicked gleam appeared in Annie's eyes. "There's a lot to be said for the element of surprise. I think that's a no."

To Annie's delight, the women high-fived one another.

"So, Nikki, dear, perhaps you should call Jack, who can then call Mr. Robinson and plant the rumor. By the time we get to Washington, that will be all the big news. In the mean-time, I will call my people to see if anything can be done. If not, we'll still have fun with the rumor," Annie said, beam-ing from head to toe.

"Annie, you are a genius. An absolute genius," Kathryn chortled.

Nikki started to laugh and couldn't stop. Finally, she asked, "Can you just see all those political types, all those D.C. social climbers, going berserk wondering if the new owners will be on their side? Priceless. Kathryn's right, Annie, you are a genius. I'm going to call Jack right now and tell him to start the rumor. Remember now, mum's the word where Charles is concerned. At least for now." She doubled over laughing again as she punched in the numbers to Jack Emery's cell phone.

Chapter 5

Jack Emery looked at the king-size sirloin on his plate and prepared to dig in when his cell phone buzzed. He sawed away, the phone crooked between his ear and shoulder. He stopped what he was doing when he heard Nikki's voice on the other end of the phone. His heart kicked up a beat when he whispered, "Hi."

"I'm in a rush, but I do want to talk to you, but later this evening, okay? Listen, Jack, I want you to do something for us. Us. Spread the rumor if you can, somehow, some way, that the *Post* is being sold. Right now the buyer or buyers prefer to remain anonymous, that kind of thing. Can you pull it off, Jack?"

Jack almost blacked out. His lady love wanted him to do something for her. He didn't stop to think, he just said yes, then he said, "I thought it was going to be something tough like reaching for the moon or the stars." His voice dropped to a mere whisper. "Actually, Robinson is sitting across from me and Harry right now. We're at a new watering hole by the World Bank, named the Fast Track. He and his sidekick Joe Espinosa are with a private dick they hired, Tick Fields. Don't know if you know him or not. Mark Lane, my old buddy from the FBI, called me earlier to tell me Ted and Espinosa hired him but wouldn't tell him why.

Mark does work for Tick from time to time. So, something is up. Can we talk later?"

"After nine will be good. Tell Harry that Yoko will call him at the same time. I love you, Jack, and don't you forget it."

He didn't mean to say the words, preferring to save them for a more intimate time, but they just bubbled up and out of his mouth. "Will you marry me?"

The indrawn breath on the other end of the phone sent a shiver of fear up Jack's spine. Then he heard the words he'd dreamed of all his life. "Damn straight."

Stunned at Nikki's response, Jack snapped the cell shut and stared at Harry. His head bobbed up and down. Harry frowned at the sappy look on his friend's face. "Did you just win the lottery or something?"

Jack blinked. Then blinked again. "Or something. She said yes, Harry. Nik said yes. I want you to be my best man. Will you do it?"

Harry grinned from ear to ear. "As long as I don't have to dude up in one of those monkey suits. And if you pay me. And if you promise to get out of this spy game shit. Yeah, yeah, I can't let you take that walk down the aisle all by yourself. Someone will have to prop you up. Just like that, she said yes?"

"Yeah, do you believe it?"

Harry waved his fork in the air, and said, "Since meeting you, Jack, I believe anything." He waved again to someone he knew. Harry knew everyone. Or, as he put it, everyone worth knowing.

"Hey, she called you. Since she didn't know you were going to propose, she must have called for something else. What?"

Jack shook his head to clear his thoughts. He leaned in closer to Harry and told him what Nikki wanted him to do. "You got a clear shot right now, Jack. They're having coffee, and it looks like they're waiting for the check. Go for it. Make me proud, Jack."

Jack, a wicked gleam in his eye, slid his chair back and walked across a narrow aisle to the booth where Ted and his friends were sipping coffee. "Well, if it isn't Dumb and Dumber. Who's your friend, Ted? Ah, let me guess, Dumbest, right? Listen, I just stopped over to offer my condolences. You guys," he said, pointing to Joe Espinosa and Ted, "will look good in the unemployment line. You sending out your résumés?"

The trio gaped at Jack. Ted finally found his tongue. "What the hell are you talking about, Emery?"

Jack playfully waved his finger. "Well, I guess if the courthouse was being sold, I'd play it cool, too. Then again, the peons are always the last to know. Guess that's why Maggie bailed, huh? How come you didn't see the handwriting on the wall like she did?"

There was an edge to Ted's voice when he said, "I don't know what the hell you're talking about."

"The *Post,* Teddie. It's being sold. New people coming in. New broom sweeps clean. How come you don't know that?"

Espinosa looked sick at what Jack was saying. He really didn't have a beef with Jack other than that Ted hated him. "Where'd you hear that? Who's doing the buying?"

Jack raised his voice several decibels so the other diners could hear him. "It's all over town. I heard it at lunchtime. Some big conglomerate is what I heard, but then I heard it was just some wealthy family in upstate New York. What I heard was it's almost a done deal. The negotiations were and are top secret and have been going on behind closed doors for the past two months. Hey, don't thank me, just too glad to help. You want anyone to lick the envelopes for your résumés, give me a call."

"What the hell did you tell those *schmucks?* They look

green around the gills," Harry said when Jack returned to their table. "Ah, they're leaving. Wow, you really stirred them up. They're tripping over their feet to get out of here."

Jack told him what he'd said verbatim. Harry burst out laughing. "How long before it hits the media?"

"Let me finish this steak, and I'll call Channel 5 and ask if it's true. That should get the ball rolling. So . . . by eleven, I'd say this whole town will be in an uproar. Including the powers that be at the *Post*. The denials will be front-page material for weeks. It will be the lead story on every news channel from here on in. I'm not sure what the girls hope to gain by this. Guess we'll have to wait until we talk to them later. This steak is delicious. If this place can keep it up, you're right, they have a gold mine."

Harry looked at his watch. "Chop-chop, Jack. If I have to drop you off in Georgetown and get back to my own digs, you're going to have to chew a lot faster than you are right now. Otherwise, we're going to miss our phone calls. No time for coffee, either."

Jack gobbled the rest of his food, paid the check, and the two men somehow managed to leave the packed room. A line of people waiting to be seated stretched all the way outside and halfway down the block.

As Harry fired up the Ducati, he mumbled and muttered about never going to the Fast Track again except on off-hours. Jack didn't bother to respond as the wind slapped him in the face. He shifted into a neutral zone and thought about Nikki's response to his proposal. God, he was going to get married. He was going to promise to love, honor, and obey forever more. How it would ever work was beyond him. Somehow. Some way. Because love would conquer all.

*   *   *

The two reporters and the private detective were on foot. They walked in silence until Joe Espinosa spoke, "If Emery is right, it explains Sullivan's pissy attitude of late. Plus, he asked you to clear Maggie's stuff out of the apartment. That can only mean someone important is coming to call. How come we're the last to know?"

"I don't believe it," Ted said. "Emery just wanted to rile us up. And we played right into his hands."

Espinosa jammed his hands into the pockets of his jeans. "To what end, Ted? Think about it. Why would he do something like that? He was too damn gleeful. What do you think, Tick?"

The skinny, stringy-looking detective looked from one reporter to the other before he spoke. "He sounded like he was telling the truth to me. At least the way he heard it. Buyouts are always like this. No one knows till it hits you in the face." Ever the businessman, he said, "You sure you guys can pay me? This could get involved and run up a good-size bill. You want to rethink all of this? It goes without saying, I'll refund your deposit."

"Who the hell would buy the *Post?*" Ted asked, ignoring Fields's comments.

"Someone who doesn't like the owners of the paper. Someone with money to burn. Some asshole, would be my opinion. Like I said, if it's for real, it explains Sullivan's pissy attitude. He's been down on everyone. He wants news! What the hell are we supposed to do when there isn't any news going on?"

"He told me to get creative," Ted said.

"I saw some suits going into his office two days ago. Never saw them around the paper before. Five bucks says Sullivan knows. Call him, Ted," Espinosa said.

"It's almost eight thirty. You want me to call him at home?"

"Well, yeah, if that's where he is. You'll get a feel for whether he's telling you the truth or not."

Ted's stomach muscles curled themselves into a hard knot as he punched in the numbers of Liam Sullivan's home phone. The EIC answered, his voice cold and angry-sounding. He hated to be called at home unless some politician bit the dust in his paramour's arms. "This better be good, Robinson."

Ted didn't mince any words. "How come you didn't tell any of us the paper is being sold? What, we come in one day and turn around and walk out when the new owners tell us our services are no longer needed? Is that the way it's going to go down? Dirty pool, Sullivan." He hated how choked up his voice sounded.

The sudden silence on the other end of the phone bothered Ted. "It would help if you'd say something here, Mr. Sullivan."

"I don't know what you're talking about," Sullivan snarled. "Have you been drinking, Robinson?"

"No, I haven't been drinking. Jack Emery, you know District Attorney Jack Emery, well he just told me he heard the news at noon today. Turn on the news, your secret is out. I expected more from you, Liam. Now what the hell are we supposed to do?"

"What did I tell you to do today, Robinson? This crap was not what I had in mind. Didn't I tell you to go out there and find some news? Aren't you supposed to be working on that and the 'Where are they now?' series you conned me into agreeing to? Stop bothering me with this nonsense."

Ted snapped his cell phone shut. "He acted a little too . . . angry. I think he knows something."

"Ha! I told you. Now what?" Espinosa demanded.

"I'm splitting, guys. My car's on the next block. Call me

if things change," Tick Fields said as he veered off to the right. Both reporters ignored him.

"What should we do, Joe?" Ted asked.

Espinosa shrugged. "What can we do? If you're looking for some instant gratification, we can go home and hit the phones. We can start with all our snitches and see whose ears have picked up what. I have a few favors I can call in. You must have a few yourself, Ted. Worst-case scenario, we turn on the news and wait to see if anyone is talking. What's your gut saying after you talked to Sullivan?"

Ted shrugged. "He sounded surprised and angry. Surprised that I knew? I'm not sure. The thing that bothers me the most is Emery saying Maggie bailed because *she knew what was going down.* I could see Maggie doing that. She always knew everything before it happened. I never could quite figure out how she did that, but damn, she was always on the money."

Espinosa stepped to the curb and hailed a cab. "Call me if you hear anything. I'll do the same." Ted nodded as he walked along. He did some of his best thinking when he was walking. Or pretending to jog. Or running. His feet picked up some speed, then he was running so fast he could barely catch his breath.

Sometimes life just plain sucked.

Ted was almost to his apartment when he remembered he hadn't cleared out Maggie's things. Gasping for breath, he waited for his heartbeat to return to normal. Suddenly, his head jerked upright. If Maggie knew about the possible sale of the paper and was getting out, why didn't she take her belongings to her new job? Assuming there was a new job in the offing. It wasn't computing. Still, if he didn't pick up Maggie's belongings, his ass would be grass with Sullivan.

With that thought hanging over his head, Ted whirled

around and walked to the corner, where he hailed a cab. He gave the driver the address of the *Post*'s apartment. When they arrived, he asked the cabbie to wait, the meter ticking.

Ted jammed things any old way into Maggie's suitcases. It took him three trips to load up the cab.

When all was said and done, Ted had his old girlfriend's belongings stored away in the spare room and was out $70. He made a note to put it on his expense account.

He was so tired he felt like he was going to fall asleep on his feet, but he couldn't give in to the tiredness. He had phone calls to make. Lots and lots of phone calls.

Each call required a different story to the person on the other end of the line. On his ninth call to a senator's aide his eyeballs popped to attention. "Yeah, yeah, I heard something about that earlier this evening," the aide said.

"Who told you?" Ted all but snarled.

"Nobody *told* me. I just overheard a conversation. About an hour ago, as a matter of fact. I thought about you when I heard it, then it just blew out of my mind. You want me to ask around?"

Did he want to perpetuate what he was convinced was a Jack Emery rumor? Not really. "Sure," he said.

Ted bit down on his lower lip. Truth or fiction? He looked at his watch. Five minutes until the eleven o'clock news came on. He used up the five minutes by making a quick trip to the bathroom, where he scared his cats half to death as he barreled into the small bathroom, and then popped a beer from his kitchen on the way back to the living room. If Emery was right, and the media had hold of the story, the possible sale of the *Post* would be the lead for the late-night news.

Ted settled himself in his ratty old Barcalounger, kicked up the footrest, and leaned back, the ice-cold beer in his hand. Feeling like a little kid, he crossed the fingers on his left hand.

Ted ogled the attractive blonde with the flawless skin and expertly made-up eyes and lips. Very kissable. Bedroom eyes. Even so, she couldn't hold a candle to Maggie Spritzer. He listened as the anchor, Sylvia-something-or-other, welcomed all the viewers who stayed up late enough to watch her. Then she moved with expertise to the news at hand.

"While we can't confirm the news I'm about to share with you at this late hour, it is rumored that the *Post* is going on the auction block. We're told—again, this has not been confirmed—that secret negotiations have been under way for the past two months." Ted groaned at the news as Sylvia-something-or-other moved on to a bill that was about to be voted on in the Senate.

"Shit!"

Emery was right!

"Son of a fucking bitch!"

Ted squeezed his eyes shut so he wouldn't cry.

Chapter 6

Charles Martin stared at his computer screen, a frown building between his brows. His stable of retired covert operatives were sending him e-mails at the speed of light. Most were giving him tidbits of information they'd picked up over the past few days in regard to the World Bank and the problems within. All were chomping at the bit to, as Charles put it, get back in the covert game. When it came right down to it, it wasn't what you knew, it was who you knew. Without these old friends willing to stick their necks out, he knew he could never mastermind his operation. He had other powerful help he could call on from time to time, too, but he preferred to deal with people like himself, people who knew how to play the game, when to hold and when to fold.

Even when money was no object, things sometimes couldn't quite come together. Right now he was instant messaging an operative he'd put in charge of securing six black Chevy Suburbans bearing untraceable government license plates with blackened windows and delivering them to the base of Big Pine Mountain. This last incoming message read:

> Only five Suburbans available, plates intact
> as specified. Can deliver all five by sundown.

> Two to mountain base, other three to areas
> as specified.

Charles looked out the window. The sun would be up shortly. He'd been working through the night but now he was seeing results. Going without sleep was one of Charles's strong points. His thoughts raced. Five Suburbans would have to do. That meant Myra and Annie would have to double up, which they would probably prefer anyway. Still, it was a snafu, and if there was one thing he hated, it was a snafu at the beginning of a mission. He typed in a message agreeing to the delivery of the Suburbans.

He then checked in with a second operative he'd put in charge of housing. No snafus there. Charles's fist shot in the air. He stretched his neck left to right, then right to left. Time to take a break. Maybe he'd go over to the kitchen and whip up a special breakfast for the girls.

He loved to cook. One time, and now it seemed a lifetime ago, he'd prepared a special breakfast for his very special dear friend in England. He still smiled when he remembered how she'd shooed out the kitchen staff, who were stunned to even see her anywhere near the kitchen. She'd sipped on tea he'd made for her while he cooked kippers and poached eggs. The two of them had actually sat at the enamel kitchen table like two ordinary people talking about nothing and everything. Just two old friends who would always be friends. The day she'd knighted him she'd winked at him. *Winked.* He'd almost fainted. Of all the people who walked the earth, Lizzie and Myra were the only two people he knew he could count on one hundred percent. He belatedly added Annie to the count.

The starry night greeted Charles when he walked out onto the plank porch. He stopped when he heard a slight rustling to his left. Murphy appeared out of the darkness and nosed his leg. He reached down to scratch the big dog behind his ears. The shepherd whined in pleasure. "Come along, big boy, and I'll make you some breakfast." At the sound of the word "breakfast," Grady, too, walked out of the darkness and waited for his ears to get scratched before he trotted along next to Murphy. Breakfast was always a good treat with Charles mixing real bacon with their dog food.

Charles worked his kitchen duties the way he did everything, with quick, economical moves, no time wasted. Within seconds he had a special banana–macadamia nut pancake mix stirred to perfection and banana syrup warming on the stove. He nuked what Myra termed a ton of bacon and set it aside. Fresh-squeezed orange juice just took minutes and went into the refrigerator to be served ice-cold with crushed ice and a sprig of mint. The last thing he did was to core a melon and slice it. He looked down at the dogs, who were waiting patiently as they sniffed at the bacon aroma wafting toward them.

Charles poured himself a cup of coffee and carried it out to the small deck off the kitchen. He left the door open so the dogs could join him when they finished eating.

This was his favorite time of the day, right before the sun came up, when it was still dark and mysterious. This was when he thought about the new day, with all its possibilities and problems.

Here, alone in the darkness, he could admit to himself that he had qualms about sending the girls back to the Nation's Capital. He also had qualms about taking on the prestigious World Bank. There were just so many things that could go wrong, no matter how many good people he had in place to head off problems. He still cringed each time he thought about the hair-raising experience of his ladies getting caught and hauled off to jail. He never wanted that to happen again.

He ran each step of his plan over in his mind. On the

face of it, it seemed foolproof but he knew there was no such thing. The human element always managed to creep in somehow, some way. All he could do was his best and hope his girls would follow through.

When he got to that point, Charles thought about money and how much of it Myra and Annie contributed. All in the name of justice. He thanked God for Myra and Annie's robust contributions to the Sisterhood cause. This little gig, as Kathryn called it, was going to net them ten million dollars, not that they would ever see a penny of it, and that was all right, too. His chest puffed out a little, knowing his girls were worth every penny of it. He remembered how he'd felt when they announced that every last penny was to go to worthy causes. They made him so proud. He made a mental note to call his royal friend on the other side of the pond to let her know. The last time they'd spoken, she said hearing about the girls was better than reading a mystery story. He'd willingly given his word to update her weekly. And, she always had one little bit of advice to offer at the end of the conversation.

Charles finished the last of the coffee in his cup and walked back to the kitchen just as the first streaks of dawn appeared on the horizon. The girls would be entering the dining hall any minute.

It was like every other breakfast Charles cooked for his little family. The talk that morning was all about Nikki's proposal and the glow she was exuding. Charles smiled to himself as he imagined Myra and Annie trying to figure out what kind of wedding they could pull off on top of a mountain. He just knew it would be a formal affair. If indeed it ever came into being. He felt sad at the thought that it might not work out the way Nikki and Jack wanted.

"Talk to us, Charles," Kathryn said, when the table was cleared and fresh coffee poured.

Charles looked around the table at the expectant faces staring at him. He knew they hated it when he made them wait for finalized details. "All I'm going to tell you right at this moment is your ETD is tomorrow at sundown. I'll have more details for you at lunchtime. Nikki, I want you to monitor the computer for e-mails. If one comes through from Avery Cromwell, wake me. I'm going to try to catch a few winks, since I was up all night. Talk among yourselves and decide what sort of disguise you will be comfortable with to invade the Nation's Capital. 'Normal' is the key word here. Alexis will accommodate all of you.

"Lunch is whatever you come up with. Dinner this evening will be a pot roast with mashed potatoes and whatever vegetables are ripe in the garden. And, of course, they have to be picked and cleaned."

Isabelle threw her napkin at Charles as he left the dining room.

"Let's have another cup of coffee so we can talk our departure to death," Annie said as she bustled over to the sideboard and the huge coffee machine. When she returned to the table, she said, "We need to talk about how we're going to invade Mr. Zenowicz's space."

From that point on, the women were off and running, ideas flowing at the speed of light, either to be voted on or vetoed. At the end of the lively discussion, the women burst out laughing when Annie came up with what they thought was the ideal punishment for one Maxwell Zenowicz.

"Now we have to concentrate on Miss Rena Gold. We can't let her walk off into the sunset, now, can we?" Isabelle asked. "And," she said, wagging a finger, "we need to know who corrupted whom. Do we know if Zenowicz started pilfering before or after he met Rena Gold?"

"Good question, Isabelle. We'll ask Charles at lunchtime," Nikki said. "Let's do some serious computer time. I say we invade Charles's lair and see if we can put names to our new employers. I always like to know who's paying the bill."

The moment the words were out of Nikki's mouth, the women were on their feet and headed for Charles's computer room.

"You know what else?" Nikki asked, as they walked across the compound in the bright summer sunshine. "That's pure bullshit about not involving them just because they're paying us. Do they think we're stupid? We go down, they go down. That's the bottom line. I'd also like to know which wealthy individuals are donating that ten million. I bet we'd all be surprised. It's coming from inside the Beltway is what I'm thinking. The US wants to be top dog where the World Bank is concerned. But, that's just my opinion."

"I think you're right," Myra and Annie said in unison. "Let's check it out," Myra said. "Everyone in Washington has their own agenda. We just have to find what those agendas are."

"What we should have done and didn't do was get fingerprints off the dishes. I wonder if Charles did that and didn't tell us. See, we messed up, and we haven't even started yet," Kathryn said three hours later, when Nikki came up dry on the computer. "But I have an idea. Alexis, can you sketch pictures of our new employers from memory? Then maybe Nikki can scan them and see if anything pops up."

Alexis nodded and reached for paper and pen.

"I don't think the people who came here are our actual employers. I think they were emissaries of the big shots. People like them are never seen because they prefer to remain in the shadows and let others do their dirty work," Yoko said.

"I agree," Kathryn said. She peered over Isabelle's shoulder to see how Alexis was doing with her first character sketch. "That's it, Alexis! You caught the weasel look. Ooh, it's just too perfect."

Alexis handed the dark-lined sketch to Nikki, who immediately put it into the scanner and started typing. Alexis was already on her second sketch, her pen making clear, sharp lines on the stark white paper.

"I'm not really clear on why we're doing this," Annie said. "Even if we get a name to match the face, what are we going to do with that information? Are we going to go after the hand that is feeding us? I just want to make sure I understand, since our trip to Washington is going to be time-sensitive."

Nikki frowned, and the others looked at Annie in surprise. She threw her hands in the air. "What? Was that a stupid question?" The others, Annie included, looked to Nikki.

"No, it's not a stupid question at all. Charles had the cameras on in the conference room. I'm sure our guests didn't realize it, but that's not our problem. These people will lead us, if we decide we need to know, to whoever wrote the checks for our ten million dollars. I thought we were clear on that. Look, I think we're all a little intimidated here because we're taking on the awesome World Bank and the people involved. We all need to change our mind-sets here, myself included. If we're intimidated, this mission is not going to work. It's just another mission, our tenth. That's how we have to look at it. Look at us, we're already spinning our wheels."

The women whirled around when they heard the sound of hands clapping. Charles stood in the open doorway. "All you had to do was ask me. I have our guests on video. I have their fingerprints on file. I know exactly who visited us on our mountain the other night. I know whom they represent. I've been waiting for you to ask me. This is a team effort, in case you've forgotten. When you leave the mountain tomorrow all that information will be at your fingertips. A word of advice: tread cautiously where these people are concerned. They have far-reaching arms and unbelievable power."

Kathryn openly bristled. "What's the worst thing they could do to us? Blow up this mountain?"

"There is that possibility," Charles said quietly. "Even though I, as well as the pilot, took precautions, there is every possibility our guests figured out our location. Like I said, tread lightly, ladies. You're dismissed now. Thank you for your artistic efforts, Alexis."

The women trooped out of the computer room, each busy with her own thoughts.

"It's lunchtime, let's all do it together," Myra said. "Something light, a chicken salad and some fruit. It will keep our minds busy."

While the women set about the tasks Myra assigned them, they kept up a running dialogue with each other, calling back and forth. Again, it was Annie who summed it all up, to their surprise.

"Don't you see what we've been trying to do? The other night when we took it upon ourselves to . . . uh . . . take out Charles and show our guests we were in charge—we were undermining him. That was the start. We think we're capable of running this mission on our own, and that simply is not true. And we all know it. So, that raises the question of why we're all feeling like we suddenly want control. Is it that we no longer trust Charles? I'm sorry, Myra, if that hurts your feelings, but I think we need to air all of this right now before things get out of hand. One at a time, voice whatever is on your mind. I'm also allowing for cabin fever, but I don't think that's our problem. One last thing, it was *NOT* Charles's fault that we got caught and are now fugitives. The blame for our capture rests solely with Ted Robinson and Maggie Spritzer. I like things clear in my own mind, so I am assuming you are all the same way. Now, goddamn it, spit out whatever it is that's bothering you."

Myra clapped her hands in approval. "I couldn't have said it better, Annie." The others looked sheepish.

In the end, when the women sat down at the table with their salads, the words flowed like wine. When they were finished, Myra summed it up succinctly by saying, "So, it's a combination of cabin fever, being fugitives, suddenly becoming guns for hire, and missing life in the fast lane that is bothering everyone. Correct me if I'm wrong." There was a bite to Myra's voice the others had never heard before.

"You're not wrong, Myra. It's just . . . What I mean is . . . No matter how I say this, it's going to come out wrong. So, speaking strictly for myself, it's easier to blame someone else rather than own up to my own shortcomings. I don't know what we were trying to prove the other night. Maybe that we're equals? I just don't know. I'm over it now. Charles is the boss as far as I'm concerned. I trust him with my life." Kathryn looked around at the others to see if they agreed with her. When she saw them nod she smiled. "Okay, we're back on track. We'll kick ass and take names later."

Annie put her fingers under her tongue and whistled the way Kathryn taught her. "I so love it when we're all on the same page. Now, let's get down to business."

"After we eat," Kathryn said as she slipped Murphy a strip of chicken from her salad. "You know Charles; we don't discuss business while we eat."

"Amen," Annie said.

Chapter 7

"**D**amn it, Harry, if you don't stop that crazy pacing, I'm going to deck you. It's too early to be in such a frenzy. The girls won't be here till around midnight, so cool it," Jack Emery said as he finished his early-morning workout.

"Easy for you to say. Admit it, Jack, you thrive on this shit, and we both know it. The crazier the scheme, the more dangerous, the better you like it. I come from a peaceful, gentle nation of people who don't do this kind of stuff."

Jack wiped at his brow with a snow-white towel. "You're screwing with me, right, Harry? You, who can kill with one finger. You, who breaks bones the way other people break pretzels. And you damn well fucking get paid for doing it by the police department. I think you need a refresher course in that Zen crap you practice every day. Kick back and relax. Listen, I have to get to work. I need to be in court at nine o'clock for a hearing. Some asshole from the Prizzi law firm has filed a motion to dismiss the case against his client on the grounds that said client was not properly Mirandized. If you have time, see if you can find out anything on Ted and his friends. Call me on my cell if anything pops up. And, if you feel like checking out the Fast Track, give it a go."

"Yeah, sure. You want me to pick up your dry cleaning or maybe do your grocery shopping while I'm at it?"

"Wiseass!" Jack threw the towel at him as he marched off to the shower. He was just as antsy as Harry, but he'd never let him know it. What the hell was Charles thinking to take on the World Bank? There was daring, and then there was *daring*. Thumbing one's nose at the FBI and every other law enforcement agency in Alphabet City, also known as the Nation's Capital, could only wreak havoc. His stomach continued to churn as he stepped out of the shower and dressed for the day.

As he shaved, Jack stared at himself in the mirror. He didn't like the worry he was seeing in his eyes. All those other times he'd been nervous but confident the Sisters could pull off their gig with him, Harry, and the others working in the background. This deal was no different, people, things, were in place, according to Charles. So what makes this time so different? he asked himself. Was it because he had finally asked Nikki to marry him, and she'd said yes? Was he afraid something was going to wreck those plans? Or was it the deep hatred he'd seen in Ted Robinson's eyes? Probably all of the above.

Jack wiped his face clean, then patted on some after-shave, a gift from Nikki, who said the scent made her think of wild, wicked things. Oh, yeah.

Harry poked his head into the lavatory, and said, "The newspeople are really running with that rumor you planted. Sullivan is protesting all over the place saying rival papers started the rumor. He's looking worse and worse with each interview he gives. And it's not even twenty-four hours since you started it. You have no idea how impressed I am with your abilities."

Jack patted his cheeks again to take the sting out. "You

know this town, it feeds on stuff like this. Do you think Robinson went underground? If so, he should be poking that ugly head of his up pretty soon to sniff the air. We need to give him another jolt. Think of something, Harry. I gotta go."

"Think of something, Harry," Harry mimicked his friend. "Up yours, Jack," he said, stomping off.

Jack laughed as he walked out of the *dojo* to the curb to hail a cab.

With no martial-arts training class with the new police recruits until ten thirty, Harry gathered his gear and locked up the *dojo*. He fired up the Ducati and streaked out to the road, where he headed for the *Post*.

Twenty minutes later, Harry parked his motorcycle and walked into the *Post* building. Normally, he called in his ads for the *dojo,* but sometimes, if he was in the neighbor-hood, he stopped to do it in person. He looked around to see if maybe he'd get lucky and see either Robinson or Espinosa. No such luck, so he took the elevator to the fifth floor and headed for the classified desk.

A fresh young thing with hair down to her buttocks looked up and waited expectantly.

"It's almost time to renew my ad, which, by the way, is a full half page for the coming year. I heard on the news that the *Post* is being sold, so I'm a little apprehensive about renewing. Thirty thousand dollars is a lot of money, and if you're being sold, I might want to rethink my options here."

The fresh young thing bristled. "It simply isn't true. I don't know how rumors like that get started. Tons of people have been calling in saying the same thing. It's shameless the way people do things these days. It's so unfair." She twinkled at Harry to make her point.

"Well, if that's true, why are your star reporters sending

out résumés? I was in the Squire's Pub and overheard two of your people saying they had sent out résumés to every paper within a two-hundred-mile radius. That doesn't sound like a rumor. Listen, you have to understand, thirty thousand dollars is a fortune to me."

"Who?" the young thing yelped. "Who did you overhear saying they were sending out résumés? Mr. Sullivan is going to be livid. He's doing his best with damage control, but the media won't leave it alone. Read my lips, sir, the *Post*-is-not-being-sold."

"Your turn. Read my lips. You're at the bottom of the totem pole. You will be one of the first to get a pink slip. No one, me included, is going to advertise in this paper. I'll take my thirty thousand dollars somewhere else." Harry liked the way his tone was just a tad more belligerent than the young girl's.

"Who? Just tell me who is sending out résumés." The young thing all but stamped her foot in frustration.

"Okay, okay, but you didn't hear it from me. Robinson and Espinosa are the ones. They said Maggie Spritzer saw the handwriting on the wall, excuse the cliché, and bailed out months ago. They also mentioned a guy named Sal Logan. I think he does the sports. I still have two months to go on my subscription, so I think I'll wait it out. You really should turn on your TV if you have one and see for yourself what they're saying in regard to the paper. People who protest too much are usually lying." Trying to look disgusted, Harry muttered something about not trusting anyone these days.

The young thing finally stamped her foot as she whirled around to speak with a coworker who had been watching them and listening to their dialogue.

Harry dusted his hands together as he rode down in the elevator. "My work here is done," he said to no one in particular. He knew Jack would be more than pleased when he reported in on his visit to the *Post*.

Harry looked at his watch and listened to his stomach for a moment. Time for breakfast. He looked around, noticed a coffee shop on the ground floor that said they served two eggs, bacon, toast, and coffee for $3.99. He hopped to it and was just being served when he felt someone jar his elbow. He looked up, his expression bland. "Good morning, Mr. Robinson. Care to join me?"

"I'd sooner eat with the Devil. You're a long way from that house of evil you hang out in. This is my turf you're invading. What the hell are you doing here, Wong?"

Harry looked around to see how much of a ruckus it would cause if he laid Robinson out cold. He nixed the idea when he saw a group of people walk into the empty coffee shop. "Well, I was going to have some breakfast, but now that I've seen you, my gastric juices are curdling. Keep your ink dry, *Kemosabe*. I don't even want to breathe the same air you do." He pushed his plate away and slapped some bills down on the table.

"Asshole!" Ted said, his middle finger shooting up in the air. Harry laughed as he made his way to the door.

The minute Harry Wong was out the door, Ted opened his cell phone. "Joe, guess who was just here in the coffee shop?" Not bothering to wait for his colleague to respond, he said, "Harry Wong. How do I know what that jerk was doing here? He was in the coffee shop in the lobby. Yeah, yeah, that's where I am now. I just stopped in for a bagel and coffee. You been watching the news?" Ted listened for a few minutes. "You know what? I've known Sullivan for years, and he looked guilty as shit when he gave the latest interview. He looked to me like he was lying. That's just my opinion. What the hell can we do? We have to wait it out. Right now I have to figure out what Wong was doing here. The *Post* is not exactly around the corner from his place. It's not like he walked out his door to get some breakfast. He had to come all the way here, so that has to mean something. Yeah, yeah, when I figure it out, I'll let you know." He listened again, then said, "Something's up, that's for sure."

Ted snapped his cell phone shut, paid for his bagel and coffee, and loped over to the elevator. He wished to hell he knew what was going on.

Jack walked out of the courthouse, then backed up. It was pouring rain, and here he was with no umbrella and wearing his best suit. Not to mention his new shoes. Maybe it was just a summer shower, and he could wait it out. He fired up a cigarette, aware that he was not the requisite twenty feet from the entrance. Like he cared. He didn't give a shit about anything.

A voice behind him said, almost in his ear, "I thought guys like you were always prepared. You know, for rain, sleet, snow, that kind of crap. By the way, just for the record, I could arrest you for smoking this close to the entrance," Bert Navarro said as he fired up a cigarette of his own.

Jack whirled around and stepped away. "Bert!" He looked around, right to left to see if anyone was listening to their conversation. "I was hoping you were in on this gig. You want to share info? Assuming there's info to share."

"Sure, but not here. Let's grab a cab."

"What are you, some kind of comedian? You can't get a cab in this city in the rain. This is my best suit, and I love these shoes."

"Watch this!"

Jack watched the FBI agent walk to the curb holding an umbrella. He held out something in his hand and a cab rolled to the curb. He opened the door, then walked back to where Jack was standing and motioned him under the umbrella. Jack started to laugh and couldn't stop. He loved this guy. Loved his chutzpah and the shield he carried. Loved the way he stepped up to the plate and used his shield and didn't think twice about looking the other way so the Sisters could mete out their own brand of justice. Yessiree, he loved this guy, and he sure as hell loved his umbrella.

Bert got right to the point the minute he settled himself and Jack gave the driver his address in Georgetown. "So, tell me stuff about Kathryn."

Jack eyed the cab driver but responded anyway. "You getting all warm and fuzzy thinking about her?"

"Hell, no. I'm getting hot and bothered thinking about her. I break out in a cold sweat every time she pops into my mind, which is all the time."

Jack smothered a laugh. "Did you tell her that?"

"You insane, Jack? Aren't you the one who said to play it cool? If I play it any cooler, I'm going to freeze my nuts off, and where will that leave me? Come on, has she said anything about me?"

An evil devil perched itself on Jack's shoulder. Time to have some fun with old Bert. "My girl," he said, opting not to use Nikki's name since the cab driver looked like he was all ears, "said that she moons about you. That means she's a daydreamer. She's been asking for advice from the girls. So, scratch whatever I told you. You don't have a prayer if the others are feeding her advice. Just roll with it and hope for the best. I'll say one thing, that one is all woman. Maybe more than you can handle, Bert," Jack said slyly.

The handsome agent looked over at Jack. He let loose with a crooked grin and laughed outright. "In your dreams, Jack. Did you ever hear of a special agent that couldn't handle any situation thrown at him?"

It was Jack's turn to laugh. "The manual doesn't say

anything about a posse of women giving advice in the *amour* department."

"So, you think I might have a problem?" the agent asked fretfully.

Jack laughed again. "Yeah, a big problem."

Both men drew into themselves and watched the driving rain out the side windows. When the cab pulled to the curb outside Jack's Georgetown house, Bert paid, got out first, and opened the umbrella. Both men raced across the sidewalk and up the steps. Minutes later they were inside. They removed their jackets and hung them up. Jack headed for the kitchen, where he popped two longnecks of Budweiser and handed one to Bert.

They walked into the living room and sat down. "Okay, tell me what you know, Bert, and I'll tell you what I know."

"I know that there was a problem with the Suburbans. They were one short, but Charles said Myra and Annie would double up. Personally speaking, I think that's a good idea anyway. We managed to get government plates that haven't been previously issued. There are two spare sets that will be changed at different times. We're good to go on that."

"They're leaving at sundown and will drive through the evening," Jack replied. "Charles said their departures would be staggered. I'm waiting for him to get back to me with their final destination. I'm assuming it's a safe house somewhere in the District, but I'm not sure. For all I know it could be this very house. Charles's theory at times is if you put it out there in someone's face, they don't see it because it's too obvious. This is Nikki's house, in case you don't know. When . . . when they got caught, she did a quit claim deed. One of the women in her old law firm backdated it, so it all worked out."

"They should be here around midnight then, right?"

"Yeah, I think so. Unless something goes wrong. Nikki

called yesterday and wanted me to start the rumor that the *Post* was going to be bought up by some nameless person. I did it, and it's been the lead story on every news channel."

"Why?" Bert asked.

Jack shrugged. "Red herring I guess. My old buddy, Mark Lane, you know him, called me yesterday and said Robinson and Espinosa hired Tick Fields. We don't know why. But ask yourself why two *Post* reporters would pool their money and hire a private dick like Tick Fields. What are they up to? Does it involve the girls? Is he privy to something we don't know about? You know this whole gig this time around involves the World Bank. Wong and I went to this watering hole called the Fast Track, which is right next to the World Bank, to grab a bite to eat and to check it out. And who else is there but Robinson, Espinosa, and Fields? My antenna went up, and so did Wong's. I know there are no leaks on our end. Reporters have sources, as you know. Robinson could have blundered onto something without realizing the Sisters set it up as their next mission. Coincidental? Your guess is as good as mine."

The doorbell took that moment to ring. Jack and Bert looked at one another.

"You expecting company, Jack?" Bert asked, his hand reaching around back to where he kept his gun.

"No. Stay out of sight but close, okay?" Jack asked as he peered out the peephole in the front door. "It's Harry!" He opened the door and waited while his friend shed his rain gear and removed his sodden sandals.

"I wouldn't be standing here soaking wet if you'd answer your damn cell phone," Harry snarled.

"Ah, shit, Harry, I'm sorry. I have to turn my cell off in court. When I was leaving, I met up with Bert and forgot to turn it back on. Come on in. If you strip down, I'll put your clothes in the dryer. Want a beer?"

"Hell yes, I want a beer. I'm okay clotheswise. The slicker covered me. What's going on?"

Jack briefed him, with Bert adding what he knew. Then it was Harry's turn, and he explained about his meeting with Robinson and the story he'd planted with the young thing in the classified office.

Jack turned his cell phone on while Bert offered to get beer refills. Two missed calls. One from Nikki and one from Charles. He listened to the one from Nikki that was purely social, saying she was counting the hours and minutes until she saw him. He saved the message so he could play it over and over at a later time. The call from Charles on the encrypted phone simply gave an address that Jack scribbled on the palm of his hand. When he clicked off the phone, he held up his palm so Bert and Harry could see what he'd written. "It rings a bell. You guys familiar with it?"

Bert grinned. "Oh, yeah."

"Well?" Jack snapped.

"It's the British Embassy. It was on the news this morning. Seems the premises suddenly became overrun with vermin. It's going to be closed for two weeks. Exterminators will be going in and out trying to control the situation."

All Jack and Harry could do was gape at the FBI agent. "How in the hell did he pull that off?" Jack asked, his voice full of awe. When there was no response, he shrugged.

"So, does that mean the girls will be ditching the Suburbans to pick up exterminator trucks?" Harry asked, his voice just as shocked as Jack's.

Bert laughed. "That would be my take on it. That guy Charles has a brass set, I'll give him that. I think this calls for another round!"

Chapter 8

The mood in the newsroom of the *Post* was sullen at best. Reporters sat with their heads down as they pecked away at their keyboards. Half the cubicles were empty, an indication colleagues were out beating the bushes in hopes of landing a job with security.

Liam Sullivan stomped his way down the corridor to the newsroom, where he took in the scene at a glance. He bellowed at the top of his lungs. "Listen up, people, this goddamn paper is not on the auction block. This is the last time I'm going to tell you that. Now, if you don't like it, don't believe me, pack your shit and walk out the door." To his surprise his top sportswriter and the columnist for the Sunday Home & Garden section got up and left. Neither said good-bye, and neither looked back.

Ted Robinson raised his head and looked directly at Sullivan, daring him to say something, which he did.

"So, what's going on with your mystery series?" Sullivan snarled.

Ted snorted. There was no reason to lie, so he didn't. "We're coming up with dead ends. I want to continue working it if that's okay. I have people on it."

"Well, until you come up with something, here's an assignment for you. Get your ass over to the British Embassy and see what they're defining as vermin. To me vermin means rats. The people in this town want to know all about it, so we can have some major hysteria at 3100 Massachusetts Avenue. I want full details. Like where is the staff staying, who moved them out, all of the etceteras. Housing two hundred fifty diplomats and six hundred staffers has to present major problems. Get some interviews, see who is pissed off and who isn't. See if you can get some pictures of the pesky little devils while you're at it, the vermin, not the staff. Be sure to get a picture of the Churchill statue. Most people don't know that one of Churchill's feet is inside the embassy and the other outside in the District of Columbia. Work in a history lesson. Play up Embassy Row and how the Brits were the first to build an embassy and that's how Massachusetts Avenue got the name Embassy Row. You should be able to get a couple of days' news out of it. You're still sitting here, Robinson."

Rats. Vermin. This was what he'd been reduced to. Seething inside, Ted grabbed his backpack and headed for the main corridor that would take him to the elevator. "Shit!" he said succinctly as he jabbed at the button on the wall.

Ted's cell phone rang just as he exited the building. He moved away from the pedestrians and leaned against the wall. "Whatcha got, Tick? Tell me you found something. Sullivan is ragging my ass, and I'm on my way over to the British Embassy to check out the vermin problem." He listened to the voice on the other end of the wire, his mood darkening by the second. "Nobody drops off the face of the earth without leaving some kind of clue. When five people disappear at the same time, there has to be a reason. Yeah, yeah, you keep telling me about the Privacy Act. We both know there are ways around that, so earn the goddamn money I paid you and come up with something. Dig deeper, Tick." Ted listened again, then sputtered some more when he asked, "What do you mean, where am I? What difference does it make where I am? You can reach either me or Joe 24/7 on our cells, but if you really need to know, I'm on my way to the British Embassy to take some pictures of rats and of the Winston Churchill statue." The sound of strangled laughter forced him to snap the phone shut but not before he heard the words, "Oh how the mighty have fallen."

And it was true. This was a shit detail if ever there was one. At least Joe lucked out with the sports beat, not that he knew anything about sports. Christ, what was the *Post* coming to these days? He'd give everything he owned to know if the paper was being sold or not. He felt like crossing his fingers the way he had when he was a kid and making three wishes. What the hell would he wish for? In the order of importance of course. For Maggie to return. For the rumor to be proven false. For Jack Emery to fall down a deep, dark hole that he couldn't get out of—along with all the members of the Sisterhood. Maybe that was three and a half or maybe even four wishes. Like he had a snowball's chance in hell of any of them coming true.

Ted planned to walk to the British Embassy for two reasons: to delay the inevitable and to get some exercise at the same time. The minute he felt the first raindrop, he headed to the curb to hail a taxi. Screw the exercise. Screw the rats. Screw Liam Sullivan and the frigging *Post*.

"I know you, you're that reporter for the *Post*," the driver said the minute Ted settled himself and strapped on his seat belt. "That's a hell of a thing about the *Post* being sold. What's this world coming to? I heard some Chinese group is buying it."

Christ. "Who told you it was the Chinese?"

"Two fares ago. The guy was all spit and polish, slicked-back hair, expensive threads. Seemed to know what he was talking about." The driver tilted his head back, giving the impression he was about to impart a secret. "The guy said he thought somehow the Saudis were behind it because they have so much money in our banks. What do you think of that, Mister Reporter?"

"I think it sucks," Ted said.

"Yeah, that's what my wife said when I called her to tell her. She's really up on the politics of this town. She used to work for a congressman, and she said he was a nutcase and his staff did all the work and all he did was go to lunch."

"Sounds about right to me," Ted said.

The rest of the trip was made in silence as the driver and passenger contemplated each other's words. When the driver pulled to the curb, Ted gave him an outrageous tip, knowing full well he'd have to go to the mat with Sullivan when he turned in his expense account. Like he gave a shit one way or the other.

Ted stood on the curb gazing up at the impressive-looking building known as the British Embassy. Just for a moment he felt a little in awe of the structure. He'd been here in July of 2005, when the U.S. Army band played "God Save The Queen" outside the embassy in remembrance of the victims of the London bombings on July 7, 2005. He remembered how choked up he was. When he'd written his account of the event, he made sure to let his readers know about the British remembrance service for the attack on September 11, 2001, when the American National Anthem was played outside Buckingham Palace. There weren't many dry eyes that day.

And now, here he was three years later, getting ready to take pictures of some rats. Sometimes, life just wasn't fair.

It took only fifteen minutes to realize he wasn't going to get inside to take any pictures at all. The place was tight as a drum. No sign of life at all. Yellow crime-scene tape was stretched across the front door. Huh? Ted shrugged. Rats must be considered criminals in the minds of the Brits.

Now what the hell was he supposed to do? What any good reporter would do who was soaking wet and had an aversion to all vermin: lunch and a call to his boss.

Liam Sullivan's voice almost blasted his eardrums. "You're supposed to be a goddamn reporter, Robinson. Figure out something. Or, how's this for a clever idea? The embassy operates consulates general in Atlanta, Boston, Chicago, Houston, Los Angeles, New York, Dallas, Denver, Miami, Seattle, and San Francisco. Maybe they can help you."

Ted's jaw dropped. "How do you know that? How do you have that information on the tip of your tongue?" His voice was full of awe at the EIC's monologue.

"I heard it on the goddamn news this morning, that's how."

Ted clamped his mouth shut, then opened it again. "There's no sign of life, Chief. No exterminator trucks or anything like that. There should be somebody here. It doesn't make sense. I think there's something fishy going on."

"Look numbnuts, they're probably taking bids on the job. It's a big place and it's going to be an expensive job and they want the most bang for their buck. The Brits never act in haste. You could try some of the other embassies to see if they have a similar problem. Stake it out, Robinson. Why the hell am I telling you how to do your job, anyway?" the EIC snarled again.

"Because you love me?" Not waiting for a reply and knowing he was pushing his luck, Ted closed his cell phone with a snap before he sauntered around the corner in the hopes of finding someplace to eat. He found a place called Ellie's Eatery and walked into a jam-packed shop with people waiting in line for take-out. While he waited for his turn and a table in the crowded room, he let his mind race. Rats. Exterminators. Almost a thousand people displaced by vermin. How strange was that? Surely the staff just didn't walk in one morning and see hundreds of rats? Wouldn't it have been a gradual process that would have been taken care of at the first sign of one of the creatures, especially since half the staff was female? He didn't know why, but his reporter's gut instinct was telling him there was something weird about the whole rat thing.

Something really weird.

The late-afternoon sunshine bathed the women in its warm glow as they waited for the cable car that would take them to the bottom of Big Pine Mountain. Charles stood off to the side talking to Myra and Annie, who were decked out in flashy tourist clothes. Outward appearances for this mission, according to Charles, were important.

They all watched as the huge cable car slid into its berth. Kathryn stepped in, a small folder tucked under her Windbreaker. She would take the lead Suburban, drive it as far as Fairfax, Virginia, where she would stop at a motel/gas station and trade in her Suburban for an Econoline Van belonging to a newly established exterminating company located in Reston, Virginia. By the time she put the Suburban in gear and the cable car was back on top of the mountain, she would be ten miles down the road. The other departures would be staggered so that their arrivals did not coincide. Each of the Suburbans would be swapped out at various locations either at the North Carolina border or in Virginia. Charles's last order was that they were to call one another in teams and leave their cell phones on in case anything went awry. Kathryn was hooked to Isabelle, Yoko to Annie, Alexis to Nikki. Myra was locked in to Charles, as she and Annie would be the last ones to leave the mountain. According to Charles, it was a spiffy plan.

The departure took a full hour before Charles was left standing alone with the two dogs for company. Both animals whined and ignored the man who controlled the cable car. "Come along, boys, and I'll fix us all a big steak. With all the fixin's, as Kathryn puts it."

The dogs' ears perked up as they trotted behind the only person left who would throw a stick, feed them, and even tussle with them if time permitted.

Charles loved to cook—the more exotic the recipe, the better he liked it. But he was also a meat-and-potatoes man at times. This was one of those times. He could feel his tongue start to water at the thought of the Kobe steaks Pappy had left in the freezer for him. Meat that cooked up so tender you could cut it with a fork. A little peppercorn marinade, a few minutes on the grill, and served with a mango-avocado salsa. A nice summer salad with chunky blue cheese and a few dinner rolls from the freezer, and the three of them would be good to go.

Surely he would get to eat his dinner in peace. Surely nothing would crop up that needed his attention before tomorrow. The plan as far as he could tell was absolutely foolproof. But in the back of his mind he was apprehensive. He knew only too well how Murphy's Law went. What could go wrong, would go wrong.

Charles placed the cell phone on the counter as he set to work to prepare his and the dogs' dinner. Things went smoothly for the next four hours. He was actually dozing in his chair while a game show he'd never seen before played out for the dogs' benefit. His second cell phone was vibrating in his pocket. He pulled it out and looked down at it. His heart kicked up a beat when he clicked it open and brought it to his ear.

* * *

Hundreds of miles away, Kathryn Lucas pulled into a seedy-looking motel and drove to the back end of the empty parking lot. It was almost midnight, and only one lone light shone down. She got out of the Suburban, announcing her intentions to Isabelle, who was not yet at her own destination. Kathryn giggled when she heard her fellow Sister say, "That's a ten-four, over and out. I still have forty miles to go. Talk later."

Kathryn walked into the dingy motel office and tapped the bell on the counter. She heard movement from the room behind the front desk as someone walked across a wooden floor. She looked up and froze, her eyes almost popping out of her head. The man coming toward her was as big as a grizzly bear and looked it, too.

"Big Sis!"

"Joe!"

They stared at one another, both suddenly speechless.

Kathryn panicked, hoping Isabelle was listening. "Listen, Joe . . ."

The big man put his finger to his lips. "Shhh, Cass and I are on your side. We saw the way it went down. You don't owe me an explanation, and I don't want to hear one if you're thinking of offering one. No one is here, Sis. You're safe, if that's what you're worried about."

Kathryn closed her eyes for a second until the panic washed away. "You're the last person I expected to see here today, Joe. How's Cass? Is this your place?"

"Cass is fine since she got her new hip. I wish I was someplace else myself, but I'm stuck with this dump. Me and Cass, we made a bad decision, but at the time we made it, it seemed right. We sold our truck stop and moved here to be closer to the kids. We made enough money to pay cash for this place, but as you can see, who in their right mind would want to stop here? We had great plans, but Angie's husband left her with three kids, so we had to pick up that slack. Joe Jr. fell from a roofing job he was on and was laid up for almost two years. We had to take on his family, too. Cass can't do much yet, but she's improving every day. We won't have to worry about this place much longer. We owe so many bills we could wallpaper this whole place. Got liens out the kazoo. Now, enough about me. C'mere, give me a big hug and tell me what the hell you're doing here. No, no, don't tell me that. Are you by any chance the one supposed to be picking up that white van some guy in dark glasses dropped off today?"

"Yeah, I'm that person. Listen, Joe, about . . ."

"No, you listen, Sis," he said, calling Kathryn by her old trucking handle of Big Sis. "I don't care about none of that. I'm just so damn glad to see you and know you're all right. Cass is never going to believe this. Can you wait a minute for me to wake her up? She'll kick me all the way to the Maryland border if you go out of here without saying hello."

Kathryn nodded as her mind raced. "Joe, do you have a computer I could use?"

"You know it. It's all I have going on. Day in, day out. Cass does a knitting class three days a week on it. Seems like playing on that damn thing is our life these days."

"Do you bank online?"

"Yeah, actually I was just doing that when you walked in. I hate doing it during the day because it seems worse in broad daylight. Nighttime it's still grim, but at least I can handle it. Go ahead, just X me out and do what you gotta do. I'll go get Cass. Give me a few minutes. You know, Cass, she'll want to pretty up a bit. Jesus, it's good to see you, Sis."

"You, too, Joe. Listen, I don't have much time. I'm on a real tight schedule."

"Gotcha. Help yourself to the computer."

Kathryn walked over to the computer and looked at the

screen. She felt sick at what she saw. "Isabelle, click off. I'm sure you heard the conversation. I have to do something about Joe and Cass."

"I hear you, Kathryn. Go for it. I'm reading your mind." A second later the line was free, and Kathryn was talking to Charles.

"Charles, I only have a minute so listen to me because I don't have the time to repeat anything. Copy down this bank account number." Kathryn rattled it off, then said, "I want you to transfer a hundred thousand dollars into this account. No, make that two hundred thousand. These people who own the motel used to own a truck stop where I stopped on a weekly basis. They recognized me. They're good people, Charles, and they've had a bit of bad luck. Take it off the top of the emergency fund."

"That's impossible, Kathryn, there is no time to be doing something like this. I'm sorry."

"You *will* do it, Charles, and you will hit those keys right now. I'm not leaving here until I see that money in their account. And by the way, the Suburban stays here, too, minus the plates. I'll take them with me. Now means *now*, Charles."

"Kathryn . . ."

"I said now. I'm hanging up, Charles. You have five minutes. If you don't comply, the deal is off, and I'm outta here." Kathryn didn't give Charles a chance to say anything else, she simply ended the call. She stared at the account information she was seeing on the screen in front of her. It was amazing, she thought, how at midnight with just a few computer strokes a family's life could be saved from disaster. She looked down at her watch, three and a half minutes had gone by. Her eyes started to water as she continued to stare at the screen in front of her. She could hear voices coming from somewhere. Just as they got louder to the point where she could distinguish the words, the numbers on the screen started to move. Her fist shot in the air. "Yessss."

And then she was being smothered in a fierce hug. "It's good to see you, Sis. Joe and I worried so about what happened. I prayed every night that you would be okay. You don't have to worry about us, you know that, right?"

"I do, Cass. I wish I could stay and shoot the breeze, but I'm on a tight schedule. Joe, take the plates off the Suburban and it's yours, but I need to take the plates with me. C'mere, see this," Kathryn said, pointing to the screen in front of her. "It's yours. There will be more to come, but the details will have to be worked out. Not as much as this, but enough so you don't have to sweat it out every month. You take care of your kids and all those grandbabies, you hear?"

Tears welled in Big Joe's eyes. "I can't . . . How . . . ?"

It was Kathryn's turn to put her fingers to her lips. "Shhh. Just use it all wisely. I really have to go. Hey, you got anything to eat in here? I'm starving." Joe laughed out loud. Every truck stop from east to west knew about Big Sis's love of food.

"Cass will fix you something while I remove those plates. This couldn't have happened at a better time. My old clunker is about to die on me."

Ten minutes later, Kathryn had a sack of food and hot coffee to go, along with the government plates. "I was never here, right?" she asked as she climbed into the Econoline.

"Never here," Joe and Cass said as they waved her off. Kathryn gave a light toot to the horn and barreled out to the highway, a satisfied smile on her face.

Chapter 9

It was one thirty in the morning, ninety minutes past the witching hour, when Jack Emery, Harry Wong, and Bert Navarro, who were on foot, walked to the rear of the British Embassy and entered the building quietly.

Nocturnal visitors to the embassy were due to arrive momentarily. Their job was to secure the entire building and make sure the women were safe. Bert's job was to hot-wire everything in the main computer room and check out the security system. Harry examined the top floors, Jack the bottom.

By two fifteen the men were in a stainless steel kitchen drinking coffee, their eyes glued to the windows for any sign of headlights. According to Charles, the Sisters' ETA could be anywhere between 2:00 and 3:00 AM.

While they waited, the men made small talk, mostly discussing sports. It was Harry who brought up Ted Robinson's name, saying that Ted had been scoping out the embassy. He'd seen him with his very own eyes in his quest to follow Jack's orders. "But," he said, holding up his hand for their attention, "on my sixth or seventh drive-by, I did see other reporters along with their camera people checking things out. So, Robinson could be a coincidence, or he could be onto something. But I have no clue how he

could have gotten wind of this so quick. Take that one step
further and realize the British Embassy closing because of
rat infestation is news, and the papers will all run with it.
It's on the TV news. Things are slow here in the summer,
so anything out of the ordinary—and rats at an embassy is
out of the ordinary—is news of a sort. What's even more
out of the ordinary is the building shutting down and all
the people being temporarily relocated. For two weeks,"
he said ominously. "Sooner or later, someone is going to
use the words 'terrorist' and 'plague' in the same sentence,
and the shit is really going to hit the fan. We need to get
this show on the road and make quick work of it before
that happens, and Homeland Security decides to raise a
fuss and get the Brits to allow them access to the embassy."

Jack and Bert looked at the martial-arts expert in awe.

"That's the most I've ever heard you say at one time,
Harry," Bert said.

"But he's right, Bert."

Bert looked glum. "Yeah, I know. I thought about it myself but didn't want to say anything. Those people at HS
are wild, and there's no dealing with them." He made a
strange sound that could have been laughter, and said,
"They might even want to duct tape the whole damn
building and hope the rats stick to it."

"Lights!" Harry said, pointing to the window.

Harry turned off the kitchen light and walked over to
the door that led outside. Yoko slipped out of the driver's
seat, turned around, and locked the door before she sprinted
forward to be swept up in Harry's arms. They rushed inside, leaving Jack and Bert alone in the kitchen.

Jack fired up a cigarette and offered one to Bert, who
said, "What the hell," and lit up.

"One down and five to go," Jack said, anxiety ringing
in his voice.

"You're like a cat on a hot griddle, Jack. What makes

this gig any more dangerous than the others you participated in?"

"I wish to hell I knew. I just have a bad feeling. Don't say anything to anyone. No sense spooking the girls. I have to be honest with you, Bert. I don't know how those women do it. Think back to when they stuffed those firecrackers up those two guys' asses and tell me on your best day you could have done that. They've got nerves of steel, that's for sure. I'm thinking I'm too old for this shit. And look at you, and the double life you lead. It takes its toll, make no mistake about it. When you're in your twenties, you still think you're infallible, but once you hit your mid-to late thirties, it's all downhill and you lose your edge. I don't mind admitting I'm a basket case."

Bert grinned in the darkness. "It's a mind-set, Jack. Did you ever really take the time to sit down with Charles to learn the way he operates?"

"Hell, no. If I had, I wouldn't be here. I just let Nikki convince me. Are you telling me you did?"

Bert said, "Of course I did. I'm an FBI agent, for Christ's sake. I listened with both ears. This is not some rinky-dink operation Charles has going on. The man has operatives all over the world who are only too glad to help him using whatever their expertise is. It's so well funded it makes your eyes water. If you really want to know what made me swing on his side of the gate, it was something he said to me. He said sometimes you have to work outside of the system to fix the system. I totally agreed with that. I've seen too much and get too angry at how situations slip through the cracks because of the antiquated legal system. Privatization is where it's at these days.

"This might surprise you, Jack, but there are tons, and I mean tons, of organizations like the one Charles fronts. Off the top of my head I can name you three. Fort Bragg,

Camp Perry, and Fort Story. SEALs. None of them have the expertise or the funding that Charles has, but they are out there, and they're on the FBI's radar screen. Not that they can do anything about it. CIA, you know. Our archenemy. I understand their methods are a little more unorthodox."

"The ends justify the means, in other words," Jack said.

"Pretty much. I see some lights coming our way."

Jack stared into the darkness, wondering why Bert's little speech didn't make him feel any better.

The second Econoline pulled up and parked next to where Yoko had parked her vehicle. Isabelle climbed out and walked toward them. "Kathryn is about fifteen miles behind me. She should be arriving shortly. Nikki is twenty miles out, and Alexis is forty miles out. She had an oil leak and had to stop. I have no news on Myra or Annie. Is there anything to eat or drink inside?"

"Fridge is loaded. These people eat real good. I saw a ham, half a turkey, and all kinds of cheese and specialty breads. Help yourself," Jack said.

Isabelle laughed. "I was thinking more along the lines of a good stiff drink before I tackled the food."

"It's in there, too. All top-of-the-line. Help yourself."

"See! They have nerves of steel. You'd think she was arriving for a pajama party or something," Jack said to Bert as Isabelle went inside. He fired up a second cigarette. Bert declined, saying he didn't want to smell like stale cigarettes when Kathryn arrived.

"You really like her, don't you?" Jack asked as he blew out a cloud of smoke. "I quit smoking a long time ago. I just smoke three a day. I'll totally quit again."

"And you think I need to know this, why?"

"I'm making conversation because I can see how jittery you are with Kathryn's impending arrival."

"You're a wiseass, Emery," Bert said, peering into the darkness.

"I've been called worse. Admit it, you're nervous."

"Okay, I admit it. Kathryn makes me feel . . . good. I never met anyone like her before. It doesn't even matter that she's a fugitive. I'm breaking the law myself, just the way you are. Somehow or other it's all going to work out."

A minute later, Jack said, "Here she comes, Bert. She's a lot of woman. You sure you can handle her?"

Bert laughed. "Would you mind disappearing for a little while? I'll call you when the others get here."

Jack stepped on his cigarette, then picked it up. He tossed it in the Dumpster before entering the building, his stomach muscles twitching and churning.

When the door closed behind him, he looked around at the empty kitchen just as his cell rang. He clicked it on. "A status report, Jack," Charles said.

Jack shrugged. Talking to Charles would help him kill some time until Nikki arrived. He told Charles about Harry's day. Charles told him about Kathryn's meeting with people from her old life. "Yoko, Isabelle, and Kathryn are here. Everything seems to be on track."

"Excellent," Charles said before the call ended.

Jack sat down and propped his feet up on one of the other chairs. He leaned back and closed his eyes as he tried to imagine, to feel the moment when he wrapped his arms around Nikki. He tried to picture married life with Nikki. Where would they live? A house somewhere with a brick walk leading to the porch. Lots of colorful flowers lining the walkway. A pretty front door. A welcoming door. With copper lights on each side that would be on at the first sign of darkness. A nice lawn. They'd both rake the leaves in the fall. Nikki would put pumpkins on the porch and one of those straw things on the front door people bought to decorate for Halloween and Thanksgiving.

A backyard with a fence for the dogs they would get. Maybe children. Maybe not. If they got out of this business, then there would be children. If not, it wouldn't be fair to bring children into the world. That in itself was one hell of a dilemma. He wondered if Nikki would want a pool. Definitely a hot tub.

The ideal scenario would see the two of them opening a law practice. Family law. He had no clue what they would do to earn a living.

At best it was a pipe dream. Asking Nikki to marry him was probably one of the stupidest things he'd ever done. He knew it and so did Nikki but she'd said yes anyway. His eyes burned with the realization that it was probably never going to happen.

When he felt a gentle touch to his cheek he bolted from the chair, his hand going to the gun in his shoulder holster. His eyes wild, he looked up to see Nikki, who had jumped to the side of the chair he had been sitting on before his wild bolt off the chair.

"Hi, Jack," she whispered.

"Oh, Jesus, I didn't hear you. I can't believe I fell asleep. I was thinking about us and how maybe there is never going to be an us." He held out his arms, the gun still in his left hand.

Nikki stepped into his arms and whispered, "There will always be an us, Jack," before her lips found his.

It was a kiss like no other.

But like all wonderful things, it came to an end. Jack looked at the woman he loved with all his heart, only to see tears in her eyes. He felt his heart flutter in his chest. *Please, somehow, some way, don't let it be a pipe dream. Let it be real.*

The back door opened, and suddenly there was a small crowd in the huge kitchen.

"Everyone present and accounted for," Annie said as she flopped down on a chair. "It's been a long time since I socialized at this hour of the morning."

"We're all tired, Annie," Jack said. "Let's call it a night and meet here early tomorrow morning."

The others looked at one another, then drifted off, with Jack leading the way to the housing quarters next to the chancery. Only Myra and Annie were left in the kitchen.

"How about a nice glass of soda pop and a sandwich, Myra?" Annie asked as she peered into the refrigerator.

"I'm not really hungry, Annie, but I will take the drink. I'm tired, and I still have to call Charles to let him know we're all safe and sound."

Annie's hands fluttered. "I think he already knows that, but go ahead. Do you want root beer or a cola?"

Myra perked up. "Root beer! I haven't had root beer in years. Barbara and Nikki used to love root beer floats."

Annie stopped what she was doing and looked over at Myra, whose eyes were filling up. "We can't go there, dear. Not right now." Myra nodded as she fingered the pearls around her neck.

Thirty minutes later the two older women were walking up the steps to the second floor. Two open doors beckoned them. They patted each other's arms and called it a night before they closed their respective doors. Tomorrow was another day.

Ted munched on a bagel loaded with cream cheese and chives. He finished it just as the cab he was riding in pulled to the curb. The time was a respectable 9:00 AM. He walked up to the British Embassy and saw two other reporters. He knew both men. They greeted each other and complained that no one was answering the door. The local security, according to one reporter, had left the premises around eight, but the second shift hadn't reported in as yet.

"Any exterminators show up yet?" Ted asked.

One of the reporters, Lincoln Monroe, a tall, lanky redhead, grimaced. "Five trucks lined up in the back. I think these people work at night. That's when rats come out, you know."

"I didn't know that," Ted said. "So, how come no one is answering the door?"

Both reporters shrugged.

"The cops wouldn't talk to us, either," Monroe said. "Well, actually, they did talk to us. They said we couldn't move past the yellow tape."

"No one answers the phones. Don't you guys think it's a little strange that the Brits don't have call forwarding?" Ted asked.

Both reporters nodded and shrugged again.

"The Brits have eleven consulates. You guys want to divvy them up? Let's call them all and see if we can get some kind of comment so we can get the hell out of here," Ted said.

The two men agreed. Ted ripped two sheets of paper out of one of his small notebooks and handed them out.

The reporters mumbled and muttered to themselves as they dialed, waited, stated their business, then waited again, only to be referred back to the main number at 3100 Massachusetts Avenue.

Monroe looked at his two colleagues. "I have an idea. Let's go to a pet store and buy a couple of rats and take pictures of them. We give them back to the pet store after we take the pictures and we can shuck this place."

Ted and the other reporter, Zack Ellis, nodded. It was definitely a plan.

"Why the hell not?" Ellis asked. "Who goes for the rats?"

"I'll do it," Monroe said. "We keep this zipped up, right? That'll be five bucks each, gentlemen."

Ellis and Robinson each handed over five dollars.

"What's the name of the exterminating company?" Ted asked.

"Reston Exterminating. I checked it out. They're out near the access road that leads to Dulles Airport. You just get a recording when you call."

Forty-five minutes later, Monroe was back, carrying a burlap sack with a lot of movement going on within. The sack was tied tight with stout string. "I have good news and bad news, gentlemen. The good news is I have in this sack three dozen rats—eighteen females and eighteen males. They produce young'uns on the hour." He laughed at the horror he saw on his colleagues' faces. "You have to buy rats in three-dozen lots. I did not know that. And you each owe me fifteen bucks. Who the hell knew rats were so expensive? The bad news is the store has a no-return policy. So, how do you want to play this?"

The three men huddled. "When you open the sack, are they just going to scurry like in a line? Or will they scatter?" Ted asked. "Christ, I can't believe I'm actually doing this. What do we do if someone comes out and sees what we're doing?"

Monroe pondered the question. "Then we lie and say we caught the damn things. What do you want from me? We play it by ear. Tell me when you're ready."

Ellis and Ted rolled their eyes. "Let it rip, buddy," Ellis said.

Monroe suddenly looked sick. He carefully untied the string, his hand clutched around the top of the sack. "I'm thinking, and I don't know this for a fact, but I'm guessing these little bastards are fast, so be prepared. The guy at the store said they might be confused since they're nocturnal. That damn sun is pretty bright. Okay, I'm going to drop this sack on the count of three. One! Two! Three!"

"Oh, Jesus!" Ted bellowed as rats scurried in all directions. He clicked his camera again and again as he tried to get out of the way.

"Oh, God! Oh, God!" Monroe bellowed. "They like me. Oh, shit, they're following me! Run!"

And run they did, the rats following in their shadows.

Looking out one of the second-floor windows was Myra, who screamed in panic at what she was seeing. Annie gasped, her face draining of all color.

Chapter 10

It was midmorning when Bert Navarro's cell phone rang. He walked a little distance away from the chattering group in the kitchen for privacy and to hear a little better. Across the kitchen, Jack watched the agent's expression go from stunned awe to outright fear. When Bert clicked off and pocketed the phone, he turned around, and said, "Sorry folks, but I have to leave. Duty calls and all that. I'll try to get back here later, but it might not be possible."

Jack looked at his friend's expression and his angry stance, and knew something awful was brewing somewhere. He followed Bert out to the back end of the parking lot and waited. "What?"

"I can't talk to you about FBI business, Jack, you know that."

"I understand that, Bert. Tell me this, does it affect the girls in any way?"

"Hell yes. The situation itself, not the girls directly," he clarified. "I'll do what I can, that's all I can tell you," Bert said.

"Thanks a lot, pal. I thought you were on our side."

"I am. Sorry, Jack, I gotta go. Director Cummings called a meeting of all us special agents. We're being called in from our postings. Does that give you a clue that this is serious?"

Jack ran alongside the black car Bert was driving. "Is it about the girls? Did someone figure it out?"

"Yes and maybe yes," Bert said, answering both questions. "I swear to God I'm going to run you over if you don't get the hell out of my way, Jack."

His head buzzing with this latest development, Jack now knew his earlier gut instincts were right. Something was already wrong, and they hadn't moved past square one. One thing he knew for certain, Bert Navarro was not an alarmist. He'd seen panic in the man's eyes. Real panic.

When he got back inside he found the women and Harry all clustered together in the kitchen, their eyes full of questions. He shrugged for their benefit, and said, "Bert won't discuss FBI business with me or anyone else." The words were no sooner out of his mouth when his cell phone rang. Charles.

"Yes, Charles, what's up?" He listened, his jaw dropping. When he could finally get his tongue to work he said, "That's goddamn impossible!" He listened some more, then barked, "What the hell do you mean we don't have a Plan B?" He listened again but didn't say another word before he closed the cell phone.

Harry swung his foot back and forth, his warning that Jack better speak quickly or he was going to get the brunt of that foot. "Charles told me why Bert just left. In a million years you aren't going to believe this. Never, never, never!" Harry's foot swung higher. "That meeting Bert is going to at the FBI building is about this building and the supposed rat infestation. There's word on the street that terrorists are attacking us with the rats to set off a plague epidemic. Seems these supposed terrorists hate the Brits as much as they hate us Americans."

"But there aren't any rats here! We made that up. Well, Charles made that up. Who . . . What . . . ?" Kathryn sputtered.

Annie's voice rose to a hysterical pitch. "But Myra and I saw a whole swarm of rats chasing those men out front just a little while ago. There *are* rats here! We actually *saw* them!" She reached out to Myra to clutch at her arm.

Myra's hold on her pearls was a death grip. "We did see rats, Jack. We were too far away to see the men's faces, but we did see the rats. Oh, dear God, now what are we going to do?"

Jack stood rooted to the floor. He didn't know what to do or think. For the first time in his life he felt witless and numb. "I don't have a clue," was all he said.

"Did Charles say anything else?" Nikki asked.

"Only that the CDC would become involved. Since they're in Atlanta, it will take a few hours to get here. We have to wait for Charles to get back to us."

"We've been compromised," Annie said, the hysteria still in her voice. "That's spook-speak for we've been fingered."

Myra's eyes rolled back in her head, but she didn't relinquish her fierce hold on the pearls.

Jack's brain finally started to function. "And who do you think we have to blame for that if it turns out to be true? Robinson, that's who! Myra, Annie, think now, is it possible the three men you saw out there were Robinson and his cronies?"

Both women shook their heads. It was Myra who spoke first. "By the time I saw the rats, the men were running. I only saw their backs. It was so bizarre I just kept staring at the rats, wondering if it was a prophecy of some kind. Then Annie and I both started to scream. The rats were chasing the men, that's certain."

Annie nodded. "They were on the other side of the yellow tape. It looked like there were hundreds of them. They *swarmed!*"

Nikki, who was normally the voice of reason, frowned. "But rats are nocturnal. They only come out at night. Bright light does something to their eyes. I read that somewhere. So, if that's true, what were rats doing outside in the bright sunshine midmorning?"

No one had an answer.

"Those exterminator trucks out there have our fingerprints all over them," Isabelle said.

No one moved.

"How is the background check going to work on Reston Exterminating?" Nikki asked.

"It should work like a charm. Bids were sent out giving each company twenty-four hours to quote a price. I understand they all came in extremely high except for Reston, which is supposedly a new start-up company eager for business. According to the incorporation papers, they've only been in business for three weeks," Jack said.

"With a fleet of six trucks?" Alexis asked.

"Small-business loan. A mom-and-pop operation. Five kids working the business. That's the background. Anyone fishing for information isn't going to get a thing out of the Brits. Those stiff upper lips know when to clamp shut," Jack said.

Harry stepped forward. "Is Homeland Security going to get involved?"

"Count on it. They're probably gearing up as we speak," Jack said.

"Then don't we need to get out of here? This place is no longer secure or safe."

"Tell me something I don't already know," Jack said. His cell phone rang and he answered it. It was his ex–FBI friend Mark Lane.

"Articulate," Jack said coolly. He listened. "Ha! I thought you were going to tell me something I didn't know. I'm standing inside the premises right now talking to you. C'mon, Lane, make me proud and tell me something that's going to help me." He listened, then closed the cell phone.

Jack waved his hands. "Guess the story is all over town by now. Before the end of the day, this whole town has a good chance of being quarantined if the gossip mill takes over. Normal people will become irrational out of fear. And here we sit."

"Those jackasses at HS will be our worst nightmare," Harry said. "Somehow or other, they'll get the Brits to agree to allow them to come in here in their Hazmat suits and take over. They might even barrel their way in without permission even though this is British soil and doing so is technically invading another country. We need to get out of here, Jack. Hey, I have an idea, why don't we all go to the World Bank and hide out?"

Jack shot him such a disgusted look, Harry clamped his lips shut.

"It was my attempt at humor," Harry said lamely. Yoko patted his arm in sympathy. "So, what are we supposed to do now?"

"Wait," Jack said succinctly.

Liam Sullivan walked out into the newsroom and was pleased to see his former star reporter busily tapping away. It was a relief to get away from the phone even if only for a few minutes. His head pounded with the news he'd been getting for the past two hours.

"So, Robinson, how is it you didn't see fit to call in the latest news here in town? It would seem to me that bubonic plague and terrorism would make for headline news. Why did I have to hear it from a competitor? You're damn well running amuck on me."

Oh shit! Either Ellis or Monroe must have jumped the gun in an effort to get a headline above the fold. Which just went to prove you couldn't trust anyone, not even a colleague you drank beer with. "I'm writing it up right now. Give me five minutes, Chief. Personally, I think it's bullshit even though those pictures of the rats are real. Those things multiply faster than rabbits. Five minutes, Chief."

"If it's bullshit, then why did close to a thousand people evacuate? There's going to be a panic in this town by sundown. We're going with a late-afternoon special edition. So, snap to it, Robinson."

Ted suddenly felt sick and dizzy. He'd never manufactured a story in his life. Well, there was a first time for everything. He fell to it and was finished in the self-allotted five minutes. He printed out his story and carried it into Sullivan's office. He was getting sicker by the minute as he watched his boss read the article twice before he nodded, and said, "Good reporting, Robinson. Real good. Those pictures are damn ugly, but I guess you know that."

"Yes, sir, rats are ugly. Do you think the *Sentinel* and the *News* are going to go with afternoon editions?"

"They'd be fools not to. We'll beat them by an hour, that's all I care about. We're doing a double circulation."

Oh, shit! Ted's hand itched to snatch his cell phone out of his pocket so he could call Ellis and Monroe.

When the EIC looked up at him, he said, "Get out of here, Robinson. Lunch is on the *Post* today. Ten bucks' worth."

Ted snorted to show what he thought of the generous offer, but at least he could get out of the office. The minute he got to his desk he called Monroe, who sounded as sick as he felt. Ellis sounded even sicker. Ted offered to buy a picnic lunch and told both reporters precisely where to meet him at the National Zoo. Both men accepted, and the meet was on in sixty minutes.

* * *

Ted was emptying the heavy carton of food: double pastrami and corn beef sandwiches on rye with tons of mustard, pickles, potato salad, chips, brownies for dessert, and a six-pack of Heineken. He was laying everything out on the picnic table complete with paper tablecloth and plastic utensils, just the way Maggie would have, when his two friends joined him, both their faces glum and wary. Ted wanted to demand to know which one of his friends started the rumor, but he bit down on his tongue. On second thought, maybe it was better that he didn't know.

"We're in some deep shit here, fellas," Monroe said.

"Only if that guy in the pet store remembers you. What are the chances of that happening?" Ellis asked as he straddled the bench. He eyed the food with approval. Two sandwiches each. Two was good. The *Post* had a better expense account than his paper had.

"Nada. He was an old geezer, and his eyes looked kind of milky. I think he might have cataracts. I told him I was a biology teacher from Sacred Heart. He bought it."

"I think we should worry, if we agree to worry, about me calling both of you on my cell phone right after I turned in my column. You guys going with afternoon editions?"

"Hell yes!" both reporters said.

Ted waved his pickle upward. "How . . . how do you feel about it? You know . . . what we did?"

Both reporters shrugged.

"Too late now," Ellis said. "The story is out there. We need to agree never to mention this. We met there by accident. You called us to go to lunch to celebrate, not the event but a late-afternoon edition. That's it. Period. Do we all agree?"

"Yeah," Ted said.

"Yeah," Monroe said.

"Good sandwiches," Ellis said.

Ted wondered why he still felt sick. The thought of having to eat both sandwiches was enough to make him want to run to the nearest bush.

Chapter 11

It was a pleasant enough oversized waiting room in the embassy, with real leather chairs, teak tables, luscious green plants, and copies of all the latest magazines. There was even a bowl of hard candies on one of the tables. The room was big enough to accommodate a large plasma television. The Sisters were all seated in the leather chairs, their eyes glued to the Fox News Channel as they waited for updates on the current situation involving the embassy.

"It's getting late, we should have heard something by now. The clock is ticking," Kathryn said ominously. To make her point, she wagged her finger in the direction of an antique clock on the wall; the time read 5:10 PM.

"I can't believe this is happening. How do you go from a rumor about exterminators and rats to terrorists and bubonic plague? Charles must be pulling out his hair," Myra said.

"This is Washington," Nikki said, as if those few words explained it all. "We all know this place is pretty much dead during the summer months, which means little or no news worth printing. *This is news!* The wrong kind, of course, but it's front and center. Even Charles couldn't have anticipated this happening. I agree, though, that he should have called us by now."

Myra continued to fiddle with the pearls at her neck. "Would you like me to try calling him again, dear?"

"Yes, Myra, I would," Nikki responded.

They all watched as Myra punched in the digits that would connect her to Charles. "It's going straight to voice mail. I assume that has to mean he is otherwise occupied."

The women continued to stare glumly at one another until they heard the chirp of Jack's cell phone. All eyes were on him when he flipped it open to take the call.

"It's Bert, Jack. Get the hell out of there *right now!* The boys and girls from CDC and Homeland Security are on the way. The president himself got the British ambassador to approve the incursion. Sorry about the short notice. You have less than eight minutes. Go!" he said and then hung up.

"We have to get out of here. Bert says we have eight minutes. That means five! Head for Rock Creek Park. We'll all meet there! You girls sure you wiped everything down?" Jack roared in frustration and anger.

Nikki held up her hands to show they'd all been wearing latex gloves since their arrival. "No prints, Jack!" she called over her shoulder as she ran from the room back through a series of corridors to the kitchen. Two minutes later the Econolines' tires were screeching and smoking as all five vehicles hit the street at full throttle.

Jack looked around, his eyes wild. "Let's go, Harry. I'm going to ride with you, so burn rubber, pal. We don't want to be anywhere near this place when those people in the Hazmat suits arrive. Thank God for Navarro."

Staff from several of the other embassies were leaving work and observed the activity at the British Embassy. Cell phones went to their ears at the speed of light. Jack saw it all in some kind of weird slow motion. "Fly, Harry, we've been spotted."

"Like they can see through these helmets and visors. I-don't-think-so! I put mud over the license plate before I came out here. Relax, Jack. I'll get you to your destination so you can meet up with your brothers and sisters."

"Shut up, Harry, I don't have any brothers and sisters."

"I was referring to all the apes and monkeys at the zoo, Jack. Oops, sorry, I forgot, we're going to the park and not the zoo. Shut up now so I can concentrate on my driving."

Jack much preferred to be the one giving the orders, not the other way around. He knew if he opened his mouth again, Harry would do a wheelie and buck him off.

The rush hour traffic was horrendous, but the Ducati was made for weaving in and out of tight spaces. Harry took every advantage, and the duo arrived at the park in forty minutes. They were the first ones to arrive. Breathless with the wild ride, Jack called Nikki, who told him she was six minutes away, the others right behind her.

When his breathing was somewhat normal, Jack tried calling Charles again, but his call also went straight to voice mail. He tried Bert, who barked a greeting and simply said, "This is not a good time, Monica. I'll call you back."

Jack broke the connection so fast he thought his finger was on fire. He looked over at a brooding Harry, and said, "I think we're on our own for the moment. You got any ideas?"

"There's always the *dojo*."

Jack looked glum. "It might come to that. Just to be on the safe side, set the wheels in motion."

Jack was about to call Charles again when his cell rang. It was Mark Lane. "Hey, buddy, Homeland Security is on the way, and so are the guys from CDC. Get your asses out of there. Like now, Jack."

"We're out, Mark. Navarro called me a little while ago, but thanks for the tip. By any chance do you know any safe houses that aren't in use?"

"I do, but they won't help you. They're all wired. With all the shit you're involved in, are you telling me you don't have a place to hole up?"

"That's what I'm telling you," Jack almost shouted. "Look, I'm sorry, I'm a little uptight right now." Out of the corner of his eye he saw Nikki pulling into a parking space.

"Well, off the top of my head I'd say you have a few options. No one knows the girls are here. So that leaves Myra's farmhouse. Then you have Judge Easter's place, not to mention Chief Justice Barnes's estate and Lizzie Fox's house. Take your pick, big guy."

Jack slapped at his head. He hadn't been thinking clearly. "You know, for a private eye, you ain't half-bad, Mark. Thanks. I owe you another one."

"And don't think for a minute I'm not keeping score. When this is all over, we'll grab a beer and talk it to death, okay?"

"You got it!"

Nikki ran over to him the minute he slipped his cell phone into his pocket. Jack wrapped her in his arms. The few people leaving the park to return to their hotels or home smiled indulgently. *If they only knew,* Jack thought. "Have you heard anything?" she asked.

"Charles still isn't answering. That's starting to worry me. He always picks up. Mark Lane called after Bert did with the same information. Guess his snitches aren't as high up the food chain as Bert is. Anyway, he called. Hey, did you take those magnetic IDs off the truck?"

"The minute I parked. It just looks like a white van now. There are thousands of white vans in town. We talked among ourselves on the way here. The girls know what to do. Kathryn has the government license plates, so we can put those on as soon as we get someplace safe and can get other plates. How the hell did this happen, Jack?"

"I honestly don't have a clue, Nik. I also don't have any idea as to what we should or shouldn't be doing. Mark did come up with a suggestion. Seems, if we have the guts, we have a variety of places to hole up. Myra's farmhouse, Judge Easter's, or even Lizzie Fox's house. He also suggested Chief Justice Barnes's estate. We just have to make a decision," Jack said, his eyes turning toward the parking lot just in time to see Kathryn and Yoko parking their vans. In the blink of an eye, they had the colorful logos identifying the vans as Reston Exterminating safely pulled off.

Phone calls to the others followed as Jack issued orders off the top of his head. Not wanting to call attention to his little group, he ordered Nikki to Myra's farmhouse, where their old motorcycles were stored in the barn. Nikki waved as she peeled out into traffic wearing oversize sunglasses and a baseball cap. It was a disguise that wouldn't fool anyone looking closely.

Jack waited just long enough to clue in the others on their arrival, at which point he and Harry left, but not before they looked around to make sure they hadn't caused any undue scrutiny. There didn't seem to be anyone paying attention to him. All he could see were harried mothers dealing with fretful children, fathers in a hurry to get home to dinner, vendors closing up their kiosks. It seemed to Jack that everyone was minding their own business, not his. He hoped he was right.

"Let's roll, Harry."

It was past twilight when the staggered caravan arrived at Myra Rutledge's farmhouse in McLean, Virginia. The evening was warm, with a slight breeze and no humidity. Birds chittered to one another as they got ready to settle down for the night. From across the fields a dog could be heard barking. Closer still, a horse whinnied.

Myra almost fainted with happiness when she opened the kitchen door to the house she'd lived in her whole life. She was home. Tears slid down her cheeks. The only thing that would make it all perfect was if Barbara, her deceased daughter, magically appeared. But that would never happen again.

"It's okay, Mom. I'm here," a voice whispered in Myra's ear.

Myra whirled around and bumped into Annie, who was right behind her. She flew into the laundry room off the kitchen and closed the door.

"Darling girl, I am so happy. Talking to you makes this homecoming almost perfect. I don't know what to say. Can you . . . channel . . . whatever it is you do . . . to tell me what's going on? I can't seem to reach Charles. This is so unlike him. For the first time, we're on our own. I don't know if it was wise to come here or not."

"Mom, easy does it. Things always work out, you know that. You guys are doing good. You're safe."

"Barbara, I miss you so. There are days . . ."

"Shhh," the mystical-sounding voice said.

"Will . . . will you come back later? I can wait in your room if that will work."

"I'll come back when you need me the most. Hey, you're my mom. You can do anything. Remember how you told me and Nik that all the time? You said moms could do anything, and moms were always right."

Myra smiled. "I did say that, didn't I? Are you telling me you didn't believe me?"

The mystical voice had a smile in it. *"Oh, we did believe it because it proved right time after time. I'll see you later, Mom."*

Myra wiped at her eyes and squared her shoulders before she walked out of the laundry room.

The others looked at her as though she would impart something truly profound. She decided to rise to the occasion. "It would appear that we're on our own for the moment. So, let's settle ourselves and get down to work. First things first, though. Move all the vehicles into the barn and padlock it. We'll adjourn to the tunnels and our old war room for the night, so we don't have to use the electricity here on the first floor. We can use the house during the daylight hours. It's just temporary, girls. And, gentlemen," she added almost as an afterthought. "I'll give Nellie a call. Since she's living on the adjoining farm and likes to go riding at dawn, I can ask her to drop provisions off at the property line. I suspect we won't be here that long, but we will need food and drinks."

"What exactly does 'that long' mean, Myra?" Alexis asked.

"Dear, I wish I could tell you, but right now I can't. We have to make a plan. If you recall, we came here to take on the president of the World Bank. Instead, we've been blindsided by a situation beyond our control. What appeared to be a foolproof plan now has to be discarded. However, the authorities will be concentrating on the embassy and their immediate problem, and there will be considerable chaos, all of which can work in our favor. The amazing thing is that it was not of our doing, and the powers that be won't be able to lay it on our doorstep. In that sense, we're still free agents and in a position to do what we came here to do. We *can* do this, girls. We are, after all, *women*."

Ever the skeptic, Kathryn wrinkled her nose, and asked, "What happens if we go full bore on our own, with our own plan, then Charles shoots us down?"

"Then we take a vote to see which way we want to go. I know we can pull this off. So, for the moment, let's consider Charles our backup and nothing more. I'll be the team leader, and I'll be—what is it you say, Kathryn?— calling the shots?"

"That'll work," Nikki said. "Have the motorcycles in the barn been gassed and maintained?"

"Absolutely. Maintenance comes under Nellie's purview. She rides over here once a week to check on things. Why do you ask, dear?"

"I'm thinking we should go out on the town tonight. Get the lay of the land, so to speak. Alexis can alter our appearance enough, and if we go in pairs, no one is going to pay attention to us."

Jack and Harry walked through the kitchen door and heard what Nikki had just suggested. "Are you crazy, Nik? No!" Jack said.

Nikki made a kissing noise with her lips. "Yes. We have to check things out. Darkness at this point in time is our best friend. Broad daylight is our enemy. Surely you understand that, Jack."

Alexis looked over at the door at her Red Bag, which she was never without. "I'm ready if you are."

"Then let's do it!" Nikki said, a wicked gleam in her eye.

Jack groaned and mumbled something that sounded like, "Women! You can't live with them, but you can't live without them. We're just putty in your hands."

The Sisters giggled all the way to the second floor, where there were blackout windows that allowed for the high-voltage lamps to be turned on.

"Okay, girls," Alexis said as she looked from one to the other. "We traveled light this trip, so makeup and hair is a must. Wardrobe is iffy. Now, let's get to it while someone comes up with a plan for the evening. Who wants to go first?"

"Me!" Yoko said. "I always like to surprise Harry. He's

not going to like seeing me on a motorcycle. He thinks he's so macho. Men!" She giggled. She gave Kathryn a playful poke to her shoulder before she sat down on a chair at Myra's vanity table.

"You're finally getting it." Kathryn laughed.

"Oh, I got it all right," Yoko said, as she thrust out her enhanced boobs, compliments of Julia Webster before her demise. "And you know what else? Harry has no clue they aren't real!" The girls burst out laughing.

"Men!" they said one by one. "You can't live with them, and you can't live without them."

"Amen," Annie said.

Chapter 12

Ted Robinson had a blinding headache. The beer he was swilling wasn't helping, either, but still he swigged at the bottle in his hand. He was in his recliner, the television on MUTE, his eyes half-closed. His two cats, Minnie and Mickey, were sitting on the top of the sofa and watching him with green-eyed intensity. When his doorbell rang, he mumbled halfheartedly, "Whoever you are, go away!"

The cats scampered down and ran to the front door, certain it was their friend Maggie coming home at long last. The doorbell pealed again. This time, Ted untangled himself and marched out to the door. "Who is it?"

"Guess!" Joe Espinosa's voice came through the door.

Ted threw open the door to see not only Espinosa but his two colleagues from the *Sentinel* and the *News*. All three men stared at him.

"Are you going to invite us in or not?" Espinosa growled.

Ted eyed his so-called partner warily as he wondered if he knew or suspected what had gone down earlier. Knowing Monroe and Ellis the way he did, he figured it was a certainty. It would certainly explain Espinosa's surly attitude.

"If you came here to drink, forget it. I just finished off

my last bottle. Have a seat, gentlemen," Ted said, waving his arm about to indicate the ratty chairs in his apartment.

Espinosa refused to sit down. "What the fuck did you three guys think you were doing?"

Ted threw his hands in the air. "Speaking strictly for myself, Sullivan railroaded me into writing that goddamn article. I wrote a straightforward piece about the rats outside. Yeah, yeah, we put the rats there so we could get a picture, but that's all we did. At least all I know that *I* did. I, Joe. *I, I, I.* I as in me. Then Sullivan came out to the newsroom and said he'd been getting calls all morning about the fucking plague, rats, and on and on he went. He said I had to write it, so I wrote it. What the hell do you want from me?"

"That's the way it went down with us, too," Monroe said. "I don't make up shit, and neither does Ellis. I know Ted doesn't, either. What we did was elaborate on a rumor. If you read the damn articles the three of us wrote, you can see that. Ted's right, I bought the rats, three dozen to be exact, and we let them loose and took pictures. That's it. Those goddamn things chased us all the way down Mass Avenue. Anybody who saw that little scene could have called the paper, the cops, or whoever the hell they called. You know what else? We did talk about it, but no one overheard us. I think it was Ted who said sooner or later someone was going to use the words 'plague' and 'terrorist' in the same sentence, and by God, that's exactly what happened. So, get the fuck off your high horse, Espinosa, and leave us alone."

Espinosa looked at Ted. "Swear to me that's the way it went down."

Ted's head pounded. "Yeah, I swear on Maggie, on Minnie and Mickey, that's the way it went down. You happy now?"

"No!"

"Then go home and leave me to my misery. You know me, Joe. I never manufactured a story in my life. We took pictures of rats. That was it. And if you believe for one goddamn minute there are rats at the British Embassy, then I'll sell you the Lincoln Memorial for five bucks. What the hell are you doing here anyway?"

Ellis adjusted his wire-rimmed glasses on the bridge of his nose. "It's like this, Ted. Misery loves company, so we came over to take you out on the town. We met Joe in the lobby and brought him up. You haven't been answering your phone, so that's why we had to come here. So, get your wallet, and let's go."

Ted looked from one to the other. "You didn't come here to blame me?" He looked incredulous at his own question.

"Hell, no. Getting those rats was my idea," Monroe said. "I thought we could hit the bar scene and see what's going down. This crap is all over the tube, it's all anyone is talking about. We can pick up some real human interest stuff tonight, so bring your recorder, too. Our editors will love us in the morning when we plop all these interviews down on their desks."

"That's sick," Ted said as he rummaged in his backpack for his minirecorder and wallet. He straightened up and looked at his three buddies. "There's no way out of this, you know that, right?"

His buddies nodded, even Espinosa.

"You know what I heard on my way over here tonight?" Espinosa asked. "Those Reston Exterminating trucks are gone from the British Embassy. CDC and Homeland Security have been calling the offices, and all they get is a recorded message. Somehow or other the check that the Brits wrote to Reston was never cashed."

"Where'd you hear that?" Ted asked, his ears perking up.

"Taco Bell, when I was standing in line. Two guys who looked like college professors, you know, tweedy-looking, were picking up their dinner. I didn't ask any questions, just eavesdropped."

"Some reporter you are. You should have been on it like fleas on a dog," Ellis said as he gave his glasses another hitch over his nose.

Ted stopped in midstride as his bullshit detector kicked into high gear. "So, are you saying this is all some kind of setup?"

The four reporters were still standing in the middle of the sidewalk, pedestrians muttering about inconsiderate people as they were forced to walk around them.

"Well, what do *you* think?" Espinosa demanded.

"You don't want to know what I think," Ted grumbled. His brain and his bullshit detector were making him light-headed.

"To what end?" Monroe asked.

"The Brits are too classy to pull shit like that," Ellis said. "What the hell are you trying to say here? Everyone knows the Brits are low-profile people, they don't stir up trouble, and they sure as hell wouldn't do something on our shores. I think you're nuts, Espinosa."

Ted broke formation and started walking forward, his mind going in every direction. Was it possible . . . ? Did that guy Charles have that kind of clout . . . ? Nah, it couldn't be. Yet he knew it was. Yet if he said anything about those goddamn women again, they'd lock him up and throw away the key. This time he'd be smarter and keep his suspicions to himself.

"So, where are we going?" Monroe asked.

"We're going bar-hopping," Ellis said happily. "I love bar-hopping. You get to meet such interesting people. Everyone has a story. I thought we'd hit the bars around Dupont Circle. There's a couple of new ones, one in particular called High Flyers, where the pretty people and the ones who want to be seen hang out. Then there's one called Eazzy Breezy, but I think it's more for the young, hip crowd, not old farts like us, but if we don't give it a whirl, we'll never know. Won't hurt for us handsome guys to be seen in the area."

Ted scowled. Like he cared if he was seen or not seen. If he had his druthers, he'd like to drop into a big black hole where he could think in peace, quiet, and darkness. But that wasn't going to happen anytime soon. Ted looked over at Espinosa. "How many Reston trucks were there?"

"Five. Why?"

Ted ignored the question. "And they're all gone?"

"Yep. Does it mean something?"

Ted shrugged. "Who knows? My take on it would be either Reston was successful, and they contained the problem, or they bombed out because the job was too much for them. Someone said it was a new start-up company. Then again, it could be a setup of some kind, but I have no clue as to why it would be a setup." He shrugged again. "I assume it was a pricey job. Funny they never cashed the check, though. The flip side to that is maybe when they realized the job was too much for them, if that's what happened, they didn't bother to cash the check. Hell, it could be anything."

"I was thinking the same thing," Espinosa said, watching Ted carefully to see his reaction. He imagined he could see the wheels turning inside his friend's head. He knew him well enough to know he was on to something. Whether he would share it was anybody's guess.

Ted shrugged for the third time. "Who gives a good rat's ass? No pun intended," he cackled inanely.

Alexis stood back to view her handiwork. She smiled and clapped her hands. "Perfect," she chortled. "These new facial prosthetics were a real find. I defy anyone to identify even one of us. I still like a little dab of latex here and there, even if it's just on the earlobes or tip of the nose. I just need five minutes to do myself, and we're good to go."

Jack and Harry stared at the women, their expressions dumbfounded.

"So, what do you think?" Nikki asked as she twirled around. "Do we look *tarty?* Or *slutty?* Or do we look like high-priced ladies of the evening? I'm hoping you say none of the above. Our aim is to look like high-income business-women out and about on a weekday evening. We're not going to use the motorcycles. We'll drive Myra's Jag and the Benz. Our affected British accents should draw people to us like bees to honey. What do you think, Jack?"

Jack thought he swallowed his tongue. "You're making me weak in the knees, Nik. I wouldn't recognize you if I passed you on the street."

Nikki blew him a kiss he pretended to catch.

Yoko pranced front and center on her five-inch heels as she whirled and twirled. Harry wet his lips and tried to speak. "So, tell me, honey, are you going to have a wet dream tonight or not?" Harry flushed a bright red. It was all the answer Yoko needed as, to Harry's dismay, she went off into peals of laughter. "Lighten up, sweetie." She went off into another bout of laughter.

It was Kathryn, though, who drew the most applause as she strutted like a runway model. She wore a cherry-red spandex dress and matching stilettos, and carried a jacket over her shoulder. Her long dark hair glistened with some-thing sparkly, as did her bare arms and thighs. Even her eyelashes glistened. She reeked of confidence and power. To his own surprise, Jack beamed and whistled approv-ingly. Harry just nodded.

Isabelle stepped forward. The audience gasped. She

looked like a scared, dowdy librarian right down to the thick glasses perched on the end of her nose.

Alexis moved forward. If it was her intention to look like a cross between Tina Turner and Beyonce, she succeeded. She looked stunning.

Myra and Annie just sat and looked glum.

"I can't believe you're all leaving us behind," Annie fretted.

"Someone has to watch the fort. Not to hurt your feelings, but you two don't look like the bar-hopping type. We'll take notes and tell you every little thing. Besides, if we get into trouble, you're the only ones we can call," Kathryn said.

"In the meantime, it's your job to keep trying to reach Charles. We're not going to have time to keep trying his number," Nikki said kindly. "And we discussed the fact that your Mercedes will only hold the five of us. We decided the Jag is a little too sporty for tonight. You'll be happy to know the Benz is now sporting government plates." At the crestfallen expressions on the faces of the two older women, she hastily added, "Look, we're not doing this to have fun. We're going on the prowl to see if we can meet up with Rena Gold. According to her dossier, she likes to stop for a martini somewhere after her gym workout on Thursday nights. This is Thursday. Maybe we'll find her, and maybe we won't. It's all we have going for us at the moment. So, are you two okay with this?"

"No," Annie said.

"Yes, dear," Myra said. "Please don't get into any trouble."

"We'll do our best," Kathryn said, peering at herself in the long mirror that Alexis had brought down from the upper floor and propped against the dishwasher.

"Tell me you have a plan at least," Annie said.

"Oh, we will, we just don't know exactly what it is yet.

We're going to work on it on the way into town," Alexis said breezily.

"Things always come together somehow when you work on the fly," Kathryn said just as nonchalantly.

Myra sent an appealing look in Jack's direction.

"We got their back, Myra. I'm going to call Bert as soon as we get out to the highway. You sure that disaster of a truck in the barn works?"

"Like a charm. Nellie said she put a new engine in it a few months ago. She said it purrs like a kitten."

"Then I guess we're good to go. Showtime, girls!" Kathryn said as she strutted toward the kitchen door, where Myra's Mercedes was waiting outside by the huge electronic security gates.

When the door slammed shut, Annie reached up into the cabinet for a bottle of Kentucky Bourbon. She poured generously. "This is no time to be shy, Myra. Bottoms up! I'm thinking we might need this false courage. At least for now."

"I think you might be right, Annie," Myra said, upending her glass. Her eyes watering, she held the glass out for a refill. Annie obliged. Twenty minutes later they both forgot about the glasses and took turns swigging from the bottle.

"This is fun, isn't it, Myra?"

"Oh, it's fun all right, dear. I love it when I can't stand up straight, and I see three of everything. It's just no end of fun when your head spins one way and your stomach goes the other way."

"You always were a poop, Myra. You need to get with the party here."

"Guess what, Annie. I am *leaving* this party. Right now."

"Go ahead. See if I care," Annie said, peering into the empty bottle. "Okay, okay, now that you rained on our

parade, I guess we should settle down and watch television."

"What makes you think we can see the television set . . .
you . . . you . . . lush."

"Oh, Myra, that was such a low blow. Say you're
sorry."

"I'm sorry, Annie."

"I know, dear, I know. Let's just sit on the sofa and hold
hands and worry together."

Chapter 13

Rena Gold liked it when women looked at her with envy in their eyes. She liked it even more when men looked at her with hungry eyes.

The workout routine she worked at religiously kept her surgically enhanced body in good shape. She hated flabby skin, be it on her knees or her elbows. At the first sign of a wrinkle, she sprinted to a plastic surgeon. Now, if there was just something she could do about her aches and pains, she'd be a hundred percent. Her years of dancing in Las Vegas had taken their toll on her back and hips. Her knees weren't that good, either. On the days when she wore pantsuits, she wore elastic braces on her knees. When she wore short skirts, she suffered and took eight Advil a day.

What she hated more than anything were the bedroom gymnastics Maxwell insisted on. Slug that he was, he made her do all the work. Secretly, she thought of him as a rutting pig in a barnyard. And to think tonight was what she referred to as her duty night. But not until she was ready. Damn good and ready. In order to be damn good and ready, she had to make a pit stop to fortify herself for what was to come. If she was lucky, she could be out by midnight and home in her own bed with her thousand-thread-count custom sheets, sheets that wouldn't smell like Maxwell Zenowicz.

Rena pulled on her elastic knee braces, slipped back into her pantsuit, fluffed her wild mane of hair, then checked to be sure her makeup was perfect. It was. She took one last look in the mirror and was more than satisfied. When her cell phone rang, she pulled it out of her Chanel bag and looked at the name of the caller. She grimaced but didn't answer. "Screw you, Max," she mumbled as she shoved the cell into the bottom of the bag. Then she yanked it back out and turned it off.

Tonight she was going to stop off at a new establishment, one that had opened recently. She hadn't even mentioned it to Max. She knew he kept tabs on her, but she'd become an expert at outwitting and evading the various tails he'd put on her. Tonight she was going to Eazzy Breezy.

As she walked along, Rena wished, the way she'd wished many times, that she had a close friend, a confidante here in the Nation's Capital. But she didn't. Max had warned her not to get involved with what he called jealous, catty women. It wasn't that he was worried about her reputation but rather his own. So, she'd done what any redblooded woman would do. She'd gotten herself several prepaid disposable cell phones that she kept hidden in the Tampax box in her bathroom. Hidden just in case Max sent someone to check out her apartment. He did that from time to time, and she knew each time her space had been invaded because she set little traps for any intruders. Not that anything was ever taken, not even when she left money on her dresser.

What galled Rena more than anything was that Max thought that because she'd been a showgirl in Vegas, she was stupid. He didn't give her credit for having any brains at all. Ha! He should only know how bright she really was. Having friends in Vegas who knew the right people had proved beyond beneficial. Her best friend, Esther, had told her she needed insurance in case old Max decided to kick her to the curb at some point. "You need a nest egg, a big nest egg for when that happens." She had listened, and on occasion she'd administered a doctored-up drink so Max would sleep the sleep of the dead and she could make copies of the contents of his briefcase. She'd also made videos of their sexual escapades. Everything was locked away in the safe in her penthouse, a safe Maxwell knew nothing about. "Stupid, my ass," she muttered under her breath. Her eyes narrowed in anger when she remembered her lover's net worth and how he doled out money to her. Well, that was all going to come to an end fairly soon. She had had enough. All those finance seminars she'd been taking on the sly while she was supposed to be working were finally going to pay off.

Rena looked down at the diamond-studded Rolex watch she'd insisted on before agreeing to a particular evening event. She knew that Max was calling every five minutes, wanting to know where she was and what she was doing. When she finally got around to turning her cell on, there would be at least a dozen calls, each more angry than the previous one.

She sighed as she approached the Eazzy Breezy. A doorman, no less. She smiled, showing a fortune in exquisite veneers. She'd had to do a lot of whining to get them.

The inside of the Eazzy Breezy was no surprise. Miami sleaze, just as she'd suspected. Oh, well, she didn't have to come back if she didn't want to. She shouldered her way through the crowd of people to the end of the bar, where a young guy with a crew cut and a dark tan offered her his stool. She waited for him to hit on her with the offer to buy her a drink, but it didn't happen. Instead, he moved off through the crowd. For a full minute she panicked. He wanted young blood. Did she have a new wrinkle? Were her hands a giveaway? Damn. She could see her reflection in the mirror behind all the liquor bottles. She looked damn good. If she looked so damn good, then why wasn't anyone hitting on her?

Rena heard a voice to her left say, "It's a young crowd, don't you think?"

Rena looked at the woman sitting next to her, who was every bit as beautiful as she herself was. No one was fawning over her, either. "I think you might be right. I wanted to check it out. My secretary said this was the place to go for a nice meet and greet, and she said the drinks were super. Of course she is all of twenty-two, so that might account for her taste. I think I'm disappointed."

Kathryn, using an alias, crossed her long legs and smiled ruefully. "Well, I'm a far cry from twenty-two, that's for sure. I don't see one man here that looks to be over thirty. Now why did I know there was going to be a pink umbrella in this drink? Delia McDermott," she said, holding out her hand.

"Rena Gold."

Kathryn looked around the crowded room again and shrugged. "So, what do you do, Rena Gold?" Kathryn tried to look interested as she continued to survey the room for a possible hookup. At least that was the impression she tried to convey while at the same time being polite.

"I work for the World Bank. How about you?"

Kathryn allowed herself to be suitably impressed. "Nothing that important or glamorous. I'm a lawyer with one of the big firms in town. I'm hoping to make partner this month. If not, then I'm going to hang out my own shingle. I'm not getting any younger." She looked around again and pasted on a look of anxiety. "Damn, are there just no available men in this town?"

"What about all those nice corporate lawyers, not to mention the ones that work for the government?" Rena asked as she followed what she perceived to be Kathryn's desperate search of the room.

"Are you kidding! I don't want to be someone's mistress. Been there, done that! They never leave their wives. They want you at their beck and call, and after they reel you in, they get really stingy. I'm actually thinking of relocating to New York if this partner thing doesn't work out. I'm a really good lawyer. The men at the firm hate me. I don't know why I'm telling you this. I guess women are just naturally more sympathetic to one another. It's such a damn uphill fight. I get so weary of it all. It's really hard to meet a man once you hit forty. Don't you agree?" Kathryn asked breathlessly, as her eyes continued to rake the room.

"I haven't hit forty yet, but you're probably right. I also think both you and I have another strike against us. We're both beautiful, and I think we intimidate men."

Well, damn, aren't we confident here. Not forty, my left foot. She'll never see forty-one or forty-two again. "Aren't you the smart one. I think the two of us are going to get along just fine. So, do you have a significant other or someone lurking in the wings?" Kathryn asked.

Rena made a face. "More or less. It's pretty much run its course. Listen, if you don't have anything to do, let's go someplace else. It's obvious there is nothing here for either one of us."

"I have all night. I got my client a big settlement today, so I don't have to show up till noon tomorrow, at which point I will crow like a peacock. What do you have in mind?"

"There's a really nice piano bar in Georgetown I like.

They even have decent food. We'll have to take a cab, is that okay?"

"Sure. I live on O Street. That'll work. Tell you what, I'll pick up the tab here, and you do the taxi."

"That'll work," Rena said happily. A friend. She'd finally found someone she liked and who was interesting. Screw Max and the horse he rode in on.

Kathryn tossed down a ten and a five on the bar, and the two women left. Two young things in skimpy attire, their hair frizzed up, immediately took their bar stools. In a nanosecond, a crowd of single-breasted suits with pristine white shirts, ties askew, surrounded them. She looked at her new best friend and thought she saw Rena cringe.

Outside in the balmy summer night, Kathryn walked toward the curb with Rena, who was already holding up her hand for a taxi. "If we can't get a taxi, I can always call my limo," she said.

Kathryn hoped she looked properly impressed when she said, "You have a limo at your disposal?"

"Yes, but I try not to abuse the privilege. The people at WB sometimes talk a little too much. Tonight was my exercise night, and I like to walk a bit afterward." Rena wasn't about to confess she didn't want to use the limo because Maxwell could track her whereabouts too easily.

"Must be nice to have perks like that. What else do you get? Go ahead, make me jealous." Kathryn laughed again to show she was teasing.

Rena laughed in return. Delia was just like her friend Esther in Vegas. She forgot all about Maxwell's dire warnings about making friends and telling her business to strangers. Screw Maxwell. Suddenly she giggled. Maxwell wouldn't be getting screwed tonight. Sometimes she was just so smart she couldn't stand herself. A cab stopped and Rena gave the address to the driver as they climbed in.

"Let's see, I get to travel a lot. I have an extremely generous expense account. I get to go to all the fashion shows in Paris. I also have a penthouse apartment."

"I'm in the wrong business," Kathryn said, settling herself in the cab. "I make good money and will make even more if I make partner, but the only perk I get is a free gym and day care. Since I don't have kids, that means zip to me. Oh, and we have gourmet coffee in the kitchen at the firm. You are one lucky lady."

Rena's mouth tightened. "Not really."

"Oh, oh, that sounds like man trouble to me," Kathryn said, laughing.

Rena leaned back on the seat and closed her eyes for a moment. That's exactly what Esther would have said. She opened her eyes and stared at Kathryn. "Are you saying there's no man in your life, even on the fringes?"

"Yep, that's what I'm saying. Been burned one too many times. I hate men!" she blurted.

"I guess one broke your heart," Rena said.

"Yes. He promised me the moon and the stars. He also promised me to get a divorce. Of course, that never happened. I think I knew it when I agreed to that first date, but I didn't listen to my gut. Shame on me," Kathryn said.

"We all make mistakes. I've made my share. Sometimes I miss Vegas. That's where I'm from. I really don't like Washington, and I detest the people here. All they do is lie and cheat and try to pull dirty tricks. Lately, I've been thinking the money just isn't worth it. I don't have enough saved to cut out yet. I was hoping for a bigger nest egg. Soon, though."

Kathryn digested this information but wisely kept quiet. Maybe a few stiff drinks would loosen Rena's tongue a little more. Like what did "soon" mean?

"So, who is your man of the hour, or is it a secret? You can tell me, I'm a lawyer and can't divulge anything you tell me. Unless, of course, it's a secret."

Rena laughed, but the laughter had a bitter sound to it. "It's supposed to be a secret, but everyone in this damn town knows. At least I think they do. I see how they look at me. You know what, Delia, I look right back at them and don't flinch. I try to get out of town as much as I can."

"What exactly do you do at the World Bank?" Kathryn asked nonchalantly.

"I'm a liaison there. More accurately, the European Commission in Belgium. It's a long way from being a showgirl in Vegas. But that was a fun job for the most part but hard on the body. I had a nice life there. Today is one of the days I regret leaving."

Kathryn reached over and patted Rena's arm. "Like you said, we all make mistakes at one time or another."

Rena leaned forward when the cab pulled to the curb. Even sitting inside with the windows up, Kathryn could hear music coming from what looked like a storefront establishment.

"This is it. I think you'll like it here. I found it by accident one time when I came over here to shop. They have a few specialty stores I really like. It's quaint in a homey kind of way. They have new piano players every few weeks. You know, classy, not like Vegas with all the noise and glitter. No one bothers you here and it is definitely not a pickup joint if you know what I mean. People are quiet and just come to listen to the music."

"Uh-huh," was all Kathryn could think of to say as Rena paid the cab driver. They got out of the cab and Kathryn followed her new friend into the bar. She was going to have to make an excuse to use the ladies' room so she could call the girls. Damn, she'd been lucky. First crack off the bat and voilà, here she was with the bait. Wait till Charles and the others heard about this.

Chapter 14

Nikki parked Myra's Mercedes in a vast parking lot at Tyson's Corners. The women exited the car and moved off to where other vehicles for their use were parked, thanks to Bert Navarro. One by one, they drove off. Their destination: Ethel's Piano Bar in Georgetown. Jack was to follow in a blue pickup.

Harry ran over to a rusty-looking Ford Mustang and climbed in. His destination: Dupont Circle and the watering holes in the vicinity. He pulled alongside the blue pickup, and said, "Call me as soon as you know where you want to meet up."

"Be careful, Harry. Kathryn said she wasn't sure it was Ted at the Eazzy Breezy. She only got a glimpse of him out of the corner of her eye. She said he looked her and Rena Gold over real good, but Ted likes to look at women. It doesn't have to mean anything. I'd be real happy if you'd call for some backup just in case."

"Okay, *Mom*." Harry put the pedal to the metal and managed to goose the Mustang to a frisky thirty miles an hour. He grimaced when Jack roared past him going at least seventy.

* * *

Forty-five minutes later, Harry parked the decrepit car and walked to the Eazzy Breezy. It took him five minutes to discover Ted wasn't anywhere to be seen. He left the hangout and headed for High Flyers. He walked in and headed straight for the bar. He ordered a Foster's and looked around while he waited for his beer. The owner had to be a pilot of some kind. Every available inch of space was covered with a picture of a plane, be it a sleek jet or a crop duster. Mobiles hung from the rafters. Small planes with rotating propellers managed to circulate the air. He was surprised to see people smoking at the bar. He vaguely recalled reading something about cigar bars being exempt from the no-smoking bans.

Before the bartender handed him the Foster's he demanded ten dollars. "For what?" Harry asked.

"This is a private cigar bar. The ten bucks is your membership. So, do you want this beer or not?"

"Why the hell not," Harry said, plunking a twenty down on the bar. He couldn't resist adding, "I don't smoke."

"Tell it to someone who cares," the bartender said, moving off to wait on another customer.

Harry looked up at the television mounted above the bar. He cringed as he listened to the news anchor giving directions on how to get out of the city if the authorities ordered a mass evacuation. The bar suddenly turned silent as one of the customers asked the bartender to turn up the volume on the set.

Drinks were forgotten, cigars grew ashen in the ashtrays as the customers sat glued to what was being said on the news. Harry saw fright and fear in those closest to where he was standing. He wanted to shout out that it was all bogus, just to wipe away the fear he was seeing. How in the goddamn hell had this crap made it to the media, and how in the hell could the media run with such scare tactics without hard proof? When this was all over, someone was going to have some real serious explaining to do.

Within minutes, tabs were being rung up and the now-quiet customers were leaving the club. Harry sat down on a vacated stool and looked around. He spotted Ted Robinson at the same moment Ted spotted him. Harry hung loose, winked roguishly, then swiveled around to face the bar, the cell phone in his hand. He punched in Jack's number, and said, "Robinson and two other guys are here at the High Flyer. No, not the dick, two other guys. I think they're reporters. I am sitting tight, *Mom*," he said as he slapped the cell closed and stuck it back in his pocket. He swiveled back around as he brought the beer bottle to his lips.

The place was almost empty now, so Ted and his two friends stuck out like sore thumbs. Only two people remained at the bar with Harry. The waitresses huddled in the back by the computer screen attached to the cash register, wondering if they should pack up and go home or wait it out to see if any other customers showed up. It was obvious to Harry that tips took precedence over worries about the possibility of the plague.

Harry felt like he was on display, and he hated the feeling. He toyed with the idea of starting a fight, but it would be so unfair. He could take on Ted and his two friends with one hand and foot tied behind him and walk away the winner. He nixed the idea almost immediately when he looked around at the pricey-looking accoutrements in the bar. *Sit tight. Yeah, right.*

Harry held up his empty beer bottle for the bartender's perusal. A fresh bottle was slapped down on the bar. He really wasn't a beer drinker but when in Rome . . .

The bartender, a big guy with a ponytail and a salt-and-pepper beard, looked desperate for conversation. It was never Harry's way to initiate a conversation. He waited patiently for the bartender to let go of his angst and say something.

The bartender jerked his head in the direction of the television, where the anchor was now talking about some guy in government having an epileptic seizure at his summer home. "What do you make of that?" he asked in a worried tone.

Harry played dumb as he nursed his beer. "What? The guy with the seizure or the plague?"

"Well, shit, man, figure it out; the guy had the seizure because of the plague. Those government people are in the know. I bet he got his family out of town to safety, then he had his seizure. That's the way shit like that happens."

And this is how rumors continue to circulate, Harry thought. Harry knew the seizure had nothing to do with the plague because there wasn't any plague. Still, he had to say something. "If you're so worried, why don't you close up and take your family to safety? Personally, I think it's a crock."

"Man, haven't you been listening to the tube? Homeland Security is over there now at the embassy, and those damn Brits are tighter than a duck's ass when it comes to saying one word they don't have to. And those exterminating people bugged out. No pun intended. That tells me they found something they weren't equipped to handle. You need to listen up, man. I can't leave here until the boss says I can. This is a chain, and you don't get paid if you don't follow orders."

"So, let me get this straight," Harry said, leaning across the bar. "You're piss-ass scared, but you won't leave to take your family to safety because whoever owns this joint won't pay you? That sucks, man," he said, mimicking the bartender. He tossed some bills on the bar, drained his beer, and slid off the stool.

Harry was halfway to the door when he walked back to

the bar. "See those three guys sitting over there?" he asked, pointing to Robinson and his friends.

"Yeah."

"They're reporters. Well, I know for certain the tall one is. He broke the story this morning on the rats and the plague. Talk to him, but don't believe anything he says because he lies."

"Huh?"

"Never mind," Harry said, waving him off. He walked outside and moved away in the darkness to see if Robinson would follow him. He stood in the doorway of a shop called Stitch and Sew and called Jack. "So, what do you want me to do?"

"Wait ten more minutes. If they don't come out, then come over here to Ethel's Piano Bar in Georgetown. You can fall asleep in this place, that's how boring it is, but the girls are all in the nest, and they've made contact with Rena Gold. We just have to wait to see how it all plays out, and before you can ask, there's been no word from Charles."

"Shit! Here they come, and they don't look like happy campers. By the way, Jack, it's dead, as in *dead*, around here. Right now I feel meaner than a snake."

"Then do something about it. Those three assholes are responsible for what's going down. Bye, son."

Shit! Shit! Shit! Harry stepped out of the doorway of Stitch and Sew and sauntered down the street, but not before he gave Robinson the finger. In the blink of an eye, he whirled around on one foot and stamped both feet to get the men's attention. They stopped in their tracks as Harry lunged for all three. Five heartbeats later all three men were flat on the sidewalk. They tried to slide backward on the gritty concrete as they looked up at Harry in stunned surprise.

"That's for starting false rumors and making this town

go on Red Alert. Don't even think about giving me bullshit that you didn't do it. I *know* you did. You're nothing but slimeballs swimming around in a sea of pus. Now get up off your asses and get out of here before I *really* hurt you."

Ted was braver than Monroe and Ellis. He got up, dusted himself off, and advanced a step. "Listen to me, you piece of shit. We have pictures of those Reston Exterminating trucks. And their license plates. You know what else? There really is no Reston Exterminating. How do we know this, you might ask? It's simple. We're reporters. You're just muscle. So, run back to Emery and tell him I know who was driving those Reston trucks that suddenly dropped off the face of the earth. *They're* back here, aren't they? Jesus! They are, aren't they? I wish you could see your face, Wong." Ted suddenly doubled over laughing. "Son of a bitch! *I knew it.*"

Harry's heart was beating so fast he thought it was going to jump right out of his chest. His fist shot out, and the laughter died in Ted's throat.

Monroe and Ellis helped Ted to his feet. Harry stamped his feet again, and they ran off like little boys caught stealing apples from a pushcart.

Harry headed for the rusty Mustang, but before he turned on the engine, he reported in to Jack. "There wasn't any sense in following them. The night's over for those guys. You still want me to come to the piano bar?"

"Yeah," Jack responded. "The girls are getting it on here. It's one big, happy party. Kathryn pretended Nikki was an acquaintance she knew from her legal practice and invited her to sit at their table. From there on it was like a domino effect. It's a little involved, but they're all sitting around a table drinking wine spritzers. Gold is rapidly getting snockered from the looks of things. I'm back in a corner, and it's dark in here. Ambience, you know."

Harry turned the key in the ignition. The old car

coughed and sputtered before it died. He waited a few seconds with Jack on hold and tried again. This time the engine caught, and he eased out of the lot and headed for one of the main arteries that would take him to Georgetown, all the while talking to Jack. "Robinson's onto the drill, Jack. I'm not sure the other two are buying into it, and this whole damn town knows Robinson has vigilantes on the brain. He sees them everywhere. Now, he didn't mention them by name, just that he put two and two together. You know what else, Jack, there's very little traffic tonight. This is getting scary. Have you been watching the news?"

"No, there's no TV here in this place. It's full, though. They close at twelve thirty. How soon will you be here? I'm going to fall asleep listening to all these Golden Oldies."

"Whenever this junk pile gets me there is when you'll see me. You did get the part about Robinson taking pictures of the license plates, right?"

"I got it all, Harry. I still can't reach Charles. I called the farm, and Myra and Annie sound like they're drunk. Annie admitted to a little libation. They haven't heard from Charles, either. Isn't this a fun night, Harry?"

"Up yours, Jack!" Harry said as he clicked his cell phone shut and tried his best to get the Mustang over thirty. It bucked, the odometer hitting thirty-five, and chugged onward. Harry cursed in every language he knew. Then he cursed out Jack and Charles Martin. He was about to start all over again when he realized he was a block away from the piano bar. He found a parking spot with no trouble and hoofed his way down the street to the bar.

Jack was right, it was dark inside. Harry waited a few minutes for his eyes to adjust to the darkness before he moved forward. He saw the girls, heard the final strains of "Moonlight Becomes You." The applause was soft but appreciative. The piano player, a short, balding man, finished his set, then ambled over to the bar. People started to talk to one another. Harry finally spotted Jack in the back, nursing a beer. He slid into the booth across from him, and said, "So, whasup? I see what you mean about falling asleep in this joint."

"The guy is okay, but he's no Bobby Short."

"Am I supposed to know who that is?" Harry asked sourly.

"No, I was just making conversation. What the hell are we going to do about Ted and his cronies?"

"Listen, Jack, I don't want to be a party to the crap that's going on. People are panicking. I would be, too, if I didn't know this is all a big setup. Someone has to do or say something. We can't let this continue."

"What? You mean like calling in anonymously to television stations or the papers? The papers are what started this in the first place. I don't feel any better about this than you do. Until we hear from Charles, our hands are tied. If we go off half-cocked, we could make things worse. *Capisce?*"

Harry shrugged. He didn't care what Jack or Charles said. First chance he got he was calling someone. "How much longer are we staying here?"

"Till the girls give me a sign the night is over. Nikki stopped on her way to the ladies' room to say Miss Gold is very talkative and loves having met new friends. She's particularly taken with dowdy Isabelle because Isabelle has a little musical background and can actually play the piano and talk about it intelligently. So far Gold hasn't given anything up other than she has what Nik called a stingy sugar daddy. They're making plans to meet up again tomorrow evening for dinner. Girls' night out after work. Gold offered up the use of her limo. That's all I know right now. I think there's one more set, and it's lights out for this place. It can't be too soon for me. By the way, Nik said that Gold is sharp as a tack."

Harry snorted. "She can't be that sharp since she hasn't figured out this is all a setup and Kathryn was a plant. I thought you said she was snockered."

"I did, and she is. I guess she said or did something before she became inebriated. What do you want from me, Harry? *They're women.* They talk in code. They only understand each other. Anyone with a brain knows women are the smarter sex. As men, we're just clay in their hands."

Harry tried to widen his slanted eyes, but it didn't work. "And you're just figuring this out? I don't want to be your friend anymore; you're too stupid."

Jack burst out laughing. "That was a good one, Harry. I needed a good laugh."

In spite of himself, Harry grinned. "Looks like the last set is ready to start. If I manage to nod off, wake me. I have a 5:00 AM workout scheduled for tomorrow."

As the piano player sat down and flexed his fingers before striking the keyboard, Jack rolled his eyes. He sipped at the last of the beer in his bottle and waved to the middle-aged waitress for the check. Harry's eyes remained closed, but Jack knew the martial-arts expert was aware of everything going on around him. He'd long ago given up trying to figure out why or how Harry did anything.

With one number left to go in the set, Jack nudged Harry. "I paid the bill. Let's go outside so it won't seem like we're waiting and watching. We'll just be two guys talking about music who are getting ready to call it a night."

When the women exited the piano bar, Harry and Jack

were standing off to the side. Jack was smoking a cigarette as he pretended to look at the ground, the trees planted curbside, and the curb itself.

"What are you looking for?" a patron coming out of the piano bar asked. "Did you lose something?"

"Rats!" Jack said loud enough for Kathryn and her party to hear.

Nikki whirled around and literally screamed. "Did you say there are rats here?"

Rena Gold turned around and lost her footing. Alexis and Isabelle caught her before she fell. "Whoa there, little lady," Alexis said, holding on to her.

"Are there rats here?" Gold asked in a shaky voice.

"They're all over the city," someone said. "Didn't you hear the news earlier? Homeland Security issued an alert. They're afraid of the plague," he said before he walked away.

"Oh, my God!" Rena Gold said.

"I don't think it's true," Harry chirped up.

"I don't believe it, either," Jack said.

Rena Gold looked from Harry to Jack and asked, "Then why did that man say what he said?" She listed to the side, but Alexis held on tightly. "Someone needs to call those vigilantes to take care of it. They can do anything. Where are they when they're needed?" And on and on she went until her cab rolled to the curb. "Someone should get in touch with them. I donated a huge sum of money to their defense. Maxwell didn't like that one little bit."

Kathryn was on it in a nanosecond. "Who is Maxwell?"

Rena Gold giggled. She leaned over and whispered in Kathryn's ear. "He's the stingy bastard that pays my bills. I'm not allowed to talk about him or mention his name."

Kathryn winked slyly to show she understood. "Your secret is safe with me. See you tomorrow evening. I'll give you a call around midday. Remember, I don't have to go to work until noon because I got my client that settlement."

"Right. Right. It was so nice meeting all of you. Tomorrow night—or is it today already?—the party is on me," Rena said happily, as her cab pulled away.

"Well, damn," was all Yoko could think of to say. "Do you think you should have gone with her, Kathryn?"

"I thought about it, but when she sobers up, she might have second thoughts. It worked out perfectly, with no suspicion that I could discern. Do you all agree?"

The women nodded and moved off. Harry and Jack followed at a discreet distance.

"And she donated to the vigilantes' defense fund," Jack cackled. "Sometimes you just step in it, and it's golden. See, we're having fun. What say you, Harry?"

Harry scowled as he peeled off and stepped to the curb to hail a cab. No way was he going to chug his way home in the rusty Mustang. "Screw you, Jack."

Chapter 15

Rena Gold woke in good spirits even though she had a throbbing headache. She brushed her teeth, showered, and dressed for another uneventful day in her life. While she waited for the coffee to finish dripping into the pot, she thought about the new friends she'd met the night before. It was the first enjoyable evening she'd had since leaving Las Vegas.

As she poured her coffee, she suddenly remembered her cell phone. She flinched slightly. There was going to be hell to pay for that little folly. She reached for her handbag on the counter, where she'd tossed it when she got in. She yanked out the phone and glared at it but didn't turn it on. As she brought the steaming cup to her lips, she realized she had to decide, right here and now, if she cared. She decided she didn't give a tinker's damn about Maxwell Zenowicz. Last night was all the proof she needed that she didn't belong here and that she hated him. Her old mother, whom she loved dearly, would say she was in a bit of a pickle.

Rena supposed maybe she *was* in a bit of a pickle, depending on how one looked at things. Maybe if she played her cards right, fought to the finish, she could walk away with a killing. She felt light-headed just thinking that maybe she was finally going to get out from under Maxwell. Vegas was looking real good and it didn't even have a state income tax. If she was smart, she could take all her plunder, assuming she got said plunder, and start a business. Something for women. Esther and a few others could help, and they'd get out of show business. Being on the fringe was almost as good as participating and a whole hell of a lot easier on the body and joints.

And all this new confidence she was feeling was thanks to a lawyer she met in a bar. She could hardly wait for tonight to meet up with all her new friends.

When the doorbell rang, Rena shuddered. One of Maxwell's security team coming to check on her. If she didn't answer the door, the man would use a key. That was just one of the things she hated about Maxwell. The second thing she hated was the way Maxwell allowed them to ogle her.

Carrying her cup, Rena walked to the foyer and opened the door. She looked up at the tall, burly man standing in the doorway. She almost laughed in the man's face when he said, "The president wants you to call him. It seems your cell phone is in the OFF mode. He said to tell you the phone is always supposed to be kept in the ON position in case he needs to reach you."

"Yes, he did say that, didn't he? Go back and tell the president I'm PMSing, and until that phase is over, the phone will be in the OFF mode. Thanks for stopping by." Rena slammed the door shut and slid the dead bolt, something she'd forgotten to do last night when she got home. Once inside, with the dead bolt on, no one could enter.

Never one to make rash decisions, Rena realized she'd just made the Queen Mother of all rash decisions. She looked around at the spacious penthouse apartment. It was lovely—exquisite, really. She had good taste, and, in the beginning, money had been no object where Maxwell was concerned. She loved the floor-to-ceiling windows. She liked looking out at the starry night and seeing the Capital's monuments, but she preferred the brighter, gaudier lights of Vegas.

Rena eyed the creamy white furniture and matching carpeting that looked like no one ever sat or walked on it. It was all contemporary and went with the rooms and the lighting, but it wasn't who she was. In her heart of hearts, when she wasn't playing a role like she was playing with Maxwell, she was a down-home girl, preferring home and hearth with a roaring fire in a big old fieldstone fireplace. Cozying in with a few good women friends and bashing men till the wee hours of the morning, more often than not drinking coffee or hot chocolate and sometimes a few bottles of good wine.

Rena walked around the rooms, checking the soil on the luscious green plants that a florist tended once a week. It was a nice perk, but she could water her own plants the way she had in Vegas, so in the end it wasn't really a perk at all. Just like all the other perks weren't really perks. When you had to pay with your body for a perk, it simply wasn't a perk. She was angry as she marched into her bedroom, which was as big as one of the reception rooms in the White House, and headed straight for her closet. She set her coffee cup down on the dresser and moved over to the huge walk-in closet. She stared down at the lush white carpeting on the floor, knowing if she dropped to her knees and peeled back the thick carpeting at the corners, she would see the safe she'd had installed in the floor six months ago. That had really taken some doing, but she'd managed it. Just the way she managed everything else once she put her mind to it.

The only thing that bothered her was Maxwell's security people. The moment they sensed that she could cause the president harm, they'd take care of her in ways she didn't want to think about. Maxwell had warned her early on what would happen if she ever crossed him. And she never had, until now.

Rena backed out of the closet, her thoughts on the group of women she'd met at the piano bar. Savvy women. Even the dowdy one had some spunk.

Friends.

Back in the kitchen, Rena poured herself a second cup of coffee. This time she sat down at a chrome-and-glass table that held fresh flowers. The fresh flowers were another little perk. She looked around for her purse and the prepaid cell she used to call Esther and a few other friends in Vegas. Then she realized it was too early to call Vegas. And the girls always slept well into the afternoon since they worked almost all night. The downside to working in Vegas was you hardly ever got to see the sun. She reached inside her bag for the World Bank cell phone Maxwell had given her. She switched it from OFF to VIBRATION mode and set it on the table, knowing it would vibrate continuously until it slid off the table and, she hoped, break into a hundred pieces on the marble floor.

To kill more time, she turned on the television and gaped at what she was seeing and hearing. She switched channels, but the same news played out on every channel. Rats, plague, frightened people, other people saying there was no cause for alarm while the camera panned the choked highways. She looked at the vibrating phone as it shimmied on the glass-top table. Maybe she should answer it and just get it over with.

Rena sucked in her breath and did a few deep-breathing exercises until she was able to manage a throaty, sensual, "Hello, darling."

It was hard to get past the snarling, high-pitched voice that was reaming her out. She got up and walked through the living room to the bedroom as she listened to the president's tirade, her eyes on the floor of her closet. She listened a little while longer, then her back stiffened. Knowing how he hated to be addressed by anything other than Maxwell or President Zenowicz, she said, "Listen up, Maxie. I've had just about all of your bullshit that I can stand. I told your . . . your person I wasn't feeling well. What part of that don't you understand? Do not talk when I am speaking, do you hear me, Maxwell? And remember this, too, Maxie, I know where all the bodies are buried. So, having said that, be extra nice to me, and I will be extra nice to you the next time I see you. To show you how kind and caring I am, I suggest you go to your doctor and get a shot to ward off the plague. You have been watching the news, haven't you? I'll call you when I'm feeling better. I certainly hope I'm not coming down with the plague."

It occurred to her to wonder exactly what the plague was and how one could catch it. Rena disconnected, then turned off the cell, knowing it would irritate Maxwell to the point where he would be sputtering and cursing and lashing out at anyone in his path. "Like I give two shits," she mumbled to herself. In five minutes he would be running to the doctor because he was a hypochondriac.

Rena looked at the coffee still in her cup. It was cold now, so she heated it again in the microwave oven. She needed to sit very still and think about Maxwell Zenowicz and what had been going on of late. She'd picked up on hostility directed at her from some of her coworkers. She'd heard some strange rumors that weren't meant for her ears. Not about herself but about Maxwell. As with everything in the world of high finance, there were two sides—their side and the other side. There were those who said Maxwell Zenowicz was the last person in the world who should be president of the World Bank. Those same people said he was a political appointee for a favor done for the administration. Other people said he bought his job with his vast wealth. His staff, according to Maxwell himself, hated him and his Gestapo-like methods. He defended his position saying that he ran a tight ship and wasn't interested in winning popularity contests. The staff said he had shoddy methods of doing things, and if they didn't clean up his messes, he'd be out on the curb, flat on his ass. She believed every word of it.

He was a womanizer, and she knew she wasn't the only woman in his stable. She was, however, the only *kept* woman. She didn't mind his dalliances one little bit because the more of them he had, the more he left her alone.

She also knew a very discreet audit was going on within the bank. Staff talk and whisper, and, if one paid attention, one could pick up all kinds of tidbits. When one had the smarts to put it all together, a story emerged that wouldn't be to anyone's liking.

She'd been planning on bolting in the near future, but the way things were going, it just might be wise to head for safer shores sooner rather than later. She could get lost in Vegas. As the saying went, "What happens in Vegas stays in Vegas." Something like that. Still, it would be a shame to leave since she'd just found new friends.

How long before those crazy alphabet agencies here in D.C. started snooping around? She'd be the first one to go since her job was just a salary on paper. One of those gigantic perks for favors rendered. They'd splash her all over the big screen. She'd be toast in seconds. She might even go to jail. The thought horrified her.

She had learned one thing from Maxwell, though. She'd learned how to send her money offshore. Not that Maxwell knew he'd helped her. She'd slipped him a really nice doctored-up cocktail one evening and he'd slept for twenty-four hours while she helped herself to his computer and his financial records. She'd simply picked the lock on his Halliburton case with an ice pick and gone to work. It had taken her three solid hours to figure out what his password was, and when she finally came up with it, she'd laughed hysterically. Six dollar signs, $$$$$$, and she had his life in front of her. A laugh tickled at her throat even now when she thought about it.

She was so frazzled she couldn't think straight. She really should start to pack. Then again, maybe she should go into the office and tidy up there if she wasn't going to go back. She would do the right thing and type up her resignation and leave it on her desk for someone to find come Monday morning. She hoped she'd remembered to lock her office door. By then she'd be long gone. *Hopefully*, she'd be long gone, and not dead in some ditch somewhere. Though, come to think of it, she hadn't seen a ditch anywhere since coming to Washington. Maybe they'd dump her somewhere on a grassy knoll out in Manassas. The thought was so depressing, Rena got up, rinsed out her cup, and left the building. She'd pack when she got back.

Rena's spirits were high. When she joined her new friends for dinner, she'd thank them all for giving her the guts to do what she needed to do. She'd offer an open invitation to all of them, even the dowdy-looking librarian, to visit her in Vegas anytime they wanted. She just knew they would be friends forever.

Rena was back in her penthouse by one o'clock. She shed her Chanel suit, popped a Lean Cuisine in the microwave, readied a new pot of coffee, and set to work packing.

By three o'clock she had all four Louis Vuitton suitcases filled. The big problem was how was she going to get them out of the building and to the airport? Her plan was to ship the suitcases separately so that when she was ready to leave, she would just walk out of the building like she was going shopping. Even if she bribed one of the staff in the building, Maxwell and his people would be on it in a nanosecond. She also knew her limo driver would give it all up in a heartbeat. She didn't know anyone else well enough to bribe. In Vegas, all she would have had to do was snap her fingers and the job would have been done, and the deal would never have seen the light of day. Maybe the girls would have an idea this evening when she met up with them and told them what was going on. Surely one of them would come up with something plausible.

She looked in her closet to see what she'd left. Just enough to get her through the next couple of days. Plus an outfit for tonight, a good pair of shoes, and that was it.

Nothing in the penthouse was in her name, so she didn't have to worry about paying anything or about bills coming due. She felt a little sad that there was nothing to cancel. She'd leave the World Bank cell on the kitchen counter. She did have to log on to her computer and move the money in her personal checking account. She also needed to hit up a few ATM machines for as much cash as she could get her hands on.

Then it was good-bye, Washington, D.C.

Rena walked around the spacious apartment again. No, she wouldn't miss this place one little bit.

Chapter 16

Charles Martin walked outside into the bright summer sunshine and took stock of his surroundings. His heart was beating so fast and hard he thought he might keel over at any moment. In the whole of his life, even during his wartime years, he had never seen such total and utter destruction.

The storm had come out of nowhere, and he'd barely had time to get the dogs and himself into the underground bunker beneath the Big House. All he could remember was a whistling sound that had set the dogs into a frenzy. He'd stayed in the bunker for seven long hours with the two dogs huddled next to him. He'd never been truly frightened for his life until the minute that the heavens exploded over the mountain. Now, on shaky legs, he surveyed the damage he was seeing. The Bell JetRanger helicopter was gone, probably swept from its moorings someplace on the mountain. The cable car hung drunkenly from its nest. There were no roofs on any of the buildings. Monster pine trees clogged and cluttered the compound. The rich resin scent engulfed him as he tried gingerly to make his way around to assess the damage.

He was cut off from the world, pure and simple. The satellite dish was nowhere in sight. The special phones were dead, the computer room a soggy, sodden mess of wires and plastic. And no one was going to come to his rescue. He couldn't even hike down the mountain because it was mined with explosives.

The dogs looked up at him, not understanding what was going on. "Boys, we have a slight problem here. Let's see if we can find something to eat in the kitchen. If we have a kitchen, that is." The dogs followed him as he made his way cautiously through the fallen trees. His main worry was the girls. He could survive here for a while. Sooner or later, the girls would know something was wrong and act accordingly. But sooner or later could be a long way off.

While he was feeding the dogs, he heard a far-off but deafening noise and rushed to what had once been a doorway. Overhead he could see five helicopters circling the mountain compound. He blinked when he saw dark-clad figures clinging to cables and dropping to the ground. Friend or foe? Charles felt his guts start to churn, but the dogs weren't kicking up a fuss. *Friendlies?* The dogs moved to his side and stood at attention, waiting to see what Charles would do.

Charles picked his way through the debris and waited for the first man on the ground to approach. "Looks like you hit a spate of trouble, eh, mate?"

Charles just looked at him, a helpless look on his face.

"Well, we're here to help. By tomorrow at this time, you'll never know a storm came through here."

Charles finally found his tongue. "How did you know? Who sent you?"

"Friends," the man said. "They said to give you this."

Charles reached for what looked like a diplomatic pouch. He needed to go somewhere private to look inside, but he waited as more men dropped to the ground. Chain saws started to whine and screech, the sounds dueling with the noise of hovering helicopters. He saw a crew of four men take up positions near the cable car. A second later giant rolls of cable dropped to the ground. Not one wasted motion as the men worked as a team. More heavy wooden boxes dropped to the ground. Ten minutes later, the helicopters moved out of range and five more took their places. More men, more supplies dropped to the ground.

"What do you want me to do?" Charles asked.

"Stay out of our way, mate. Just let us do our job, and we'll have you operational before you can say 'Queen Mum.'" Charles blinked, then blinked again. No! Impossible! Well, perhaps with modern technology what it was, anything was possible.

Charles, the dogs at his side, moved off toward what was left of the back of the Big House. He looked around for something to sit on, but there was nothing. It was Murphy who led him to a log at the far end of the pool, which had collapsed inward. All he could see was a foot of water on the bottom. It looked like the colorful tiles had exploded from the sides. They were everywhere.

The dogs were breathing heavily. He wasn't sure if they were frightened for themselves or him. Probably both, he decided. He talked calmly to both of them as he stroked their heads. Within minutes, both animals were lying at his feet, their heads between their paws. They'd been reassured, and now they could relax.

Charles opened the pouch that was as big as a bread box. He grew light-headed at the contents. A laptop. Two special cell phones. A brown envelope with a huge red seal over the enclosure and a thick red stamp in large block letters that said, "TOP SECRET."

Charles ran his tongue over his lips as he drew a deep breath. A sudden rage, unlike anything he'd ever experienced, riveted through him. Rage at his circumstances, rage that other people had to bail *him* out. He looked down at his hands and saw how badly they were shaking. *His hands were shaking.* This was another first. How had it come to this? Murphy whined as Grady pawed at his leg. Both shaking hands went down to soothe the anxious dogs, who waited moments before lying back down. This time their ears stayed up, their eyes alert.

Charles ripped at the envelope and pulled out the contents. The relief he felt, the total surrender to calmness, left him in a euphoric state. He'd been so sure the pouch was from his friend Lizzie. Instead, the name at the end of the letter was Kollar. The letter wasn't long, but it said everything he needed to know.

Sir Charles,

I'm sorry about your current situation. The same thing happened to my father and me in our third year at Big Pine Mountain. I've sent help. You should be up and running in three days' time, operational by this time tomorrow. My people saw the destruction via satellite. The Bell JetRanger is midway down the mountain. It exploded on impact. It might take an extra week to clear away the debris. A replacement will be sent shortly. The way I see it, you have a three-day vacation. Call me if I can be of any further assistance. I've programmed in my special number. Stay well, Sir Charles.

Charles closed his eyes for a moment while he thought about the contents of the letter. Kathryn would have said, *"Three-day vacation, my ass. Get on the stick and pull this mess together. We don't want to hear about your little problem on the mountain. It's just a pimple on your ass, Charles."* He laughed then, a genuine sound of mirth that woke the dogs.

Charles looked down at the laptop as he waited for it to power up. He thanked God now for the long talks he and Kollar had had prior to the decision to switch mountains. He'd sent all his encrypted files to Kollar, and they were stored on the mountaintop in Barcelona. Kollar's originals were here and so now lost. But there were copies of his in Spain, too. Foresight.

In the world of espionage and counterespionage, you could never be too careful or too safe. Right now it was win-win, and for that he would be forever grateful.

Charles shoved in one of the memory sticks, and the screen in front of him came to life. He tapped furiously and clicked the SEND button so many times his finger got a blister on it. A blister was the least of his problems. While he waited for the return responses to come through, he punched in Jack Emery's number. When the DA came on the line, surly as usual, Charles barked orders.

"Hold on there, hotshot," Jack said. "You need to hear our problems first. This is not going well, Charles. The shit hit the fan, and it is splattering in all directions. Right now the girls are holed up in McLean at Myra's farmhouse. Everything is in play with a few side problems. It seems the city is on high alert due to rat infestation at the British Embassy. Reston Exterminating is out of business. Ted Robinson is onto us. There really are rats at the embassy. The Brits are being close-mouthed—there hasn't been a peep out of them. As we speak, there is a mass exodus from the District as everyone is afraid of the plague and the so-called terrorists who are behind it. Traffic going out of the city is unbelievable. Even with opening up the incoming lanes to outbound traffic, there are some places where the roads are one big parking lot. On top of that, the rumor mill is reporting the pending sale of the *Post*. Our very own Annie is supposedly buying it. Is that true? I don't have a clue.

"The girls made contact with Rena Gold. They're back on for this evening. Right out in the open, Charles. Do you have any idea how frightening that is for Harry, Bert, and me? By the way, the CDC is at the embassy in their Hazmat suits. Apparently the Brits were 'persuaded' to agree to let them in. Now, that's scary for these Washingtonians. They're into designer labels, not biogear. Homeland Security is trying to take center stage, and the two are warring with each other. You can talk now, Charles. I won't guarantee to listen. Where the hell were you when we needed you?"

Something sparked in Charles as he listened to Jack's tirade. He deserved the district attorney's wrath. He struggled to remain calm as he looked around at the destruction on the mountaintop. "Actually, Jack, I was holed up in the bunker under the Big House with the dogs for seven hours. A storm hit the mountain and destroyed everything. It might have been a tornado for all I know. I've never personally seen or lived through one of them. The high winds blew the helicopter off the mountain, and it exploded. The cable car is hanging uselessly. The only access now is by helicopter. Kollar sent people who are now working nonstop to rebuild everything. The communications room is waterlogged. The satellite dish is gone. I just now got a laptop and a new phone, thanks to Pappy. I'm working as we speak. For the next few hours, until I get things in place and get thorough briefings, you are on your own. Can you handle it, Jack? Just say yes or no."

Jack played Charles's words over in his mind. Suddenly he felt lower than a snake's belly, and rightly so. "Yes, we can handle it. Do you mean the whole mountain?"

"Just about. All the roofs are gone. The pool caved in. The tall pines snapped, and there's no place to walk. We have it under control, but like I said, I'm going to need a few more hours. The plague, eh? Even I couldn't have come up with that one. I'll get back to you, Jack."

Jack powered down and thought about the call for a good five minutes. He wondered why he hadn't seen anything on the news about a storm of the magnitude Charles described hitting Big Pine Mountain. Then he gave himself a slap on the head. Big Pine Mountain was not on anyone's radar, so how could they report on it? But then how did that Greek guy who owned the mountain find out? He snorted then at his own stupidity. Those guys were hooked into the spook business, and the satellites in orbit would have tracked the mountain and told the Greek precisely what had happened there. Damn, he was stupid sometimes. Maybe he needed to get a book on the spy game instead of winging it by the seat of his pants. But, all things considered, working on the fly had worked out pretty well.

Jack next called Myra. He relayed Charles's message. He heard her sigh of relief and Annie's whoop of pleasure now that things were going to be all right. He told them to alert the girls because he had other things to do. What those things were, he didn't know at the moment. What he did know was that he was going to have to go into the office and pretend he still worked there if he wanted to ever draw another paycheck.

When Jack arrived at his office he looked around. He yanked at the arm of one of his assistants and demanded to know what was going on.

"We're being relocated, Jack. Didn't you get the memo? Court's dark. It's that plague thing. We're all supposed to go to the clinic and get some kind of booster shots."

"Who gave that order?" Jack asked testily.

The ADA looked at Jack, and barked, "Who the hell do

you think gave the order? Your boss, that's who. I just heard on the news every judge in town has been taken off to some undisclosed location."

"Where are we supposed to go?" Jack asked.

"I don't know where *you're* supposed to go. I'm being relocated to Chevy Chase, Maryland, with all the other peons and office staff."

"This is bullshit," Jack muttered as he marched into his boss's office.

Brandon Hollister, Bud to his colleagues and friends, looked up at Jack. "What are you doing here, Emery?"

Jack waved his arms about. "I just heard about all this. What's going on, Bud?"

"Orders from on high. Show the politicians a picture of a rat, and they immediately identify. They're the ones calling the shots. That jerk-off from HS is scaring the crap out of this whole damn town. They sure are mum as to what they found at the embassy, and those tight-lipped Brits are not helping matters one bit. By the way, you're going to McLean, Virginia. Court's dark for the next ten days. That order just came in an hour ago. Give you a chance to catch up on your paperwork."

Jack planted his feet more firmly on the ground and took a deep breath. "Bud, I do not think there is a plague in this town. I think those three reporters stirred this all up because there's no news going down. I've heard so many damn rumors in the past twenty-four hours my head is spinning. I heard the vigilantes are back in town. I heard the plague is going to wipe out this city. I heard the *Post* is up for sale. And, ask yourself this: Why are the Brits being so close-mouthed about all of this? The embassy, after all, does belong to them. Technically, it's British territory, and they must have given the CDC permission to go in. Personally, I think it's all a big setup. On top of that, what's this garbage circulating about the World Bank? C'mon, Bud, look at the whole picture."

Bud Hollister eyeballed his best prosecutor and winced slightly. Everything Jack had said made sense. In the end, all he could do was shrug, and say, "I have to follow orders, Jack, you know that."

"It's all a crock, Bud."

"So, who's buying the *Post?*"

Jack looked his boss right in the eye, and said, "One of the vigilantes. The rich one, the Countess something or other. That's the rumor. Of course, with all the layers in place, how is anyone going to prove that?"

"Jesus! Where *do* you come up with this stuff?"

Jack forced a laugh he was far from feeling. "In bars, where else?"

"Figures," Hollister said as he resumed his packing. Almost as an afterthought, he asked, "What was that about the World Bank?"

"Some shifty stuff going on over there. We'll probably be trying the whole lot of them at some point."

"Jesus!" Hollister said again.

"So, boss, if it's all the same to you, I'd prefer to stay in my own house, and my paperwork is all caught up. Call me if you need me, okay?"

Hollister nodded as he continued packing up his things.

Chapter 17

Ted Robinson looked down at his watch to see the time: 7:10. He considered leaving the *Post* and going home. Or maybe he should stop somewhere and get a drink. He looked around to see where Joe Espinosa was. Espinosa hated sports and didn't know a football from a baseball, and yet here he was writing a sports column. The world was fast going to hell in Robinson's opinion.

He slumped in his chair while he waited for Espinosa to close up shop. His thoughts as always went to Maggie and how much he missed her. He knew now, in his newfound wisdom, that if he could turn back the clock and undo what he'd done, he'd do so in a second. Since that wasn't going to happen, all he could do was suck it up and move forward. Forward to where?

Tick Fields had come up dry, so dry, he was gasping for breath. He and Joe had plunked down another thousand bucks for Tick to bribe someone to see if he could tap into credit card usage for Maggie and Lizzie Fox. A thousand dollars to find out neither woman had used her cards since they'd disappeared, another five hundred bucks to another source to find out their cell phones hadn't been used, either. "Privacy Act, my ass," Ted muttered to no one in particular. If you had the goddamn dollars, there was always someone willing to take a risk and scoop up the money. Which just left him $750 more out of pocket. And all for nothing. Fields, who was a greedy bastard to begin with, had said there was nothing more he could do in his quest to find the missing women. Then he'd added insult to injury, and said, "Face it, Ted, she doesn't want anything to do with you, so get over it and forget about whatever you hoped might or might not happen."

Yeah, right. Easier said than done. He loved Maggie. Would always love her.

"Hey, sport, let's bug out of this place," Joe Espinosa said, coming up behind Ted and knocking his feet to the floor. "What say we hit the Bamboo Grill and get a couple of beers? There's a hottie there I'd like to get to know better. Unless you have other plans."

"Nah." Ted bent down to yank at the backpack under his desk. When he looked up again, he whistled softly. "Do you see what I see, Joe?"

Espinosa dropped to his haunches. "Yeah. Jesus Christ, this is like a summit meeting. What the hell is going on?"

Still on his haunches, Espinosa looked up at Ted. "Why are Director Cummings, Navarro, and, I assume, two other agents, and Roger Nolan, head of Homeland Security, here? Who's that dude in the drop-dead suit?"

Still bent over, Ted inched his head up for a second look. His eyes almost popped out of their sockets. "Well, bless my soul if it isn't Nigel Summers, the head dude from the British Embassy. I interviewed him last year. Nice guy. Stiff but nice. I can't be sure, but I think it is the guy from the Centers for Disease Control. His name is Wylie. Dave Wylie. I think I saw a picture of him not too long ago. Sure looks like him. You should know him now that you're on sports. He used to be a linebacker for the Rams. What the hell are they all doing here at the *Post?*"

"Is that a rhetorical question, or do you really think since I took over the sports desk yesterday that this would come under my purview, Ted?" Espinosa hissed.

Ted ignored his colleague. "Seven o'clock at night is a weird time of day to hold a meeting of this kind, wouldn't you say?"

"This kind, this time? What the hell does that mean? We're hiding under your desk, Ted. You realize that, right? Shouldn't we bug out of here before they see us? Do you think this is serious?"

"So, what if they see us? So what, Joe? Hell yes, this is about as serious as it gets. Levy is still here over in the corner. Jackson was here a few minutes ago. The place isn't entirely empty. I saw Jessie Greer heading to the kitchen not five minutes ago, so it can't be a *secret* meeting. We aren't exactly hiding, we're just bent over . . . doing nothing. The only way we're going to find out what's going on is to ask. That means we march right up to Sullivan's office and ask. We're reporters, for God's sake. That means we have a right to be nosy. And we're on our home turf, so that gives us the right. On the count of three, get up. One! Two! Three!"

Both men were on their feet when Ted gasped. "Chief!"

"In my office!" the EIC bellowed. "You, too, Espinosa."

"It's magic," Ted said out of the corner of his mouth.

"Magic, my ass. Those guys are here to nail you to the wall, and me, too," he added as an afterthought. "Guilt by association. I bet if we wait five minutes, someone from the *Sentinel* and the *News* will be here," Espinosa mumbled.

"Careful what you wish for, buddy."

Inside Sullivan's office, Ted looked from one man to the other, then at his boss. It was a hell of an intimidating group. Ted squared his shoulders. Espinosa did the same. Introductions were made. Handshakes offered. Sullivan then led the parade of men to what was laughingly called the conference room. It was a conference room because it had a long table and chairs, but the twelve chairs were mismatched and the table was scarred and covered in dust. Ted was tempted to bend over and blow at the dust to see what effect if any it would have on the men in the room. Sullivan motioned to the chairs, and everyone took a seat.

"We'll wait five more minutes, and if the others aren't here by then, we'll simply go ahead of them, and they can play catch-up."

No sooner were the words out of his mouth than Jessie Greer arrived, escorting four men into the room, then quietly closing the door. Ted felt light-headed when he saw Monroe and Ellis, along with their bosses. He was afraid to look at Espinosa because he knew, just knew, the guy was hyperventilating. Which was what Ted was going to do any second himself.

To Ted's mind, Liam Sullivan was the most imposing man in the room. Freedom of the press, that kind of thing. In his gut, Ted knew that not one of the men in the room would or could intimidate Sullivan or the two EICs from the rival papers. No way, no how. He felt a little better with that thought under his belt.

Sullivan took the floor, his wild white hair standing on end. Ted thought he looked like a ferocious, aging lion who was about to roar. And he did. In his own way.

"It looks like everyone came to the party even on short notice. Neither I nor the owners of this paper nor my employees want to be involved in whatever business you're in. We run and publish a paper, we report news. That's the bottom line. In addition to that, we do not ever, as in *EVER*, reveal our sources. Having said that, I'd like to get home to my family, so make this, whatever *this* is, quick."

Roger Nolan from Homeland Security spoke first. "The

president wants a lid put on the rat plague mess immediately. He's been taken to a secure location, the VP to another undisclosed location. I'm here to ask you nicely to refrain from publishing any more articles on this mess. And make no mistake, it is a mess."

"Take your bullshit somewhere else, Nolan. Weren't you listening to me? I'm here to publish news. This mess that you refer to is news. You have people sitting hours on end in traffic, all the highways are choked. People are scared out of their wits. For what? I have yet to see or hear one damn thing that this town is anywhere near a plague status. We have pictures of rats. Rats running *away* from the embassy. Running away, not *toward* it. That's all we have. Now, if you want to manufacture news, go somewhere else. You can't shut this paper down."

"No, but I can," Elias Cummings said, so quietly the others in the room had to strain to hear what he'd said.

The three EICs looked at Cummings and rose as one. They looked at their reporters, and barked, "Get our lawyers in here, *now!*"

Sullivan's eyes narrowed as he focused on the director of the FBI. "I don't think you want to go there, Elias. Your organization has taken a few too many hits lately. I have freedom of the press on my side. Don't even think about telling me the news stations are going to go along with threats. The people have the right to know what's going on. Now, if you're trying to cover up some kind of hoax, that's a whole other ball game."

"We're talking national security here. The president and the VP have been relocated. That should show you how serious this is," Nolan said.

"I think it's all bullshit to cover up more bullshit," Sullivan growled. "What do you have to say?" he asked, fixing his gaze on Dave Wylie of the CDC. "Go ahead, tell me you found one case, one smidgen of something that would lead you to believe the plague is a possibility. Go ahead, tell me so I can quote you. Did you even find any rat poop? If so, I want to see it."

"I can't tell you that. Yet. We're working around the clock. I have dedicated people working to keep this city safe. We don't work on a timetable."

"Well, I work on deadlines. You know what, Wylie? This city was a hell of a lot safer before you guys got here," Sullivan said. "I'm going to put out a special edition, and I'm sure the *Sentinel* and *News* will do the same thing."

The other two EICs agreed, then both of them banged their fists on the table to show they meant business. Dust flew.

Ted's colleagues rushed back into the room, their faces full of excitement. This little meeting was the closest thing to excitement the *Post* had seen in years. "The lawyers are on the way, ten minutes tops," he said to his boss.

Cummings spoke for the second time. "We had men comb this city, and would you believe we came across a man who says he sold three dozen rats to a man of Middle Eastern descent. We think those rats were injected with a plague virus."

"What man?" Sullivan barked. "Give me a name. Give me a date and time the rats were purchased. Did the guy give your people a description other than to say the person was of Middle Eastern descent? That description alone fits thousands of people here in town. Did you use a sketch artist? If so, why wasn't *that* on the news?"

"It's all you need-to-know, Liam. You know I can't disclose FBI information to you. It's real. We have his affidavit, and that's all I will tell you. We need you to cooperate."

"When pigs fly."

Nigel Summers took that moment to speak up. "I think this is all rubbish. I have orders to move my people back into the embassy tomorrow. It would appear our vermin sightings were just that. The situation was nowhere near as critical as we first thought. Reston Exterminating set glue traps in all the ductwork, and the situation is under control. Since it is the British Embassy, and therefore British soil, I must ask you all to step down and let us get on with our business. The permission I reluctantly granted for you to enter the premises is rescinded as of this moment. Any further interference with my country's right to exercise sovereignty over its own territory will be considered a hostile act against a sovereign nation. You can go to war with yourselves, but please exclude my people and myself. What that means to all of you is, have your people call our people. Good evening, gentlemen."

Ted's eyebrows shot up to his hairline. Well, this was one hell of a fine mess. He looked over at his three colleagues and saw the same expression on their faces he knew was on his own.

The Brit, his shoulders stiff in his custom suit, walked from the room, angry comments following him. He ignored them all and headed through the newsroom to the elevator.

Ted thought he was going to be sick. He felt even sicker when he saw Navarro and Cummings whispering. Navarro in turn literally ran from the room to follow Summers. Ted looked around and swore later he never in his life saw a more pissed-off group of men standing in the same room and glowering at each other. No winner was going to emerge anytime soon. He wished he had the guts to follow Navarro and the Brit, but until Sullivan dismissed him, he figured he had better remain glued to the floor.

Ten minutes later the door to the conference room opened and a gaggle of lawyers with bulging briefcases entered.

And then it was a free-for-all as the men went at it with legal mumbo jumbo that made Liam Sullivan look like a pussycat. Ted and the other reporters moved their chairs to the far corner of the room. At a signal from Sullivan, Ted stuck his hand in his pocket and clicked on his minirecorder. The others watched him, then did the same thing.

The reporters whispered among themselves as each of them wondered where this meeting was all going and how it was going to end.

"Monroe, you said the guy you bought the rats from couldn't see, you said his eyes were milky white. You sticking with that story?" Ted whispered.

"Yeah, and . . . Did you hear the description he gave of me? Said I looked like a Middle Eastern man. What's that tell you? I bet those cruds just made that up. They have to save their asses for this . . . Jesus, I don't know what to call it at this point."

Ellis leaned forward, and whispered, "I have a good friend at the Fox Network, and she told me some guy called in and said it was all a big hoax. She called me right before my boss did his snatch and grab and brought me here. Actually, he dragged me here. She said they're going with it on the eleven o'clock news. Whoever took the call recorded it. She said it sounds legit, whatever the hell that means."

The reporters spent another fifteen minutes kicking around the question of whether the FBI could shut down the papers or not. They finally had to give up on their speculation when they couldn't come up with an answer. They continued to listen to the squabbling, which was starting to sound mean.

"Oh, shit, look at what's coming in the door," Ted said. "Judges!"

The meeting then escalated to such a high pitch, the reporters tried to move farther away, but there was nowhere else to go. Besides, they had their orders. Stay and record.

Chapter 18

Nikki looked at her watch. Then she looked the other Sisters over and nodded approval at their makeover. "Okay, heads up, girls! Same drill as yesterday. We all meet up at the piano bar and take on Miz Rena Gold. Kathryn, you're the lead on this since you made the original contact. You have a better feel for her than the rest of us. We'll follow your cues. Everyone okay with that?"

The others nodded.

"You know what, Nikki? I liked her. I think she's made of some good stuff. I can even understand how she got suckered into this mess with Zenowicz. We'll play it by ear and hope for the best. I can't help it, but I don't want anything bad to happen to her."

Annie was fidgeting in the corner. She was annoyed that this was the second time she and Myra were being left behind to hold the fort. There was no action going on at the old farmhouse. After last night's fiasco with the Kentucky Bourbon, Myra said they had to drink soda pop. She looked over at Myra, who was playing with her pearls. The urge to snatch them right off her friend's neck was so strong she clenched her fists. Boredom was a terrible thing.

The women all quieted down and jumped to attention when Myra's cell phone rang. Conversation came to an abrupt halt. The kitchen door opened, and Jack and Harry entered the room, saw Myra on the phone, and stopped in their tracks. They knew as well as the girls that the only person Myra talked to on the special cell was Charles. There was no need for Nikki to put her finger to her lips for silence, but she did it anyway.

Jack jerked his head backward and pointed to his head, which was soaking wet, an indication that it was pouring rain outside. Again. Nikki made a face, then winked at him and mouthed the word "umbrella." Jack nodded.

Myra whirled around, and announced, "That was Charles. Listen carefully. This is what he said. Less than thirty minutes ago a group of men walked into the *Post* for a meeting. The men were Dave Wylie from the Centers for Disease Control, Roger Nolan from Homeland Security, Elias Cummings, Navarro and some other senior agent, and Nigel Summers from the British Embassy. Shortly after their arrival, the editors in chief from the *Sentinel* and the *News* arrived with their star reporters, Monroe and Ellis. It seems that Ted Robinson and Joe Espinosa were already on the premises. Then a bunch of lawyers arrived, followed by four judges."

"That's it? Did Charles say anything else, like what the meeting was all about?" Jack asked.

Myra fingered the pearls at her neck. "It would seem that Mr. Nigel Summers from the British Embassy got a little . . . uh . . . pissy and stormed out, saying that he was rescinding British permission for American personnel to enter the embassy as of that moment and moving his people back into the embassy tomorrow. He said the rat situation was taken care of. And, it also seems that some anonymous person, who is deemed credible, called into the Fox News Channel and said the whole rat-plague thing was a gigantic hoax perpetrated by the FBI. They're going to run the interview on the eleven o'clock news. I imagine it will be a teaser at the top of every hour until then. They're all still going at it. Director Cummings wants the papers to put a lid on it. Said the orders came from the president himself—and by the way, both the president and the VP have been taken to secure locations. I wonder who called Fox," Myra said.

Harry Wong raised his hand. "That would be me, Myra. There are a lot of things I will do for all of you, then there are some things I will not do, and contributing to mass hysteria is one of those things."

Yoko beamed at him and blew him a kiss. "Good for you, honey," she said.

Harry turned crimson but stood his ground.

"Harry, we had nothing to do with the rat-and-plague situation, you know that," Myra said. "The story the FBI is going public with is that someone, some man of Middle Eastern descent, purchased three dozen rats and injected them with the plague. Supposedly those rats are running all over the city, and they multiply at the speed of light. Incidentally, that information has not been made public. Our cover story to get us back into the District just got out of hand. I don't think any of us fault Harry for calling in to the station."

The others agreed. Yoko blew Harry a second kiss.

"So, what are we supposed to do now?" Alexis asked. "Are we still on for this evening with Rena Gold?"

"Yes," Myra said. "Charles wants us to work quickly. He's afraid that Zenowicz might panic and take off for safer climes. He indicated that the creep is some kind of health nut."

"Then we need to stake him out," Annie said. "Myra and I can do that, can't we, dear?"

Myra bristled. "No, dear, we can't do that. Charles wants Harry or Jack to put someone on that. We're to remain here at our base to take calls."

"That just plain sucks, Myra. We're missing everything."

"Coordination is everything, Annie. Besides, it's raining very hard, and you know how your hair frizzes up in the rain. We can watch the soaps."

"What's going to happen now?" Kathryn asked.

Jack shrugged. "This is just my opinion, but I think those guys at the *Post* are trying to come up with some kind of story that will cover their asses so the public won't go after them when they learn this is all a big hoax. They're all going to look like a bunch of fools, the entire administration right down to the president and the VP. We can't worry about any of them. They created their own mess. It's a given they'll all self-destruct. We have to do what we came here to do, and the sooner we do it, the better off we'll all be. What I can do is jerk Ted Robinson's chain to see if I get anywhere."

"That sounds like a plan," Harry said as he watched Yoko blowing him more kisses. He groaned, to her delight. To further torment him, she reached into her pocket and tossed him a fortune cookie. He caught it deftly, snapped it in two, and read the message:

Someone who is near loves you very much.

In spite of himself, he grinned from ear to ear as he crunched down on the crisp cookie. Little did he know Yoko kept a supply of fortune cookies close at hand, all with the same message. She giggled at Harry's expression.

Outside, a streak of lightning zipped across the sky, lighting up the grounds outside the farmhouse, followed by a vicious clap of thunder that sounded like it was directly overhead. Rain gushed down from the sky and slammed against the kitchen windows.

"And you want to stake out that . . . that person in this

weather," Myra said, directing her comment to Annie, who looked chagrined.

"I was looking more along the lines of starting tomorrow, Myra," she said defensively, as another streak lit up the sky. A second bolt of thunder literally rocked the old house. She shivered as she moved over to the cabinet that held liquor bottles. She waited until the little group donned their rain gear and headed out into the summer storm before she reached inside and brought out a bottle of scotch. "Screw the soaps, Myra. We need a refill on our false courage."

"I see that, dear. I'll take mine straight up if you don't mind."

"I don't mind at all. Do we really want to mess with glasses, or should we do what we did last night, slug it right from the bottle?"

"I never did like washing dishes, and all those buttons on the dishwasher confuse me."

"I guess that means we're slugging from the bottle. I think it's a sin that the others don't want us with them. It's our age, Myra, and don't lie to me and say it isn't."

Myra patted Annie's hand. "I won't lie to you, dear. I really don't like watching the soaps, Annie."

"I don't like them, either. It was just something to say. We can sit and talk of other things. And drink. I was never much of a drinker, Myra."

Myra pretended to be shocked. "Well, you certainly fooled me last night, Annie."

"Guess what? I fooled myself. Tonight we'll sip instead of gulping."

"What would you like to talk about, Annie?" Myra asked, settling herself in her favorite lounging chair. "The stock market, your possible purchase of the *Post,* Charles's problems on the mountain, the girls, or your astronomical wealth?"

"I was thinking more along the lines of a sex chat. And how someone my age goes about finding the man of her dreams."

Myra took a generous hit from the bottle, forgetting that she was supposed to sip. "I don't think we should go there, dear."

"I knew you were going to say that, Myra. I just knew it. Just because there's snow on the roof doesn't mean there isn't a fire in the furnace. Look at you and Charles. You two are the living proof. I want what you have. It's not that I don't love you and the girls and Harry and Jack. I do. I just want someone of my own. And don't you dare tell me to get some goldfish."

Myra threw a pillow at Annie, then leaned back and closed her eyes. She opened them almost immediately. Sometimes it was hard to tell when Annie was serious or just saying words.

"Annie, if it's meant to be, it will be. I wish I knew someone who could . . . fill your needs, but under our present circumstances, it's not doable. At least at the moment. Nice, available gentlemen in our age group are more scarce than a hen's teeth. But I promise you I'm going to work on it."

"I don't want some nice old fart, Myra. I want someone with some dash and zip. I want someone who will make my toes curl up. I absolutely do not want someone my own age. Men our age will have forgotten everything they ever learned in the bedroom department by now. And all they're looking for is someone to take care of them. I have no desire to play Florence Nightingale. Get me some boy toy who has some gusto."

"Oh, dear God!" Myra gulped from the bottle until her eyes watered.

*   *   *

Jack drove all the way into the District with his heart slamming against his chest. He couldn't ever remember being on the road during such a storm. The one upside was there was so little traffic going into the District that he had the highway virtually to himself.

The minute he parked his car in the lot behind the piano bar, he heaved a sigh of relief and reached for his cell phone. He looked at Harry in the dim light coming off the dashboard as he scrolled down and dialed Ted Robinson's cell phone number. He admitted later he didn't think Robinson would pick up, but he did.

Jack took the lead the moment he knew the connection was made. "Hey, jerk-off, what are you guys doing down there at the *Post?* That's a hell of a headline you got going for yourself tomorrow morning. All those big wheels trying to tell you guys how to run the paper? Guess Summers told you all where to get off, huh? Aren't you all going to look silly tomorrow when the world finds out the Brits are moving back into their embassy? Just so you know, I spread the word via the court pipeline. Those judges you're diddling around with there in the office are going to look just as silly. Take a bow, Robinson."

Ted gasped as he looked around frantically. Did Emery have an informer here in the offices? Who? Where the hell was he? How the hell did he know what was going on, and, more to the point, who was his snitch? He grappled for a suitable comeback, but nothing came to mind.

"Aw, gee whiz, Teddy, cat got your tongue? Guess what else? I heard, mind you, I just *heard*, that the guy who sold the rats is recanting. Actually, he had to recant because the poor guy is half-blind with cataracts. He said he made up that whole story because he was afraid he'd get in trouble. I think your dick just got tied into a knot, Teddy boy."

When there was still no comment from Robinson, Jack

went at it again. "I get it. You're telling all those assholes in there that the vigilantes did it all. Ya know what? This time you're on the money, and there's not a damn thing you can do about it. See ya around. Well, maybe I won't be seeing you, since you'll be out there pounding the pavement looking for suitable employment. Hey, asshole, are you *ever* going to say anything? Well, shit, if that's the way you feel about it, I'm sorry I wasted all these minutes talking to you. Bye-bye."

Harry looked at Jack and shook his head. "And you did this . . . because?"

Jack guffawed. "Because I could. The son of a bitch didn't say a word. He's between a rock and a hard place right now. He's not sure if there's a spy in the group or if I planted a camera or a listening device inside. His stomach is in a knot for sure."

Harry shook his head again. "And it was wise to mention the vigilantes . . . why?"

"Just to jerk his chain, to make him spin his wheels. No one is going to believe him if he starts spouting off about them again. Right now five will get you ten he's remembering the night backstage when the G-String Girls were performing and I told him the vigilantes walked right past him. It's a game, Harry. I play to win. Trust me. If you'd ever played poker with Ted, you'd know what I'm talking about. He doesn't have a clue."

"If you say so."

"I say so. I think Miz Gold just arrived. By taxi. Didn't someone say she was going to be using her limousine this evening?" Jack asked.

"Who cares? She's here. Bet there aren't going to be too many patrons tonight with everything that's going on. Wanna bet?"

"Not with you I don't. How much longer are we going to sit out here?" Harry demanded.

"At least another half hour. We don't want anything looking contrived. Settle down and think about sweet nothings. What did that fortune cookie say?" Jack asked.

"None of your damn business," Harry snapped.

"What do you think Myra and Annie are doing, Harry?"

"How the hell should I know? Making cookies, maybe."

Jack frowned. "Do ya think? I'm not sure if either one of them can cook."

"Well, then, maybe they're watching some game show on television. Why do you care?"

Jack frowned again. "It's not that I care. Well, I do, but I like to know where everyone is and what they're doing when a mission is going down. Annie is a wild card. She can get Myra to do things she normally wouldn't do. Sometimes she scares me."

It was Harry's turn to frown. "You know something, Jack, for once we're on the same page. Annie scares me, too."

If either Jack or Harry had known what the precocious Annie was doing at that precise moment, they would have been stunned.

Myra knew she had a pleasant buzz on, and she didn't care. When Annie motioned her to turn down the volume on the television, she pressed the MUTE button. "Who are you calling at this time of night, Annie?"

"An important person. Shhh."

Myra clamped her lips shut but leaned closer to hear the conversation.

"Arthur, you know who this is, right? Good, good. Never mention names, so nothing comes back to haunt you. How is the family? Really? I am so sorry to hear that. You were married a long time. Your wife found a younger man who makes her feel young. You make her feel old? That is so sad. I believe persons of that ilk are called boy toys. Well, you need to forge ahead and fight to keep your money so the boy toy doesn't squander it. I called you for a reason, Arthur. I want to buy the *Post.*"

Myra gasped. Annie held up her finger to shush her. "Of course I'm serious. This will give you something to do, Arthur, to get your mind off your . . . uh, current domestic problem. In the end, dear, it's probably for the best if she's disenchanted with you. Yes, yes, I know I'm a fugitive and a criminal. So are a lot of other people. Don't let that bother you. I want this done quickly. Whatever it costs. Mercy, Arthur, you are dense this evening. Gather all my boys together and make it happen. Call me when it's a done deal. Do we understand each other, Arthur?

"How's this for an incentive, Arthur? You make this happen very, very quickly, and I will provide a bonus and make sure you get to keep the life you are accustomed to living when your wife takes you to the cleaners. Oh, she will. I'm a woman, I know how these things work. Before you know it, she'll have you paying for all kinds of plastic surgery to make herself look young for her boy toy. Then she's going to want a love nest. The multimillion-dollar kind. And a vacation home for . . . trysts. She'll want the yacht you have, and she'll rechristen it with the boy toy's name. Then she'll sock you with her legal bills. That's the way it works, Arthur. The alimony will be over the moon. You're fried. See, see, I'm your best bet for a long, happy life. Good night, Arthur, and don't worry about a thing. You're going to be so happy your wife left you, you'll take up rumba lessons."

"Rumba lessons? Is that what you said?" Myra demanded when Annie powered down her cell phone.

"What was I supposed to say? The poor man is devastated. I was just trying to help. Someday he'll thank me. He's not really a good catch, but with a little work, I think I could whip him into shape. You met him, Myra, what do you think of him?"

"He's a dud."

"That, too," Annie said. "Oh, well, if it doesn't work out, I'll think of something else. Isn't it exciting that I'm buying the paper? Do you think we should change the name of it to something else?"

"You should call Fox News and tell them so everyone can get in an uproar all over again," Myra said as she belatedly caught Annie's fever.

"I can do that, but who should I say is buying it?"

"Just say seven anonymous investors. Are we going to keep this a secret, or are we going to tell . . . you know . . . *our side?*"

"We'll work on that, dear," Annie said as she dialed 411 to get the phone number for Fox News. "I'm going to ask for Geraldo Rivera. I like him. He looks so tidy these days, with his new haircut. I don't care what anyone says about him, the man has a heart. He runs with things. Why are you looking at me like that, Myra? You said yourself I could afford to buy the paper. It is one way to get rid of Ted Robinson. The only other way is to kill him, and we do not kill people. You said that, too."

"God help me, I did say that."

"You know what else, Myra? When this is all over and done with, and we're free women again, we'll have a place to go to work. There is nothing better than owning a newspaper with a vast circulation. I'm thinking of all of us and our futures."

Myra wanted to tell her best friend that their futures were murky at best, but she didn't have the heart to rain on Annie's parade.

"Let's go to bed, Annie."

"But we didn't finish the bottle," Annie said, holding up the bottle of scotch.

"Tomorrow is another day, Annie."

"You're right as usual, Myra. Okay, let's call it a night."

Chapter 19

Kathryn, aka Delia McDermott, shook the rain from her raincoat and hung it up on a coatrack next to the door. Her bright red umbrella went into a stand with three others, all of which were black. She looked around the piano bar to see who else had braved the elements to come out on such a nasty night. Jack and Harry were seated at the bar, and only two other men were seated at the opposite end. Isabelle, in her dowdy-librarian disguise, was at a table that would hold eight. There was no sign of Rena Gold.

Outside, the wind and torrential rain lashed at the plate glass windows of the bar. Kathryn shuddered. Just the short walk from the curb to the entrance had left her feet soaking wet. She was dressed in a slate-gray power suit with a short skirt that showed off her long legs. The slit up the side was, as Alexis said, absolutely sinful.

I wonder if I could ever get used to dressing like this day after day, she mused.

Kathryn was deep in her own thoughts when she felt someone touch her shoulder. She whirled around, her hands clenched into fists ready to strike as she looked up to see who it was. The owner? Perhaps the manager?

"I'm sorry, I didn't mean to startle you, but I wanted to

tell you Mr. Lymen won't be playing this evening. He just called to cancel," the manager said. "Seems the streets are too flooded. The owner instructed me to close up shop. I'm really sorry. But, I did take the liberty of calling the Georgetown Grill, which is just three doors down, and they're open, with no plans of closing early, in case you wanted dinner."

Kathryn nodded as the man walked over to where Jack and Harry were sitting to relay the same message.

Isabelle, who was sitting at Kathryn's table, shrugged, and said, "We have to wait for Rena Gold."

Kathryn nodded. Out of the corner of her eye, she saw Jack and Harry get up and head toward the door. Just as they reached it, the door blew open with a gust of wind and rain. Rena Gold and Nikki ran into the waiting area and immediately shed their raincoats.

Kathryn popped off her seat and ran to the door to announce relocation plans. They all donned their rain gear and headed out to run to the Georgetown Grill. Jack and Harry hung back so they could wait for Yoko and Alexis.

"This is soooo much fun, isn't it?" Rena shouted to be heard over the pounding rain. "I used to love to play in the rain when I was a little kid. I don't like the lightning, though," she gasped as she flung open the door of the Georgetown Grill.

A waiter was standing at the reservation desk with snow-white towels. The women giggled and jiggled as they struggled to get out of their wet things. In the end, they all removed their shoes and carried them to a long table that could comfortably seat twelve guests. The bar held only a few customers, and only two tables in the far back of the room were occupied.

Just as the women seated themselves, the door opened, and Yoko and Alexis entered, Jack and Harry on their heels. Kathryn watched as the two men toweled off and headed for the bar. Alexis and Yoko joined the chattering girls, who were looking at glossy menus.

Jack nudged Harry's arm. "Perfect setup, wouldn't you say? We can see the girls in the bar mirror, and if we lean back, we can hear their conversation. I'm thinking at some point they might even invite us to join them."

"Ever the optimist, eh, Jack? What are you drinking this fine night?"

"A Corona. I've eaten here before with Nik. Seems like a lifetime ago. Hell, I could walk here from her house. They have Kobe beef, but it comes with a high price tag. It cuts like butter. What's your delight tonight, Harry?"

"I'll give it a whirl since you're paying. Twice-baked potato, the cucumber salad, and a whole loaf of that bread with the hard crust."

Jack couldn't remember offering to pick up the tab. Sometimes Harry could be tighter than a duck's ass, and other times he was so generous it boggled the mind. For all his cantankerous ways, Harry Wong was a guy you wanted in your corner. Jack didn't care one way or the other about picking up the tab, since Charles sent him a check once a month to cover his out-of-pocket expenses. They gave their order to the bartender and stared at the chattering girls, who were ordering their dinner and giggling like schoolkids. Isabelle was pouring wine with gay abandon. The object, Jack knew, was to get Rena Gold drunk as soon as possible, so her tongue would loosen up.

Jack felt his cell phone vibrate in his pocket. He fished it out and looked at the name of the caller. Bert. He powered on, aware that Nikki was watching his back. He could see her clearly in the bar mirror. He moved off the stool and headed toward the men's room. He knew Nikki would follow shortly.

"Talk to me, big guy. What the hell is going on?"

"Big stuff, Jack. Listen, I only have a few minutes. My

boss is watching me like a hawk, so if you suddenly hear me say something stupid or if I laugh, understand. The shit is hitting the fan. Everyone is scrambling. I called Charles a little while ago, but this time you're going to have to get back to him. I can't risk another call. I swear to God I cannot believe these assholes are running this country. What that means is they know this whole rat-plague thing is a hoax, but they're scrambling now to save their asses, my boss included. The Bureau has so many black eyes lately I lost count, but the guy from HS is a loose cannon. He's the one who raised the alert level, and he's the one who caused the panic. It's as if he has orders from the administration to create as much fear and panic as he can. And he's not about to give up, either. He's doing his best to keep fueling this goddamn mess. The guy from the CDC is leaving in the morning and will give an interview to the media before he leaves.

"I wouldn't be at all surprised to hear that he disappears and never gets on his plane. That's how whacked out that guy is from HS. My boss is fit to be tied. The press will not comply, and that's making everyone crazy. I never saw so many spitting, snarling lawyers and judges in one group. It's a goddamn free-for-all.

"But that's not really why I'm calling. Robinson, that old friend of yours, is spouting off about the vigilantes— saying this is the kind of scenario/diversion they create when they're ready to pull a fast one. Mind you, he did not volunteer this information. His boss called on him to wax poetic. He was only too happy to do so. My boss was all ears, I can tell you that. Nolan from HS pooh-poohed it all away, saying the women were too smart to mess around with something as serious as the plague. I swear to God, Jack, that's what he said. So, there you have it in a nutshell. I think the president and the VP are on their way back from wherever they were stashed. Now, I don't know that for a fact, but I more or less heard my boss talking to the national security advisor.

"Another thing, Robinson almost had me convinced. They're paying attention to him, Jack, and that scares me. Where are you and what's going on?"

Jack told him.

"Mom, I really have to go. I'll call you in the morning. Mom, just tell Dad to take his medicine on time, and he'll be fine. Timing is so important. You know what the doctor said. Sometimes time is crucial. Mom, Dad is not going to die from restless leg syndrome. Two days is pushing it, but he'll be fine. Remember, I spoke to the doctor myself. I really have to go, Mom. Yes, I love you, too."

"Shit!" Jack muttered as he clicked off. He whirled around and saw Nikki. He wanted to kiss her so bad his teeth started to chatter. Instead, he relayed what Bert had just said.

"Does that mean we only have two days?" Nikki asked anxiously.

"Call me stupid, but, yeah, that's what I think it means. How's it going out there?"

"She's drinking and she's chatty but nothing earth-shattering yet. Damn, I wish this weather would let up. I don't know if it's important or not, but her cell phone is turned off. She said she has to do that from time to time to save her sanity. I like her, Jack. We all do."

Jack nodded. "Let me go back first. Wait a few minutes before you return to your table. I love you, Nik."

"Yeah, me, too. It's all going to work out, Jack."

"Yeah, right. You didn't hear Bert, I did."

Nikki laughed. "Who you gonna believe, Bert or me?"

Jack groaned as he made his way back to the bar. The moment he was settled on his stool, he hunkered over and clued Harry in on Bert's phone call.

"See what happens when you don't listen to me, Jack? I

said we should take out that jerk, but you said no. Right now, this very minute, Robinson could be resting in the hospital done up in splints. So, eat shit, Jack. Your chickens are coming home to roost. I don't like that two-day thing. Does today count? Did you even ask that? Or is it two days from tomorrow? Call Charles and ask him."

"He won't know. I'm supposed to relay Bert's message to him. Well, we can do that after we eat. Our food is here. You eat first, I'll watch the girls, and when you're done, I'll eat."

"Will you eat, for Christ's sake? Nothing is going to happen while you chew and swallow. Sometimes I hate you, Jack."

Jack didn't rise to the bait the way he normally did. He did eat, but his eyes were on the mirror the whole time in case Nikki or one of the other girls gave him a signal. To do what, he had no clue.

Across the room, the wine continued to flow.

Kathryn squirmed in her chair. "I hope we can all get home tonight," she said.

Rena waved an arm. "My gosh, Delia, it's just rain. We can always take a taxi or I can call my limo. I wish I had done that to get me here, but I didn't want the driver reporting my whereabouts to you know who." She giggled to show what she thought of that.

"Who is who?" Alexis asked in a sing-song voice.

Rena waved her fork in the air. "*Who* is someone I'm not allowed to talk about. You know what, I don't care. I'm leaving tomorrow anyway. Well, maybe I'm leaving, if I can figure out how to get my suitcases to the airport."

The girls as one sat up straighter. Kathryn was the first to speak. "What do you mean you're leaving? We just met each other. Where are you going?" she asked fretfully.

The others jumped in, saying things like, "*Soon as you meet someone you can have fun with in this damn city,*

what do they do but up and leave." And on and on it went
until Rena had tears in her eyes.

"I know, I know, but I have to get out of here. If I don't,
I'm going to get caught up in a real . . . in a real mess. If I
tell you all where I'm going, you can come and visit me,
but you can't tell anyone where I am, okay?"

Isabelle, in her dowdy-librarian disguise, tittered. "How
can we tell anyone when we don't know where you're
going? I'm going to miss you. You're such fun."

"Oh, Margie," Rena said, using Isabelle's pseudonym,
"thank you for that nice compliment." She leaned across
the table, and whispered, "I'm going back to Las Vegas.
Believe it or not, I can get lost there."

Isabelle played stupid. "Why do you want to get lost?
How can you give up that wonderful job you have with
that astronomical salary?"

Rena made a very unladylike sound. "That salary is just
on paper. I make 58K. My . . . that guy I got tangled up
with takes the rest. I have to pay taxes on the 58K. I can't
live here without the perks. I don't want to live like this
anymore. I don't want to be with *him* anymore."

"Who is him?" Nikki asked softly. "Is he someone important? Are you afraid he'll harm you?"

Rena took a great big gulp of wine, and said, "*Him* is
indeed a very important man, and I don't know if he
would harm me or not. He's threatened to if I ever mentioned his name or did anything to bring him notoriety. He
keeps a tight rein on me. Even the doorman at the building
I live in spies for him. That's why I have to find someone
to take my bags to the airport. If the doorman sees me
leaving, he'll call and report to . . . him."

"That's terrible," Yoko said gently. "How can you live
like that?"

"That's just it, I can't. I've been trying to get up the
nerve for a while now, but I could never . . . you know . . .

pull it together. Then, when I met Delia last night and talked to her, it just seemed that now was the time to do it. I need a nest egg. I have a little money but not enough. I'm going to hawk the jewelry he gave me, but something tells me it's not real, just very good paste. He's stingy but likes to make a big show." Rena drained the wine in her glass and held it out for a refill. Kathryn obliged.

"Let me get this straight, Rena," Nikki said. "You're leaving even though you're afraid. You don't have enough money to do that, but you're going to leave anyway and sell off what you can. You need someone to move your suitcases. How am I doing so far?"

"You're doing good."

"How are you so sure he won't find you when you get to Vegas?" Nikki asked.

"I have friends there. The kind that aren't front and center like *him*. They could make him disappear like that," she said, snapping her fingers. "You know, a while back I tried every way I could to get in touch with those women, you know, the vigilantes. I even went to a reporter at the *Post* and asked him to help me, but he refused when he wanted me to tell him details and I wouldn't. You know how reporters are. I contributed to their defense fund, so I thought they might help me. Well, that didn't happen. This wine is really good."

"Yes, it is good," Nikki said, pretending to sip at her own glass. "What did you want them to do for you, Rena?"

Rena looked around, her eyes glazed. "For me, nothing. I wanted them to . . . you know, take care of him. I was prepared to . . . I don't know, maybe cripple him or make him resign and go away, far away. My problem is I know . . . stuff. Then I got afraid." She leaned into the table as did the others. "I had a friend visit from Vegas, and he built a safe in the floor of my closet. What do you think of *that?*" she asked triumphantly, wine sloshing out of her glass.

Yoko hastened to refill it and mop up the excess at the same time.

"Wow!" Kathryn said. "What do you keep in it? Your jewels?"

"*The stuff.* I knew the day would come when I'd need . . . just stuff," Rena said vaguely as she twirled the wine in her glass. She swallowed the rest in one long gulp. "If this town knew half of what I know, that bastard would go up in flames. So, do you girls know anyone who can take my suitcases to the airport?"

"Actually, I do," Nikki said. "When do you want to do that?"

"Do you really? Would you really do that for me? I'll be more than glad to pay them for doing it."

"Well, sure. One good favor deserves another. Just tell us that prick's name, so we never get involved with him."

Rena Gold looked around the table. All she saw were sympathetic faces. Tears glistened in her eyes. "The president of the World Bank, Maxwell Zenowicz." The moment she said the words aloud, she clapped her hands over her mouth. Her glassy eyes filled with fear at her outburst.

The girls sat in pretended astonishment, their jaws dropping for Rena's benefit.

Alexis was the first to speak. "Girlfriend, you sure know how to pick friends in high places. So, he's a crud, huh?"

"The worst. God, you aren't going to tell anyone I told you, are you?"

"Hell no. We're your friends. We'll protect you with our lives. Not to worry, your secret is safe with us. So, what's that *stuff* you got on the jerk?" Alexis probed.

"All his personal records. Financial and the bank stuff.

All the shenanigans he's pulled since he took over. I slipped him a Mickey one night and copied everything. My friend from Vegas brought it with him. The stuff to put in his drink," Rena clarified. She drank more wine, her eyes getting glassier by the minute.

"What did you think you were going to do with your information? Was it your plan to blackmail him?" Nikki asked carefully.

"Kind of. Then I got afraid. I was just going to help myself to some of his money so I could start up a small business of some kind in Vegas with a few of my friends. Show business is a hard business. You get used up real quick." Rena started to cry then.

The girls rushed to her side, cooing and offering words of encouragement. Jack and Harry found their ears burning when they heard words like, "All men are dickheads, you can't trust one any farther than you can throw them, small minds, small *everything*. And don't forget the Viagra that has to make it all work."

"They're not talking about us, Harry, relax," Jack said, tongue in cheek.

Harry stared into the mirror. "They look pretty damn gleeful to me, Jack."

Jack grimaced. Damn if old Harry wasn't right. They did look gleeful.

"I don't know why I say this, but I'm thinking we're the guys who are going to take the suitcases to the airport," Harry grumbled.

In spite of himself, Jack burst out laughing. He shoved his plate across the bar and held up his beer bottle for a refill. Harry did the same.

Outside, the wind and rain continued to batter the building. Since their arrival, no other customers had come into the Grill. Which was a good thing for all of them. Now, if the manager decided to close early, they were going to have a problem.

Fifteen minutes later, Jack's cell phone vibrated in his pocket. He turned it on and listened intently.

"It's me, Jack. I commandeered a van from the motor pool, and I'm sitting outside at the curb. When you're all ready to leave, just head for me, and I'll drive all of you to wherever you want to go. By the way, Charles sent me," Bert Navarro said.

Jack had long ago given up trying to figure out how Charles did what he did. "Okay. I'm thinking maybe another fifteen minutes, and they'll be ready to go. Miss Gold is looking for someone to take her suitcases to the airport. Looks like you get the honor, Bert."

"You're out of your mind. This is an FBI vehicle. Tell her to call a taxi."

"Can't do that, buddy; those suitcases need a personal escort. I'll explain it all later. Sit tight, okay?"

Jack headed for the men's room. Nikki followed him. He brought her up-to-date. "How sloshed is she, Nik?"

"She's babbling, and I'm thinking she's seeing two of everything about now. I'm going to pay the bill, and we'll head out and take her home. We can drive in through the basement parking garage and take the elevator to one of the top floors and walk up the last couple of flights to the penthouse. No sense giving the doorman more information than he needs. He's probably bored and watching the numbers on the elevator. She's really scared of this World Bank guy, Jack. I can't wait to get him in my clutches."

Jack winced at her words, glad he was on her side.

Chapter 20

The inside of the FBI van steamed. Outside, the rain continued to river downward. The water on the roads was almost to the top of the wheels of the van. "I can barely see ahead of me," Navarro said through clenched teeth. "You guys better have a plan in mind. You do, don't you?"

"We're working on it," Nikki said. She tried looking out the small windows at the back of the van to see if Jack and Harry were following them. She couldn't see a thing.

Rena Gold was singing merrily, unaware she was surrounded by the vigilantes she so admired. She stopped singing long enough to say, "I love Wayne Newton. He's Mr. Las Vegas. Did you all know that? I even met him once. Nice. Really nice. But, he's getting fat. I think he wears a girdle. Maybe he doesn't. But I think he does. Esther thinks so, too."

"I think," Nikki whispered to Kathryn, "when we get to the apartment building Rena lives in, one of us should engage the doorman so that he isn't watching the monitors when we come in. I'm sure one of the guys will know how to rewind the tapes on the cameras so that we were never there."

"Good idea," Kathryn said.

The rest of the ride to Rena's apartment was made in silence, the only sound the lashing of the heavy rain on the top of the van.

After another seventy minutes of crawling along at a snail's pace, the van pulled up to the entrance of the underground garage. Kathryn leaped out of the van and headed to the main entrance. Bert waited ten full minutes before he steered the van down the ramp, slid Rena's parking key card into the slot, and waited for the heavy metal gate to open wide before driving into the cavernous garage. The silence inside was deafening.

"Okay, ladies, this is your gig. Do you or don't you have a plan?" Bert asked.

"For the moment, find a place to park," Nikki said. "Right now we have to wait for Jack and Harry. Yoko, stand by the gate so you can open it from this side when they get here." Yoko was out of the van and sprinting toward the gate before Nikki could finish speaking.

Another fifteen minutes was spent inside the steaming van. Rena Gold was sound asleep. A hurried discussion ensued the moment Jack and Harry marched over to the waiting van. While no one, it seemed, knew how to dismantle the security cameras, Harry said he would take a stab at it. But only after he conferred with several people he just happened to know, who, by chance, were in the business of breaking and entering. "It's going to cost some money for the information," he said sourly.

"No problem, Harry. I'll write you a check. You know I'm good for it. Now, let's get this show on the road before company arrives. We don't want any late-hour tenants thinking we're up to no good." Jack laughed at his own joke but wasn't surprised when no one else joined in.

While the little group made their way to the service elevator, Kathryn ran back around to the main entrance and engaged the doorman, who also doubled as a security guard. She did her best to convince the sleepy guard that her best friend in the whole wide world did live in the building and was waiting for her. "She just moved here. Maybe your tenant list hasn't been updated yet, sir," she said desperately, trying to keep his back to the monitors while in turn trying to see them herself so she would know when her friends entered the penthouse apartment. "Look, sir, I'm soaking wet, I need to get out of these clothes, and I was planning on doing that in my friend's apartment. Now what am I supposed to do?" she asked, seemingly on the verge of tears.

"Go to a hotel. I'm sorry, but there is no one here by the name of Chloe Dupre. I wish there was, so I could help you, but my hands are tied. I'll even double-check the tenant list if that will make you feel better." The guard was about to turn around to open the desk drawer when Kathryn spotted her group heading up the steps to the penthouse.

"No!" she yelped as she grasped his arm. "You've been more than kind. If you would just loan me your umbrella, I'll see about catching a cab. On second thought, never mind the umbrella, I'm already soaked," she said when she realized the doorman would have to turn around for the umbrella. She almost fainted when she saw the penthouse door close. "Thank you for your time, sir. I'm sorry I troubled you."

"No problem, little lady. I like a diversion from time to time." He pointed to the bank of monitors, and said, "It gets pretty dull around here watching blank screens all evening long, especially on a night like this when nothing is going on."

"I guess so," Kathryn said, walking toward the front door. "Stay," she said, motioning the doorman to stay where he was. "No sense you getting wet, too. Again, thank you for your time."

Kathryn sprinted around the corner and down the ramp to the garage. Harry was waiting for her and pressed the button that would allow her entry into the garage.

She dripped water from head to toe. "What's going on?"

"You're an engineer, right, Kathryn?"

"Yeah. In my other life when I wasn't a truck driver. Why?"

"I'm supposed to dismantle the security monitors and turn them back so that when viewed, we were never here. I hate to admit this, but I am not mechanically inclined. I tried to call a few people but haven't been able to reach anyone."

Kathryn continued to drip water. "Let's take a look."

It took twenty minutes, but Kathryn was able to back up the tape to earlier in the evening, then short it out. "Everything is fried for the night," she said cheerfully. "The security company will think it has to do with the storm. At least in the beginning."

"After the beginning?" Harry asked, his eyebrows arched.

"Then they'll know some asshole fried the hell out of their equipment and dirty work was afoot. I don't think the tenants or their boyfriends will be told. No one wants to undermine security."

"So, in the end you didn't know what you were doing?"

"That about sums it up, Harry. Come on, let's go upstairs. With this weather, I don't think any maintenance or security people will get here before tomorrow, but you never know. Better safe than sorry."

"Yeah, yeah, that's what I always say, better safe than sorry," Harry muttered as he trudged along behind Kathryn.

*   *   *

Inside the luxurious penthouse, the girls looked around in approval. Even Jack nodded.

"The lady has good taste," Alexis said. "A shame it doesn't belong to her. I like things that belong to me even if it's just a scarf or a knickknack. While this place is beautiful, it has a temporary feel to it, like she's just passing through or something. It kind of gives me the creeps."

"That's exactly what it is, Alexis. I'm glad Rena finally got wise to that jerk," Nikki said. "Not to worry, we're going to take care of her one way or another. And him. After all, Rena is making our job easier for us. She's fearful, but I think we can allay her fears when we tell her who we really are."

"She's waking up," Isabelle said.

The tap on the penthouse door sent Jack scurrying to open it. Kathryn and Harry rushed inside. They dripped huge puddles all over the marble floor in the foyer. Both ignored them and continued into the living room, where Rena Gold was just stirring.

"I think we need some coffee, black and strong," Nikki said.

"I'll make the coffee if you tell me where the kitchen is. My bones are cold. This AC isn't helping, either. Can someone please turn the temperature up a little? Want to help, Bert?" Kathryn asked shyly.

The others had smiles on their faces as Bert beamed his pleasure at being asked to help in the kitchen. The women, even Jack, wore indulgent expressions as they looked at one another. It was obvious to all of them that the acerbic, cranky Kathryn was finally on the road to romance.

Rena Gold was sufficiently awake to ask if they were having a party. It was clear she was still under the influence of all the wine she'd consumed earlier. She looked at Jack and Harry with questions in her eyes.

"They're going to take your bags to the airport. Remember, you asked us if we knew anyone who would do that for you? They volunteered," Nikki said.

"How sweet of you gentlemen to do that for me. I'll pay you, of course. I'm such a terrible hostess. Can I offer you all something to drink? Believe it or not, this is the first time I've had guests, other than that one time my friend came from Las Vegas, and even then it was more of a . . . business call, not really social."

"We're fine, Rena. Delia is making coffee. We can all use some right now," Isabelle said quietly. "We brought you home so we could help you, but you need to be sober before that can happen."

Nikki motioned Jack to follow her to the bedroom, where the four large Louis Vuitton bags were waiting to be picked up. "Now would be a good time to take them downstairs into the van while the cameras are out. We can decide later who takes them to the airport. You okay with that, Jack?"

"Guess so." He gave her a quick kiss and bellowed for Harry, who came on the run. "Lug these bags out to the foyer and I'll take the service elevator to the garage and bring up a dolly. No sense in either one of us throwing our backs out."

"That'll work," Harry said as he lifted the suitcases. Returning, he asked, "Damn, what does that woman have in there?"

"A couple of years of plunder would be my guess, and she's not about to leave it behind," Nikki said.

Kathryn was grinning from ear to ear and Bert had a sappy expression on his face as they came into the living room. He carried one tray, and Kathryn carried the other. She motioned for him to join Harry and Jack, then took her seat on the sofa, apologizing for her wet clothing.

"Don't worry about it, it's not mine," Rena said. She

looked around at the women, who were watching her. "Should we play cards, or should we just sit here and talk?"

"Actually, Rena, we had something else in mind," Nikki said.

Rena brought her coffee cup to her lips with a wobbly hand. She suddenly looked so fearful that Nikki hastened to reassure her with soft murmurings.

Kathryn leaned closer. "Rena, if you help us, we'll help you. That's a promise."

Rena sat her coffee cup and saucer down on the glass-top table. Alexis had to reach out to steady the cup or it would have fallen off the edge. "What . . . what do you want me to do?"

"Show us what's in your safe. We'll take it from there. Are you comfortable doing that?"

"If I do that, my . . . He'll find out some way. I have to get out of here. He's not a nice person. Well, sometimes he's nice."

"Do you mean like when he steals your paycheck?" Yoko demanded.

Rena winced. "He's greedy. The man is every negative you can think of. Tell me what you'll do with the information."

"We'll use it to . . . uh . . . take care of Mr. Zenowicz," Nikki said.

The women watched as recognition finally dawned in Rena Gold's eyes. Her jaw dropped, and her eyes rolled back in her head. Alexis, the closest, reached out again to hold her upright.

Nikki mouthed more comforting words ending with, "You can trust us, Rena. But things have to be done our way. Decide now if you want our help. If you don't, we're outta here, and you can take your chances with . . . him."

Rena was suddenly stone-cold sober. "So, you aren't my

friends after all. This was all a setup to get to . . . him."
She fixed her steely gaze on Kathryn as her eyes filled with
tears.

"In a way, it was like that, but I've truly enjoyed your
company. We all did," Kathryn said, waving her arms
about to indicate the others. "We meant it when we said
we would help you. Hey, you're the one who wanted to
get in touch with us. Look at it this way—we came to you
out of the blue. We're going to make your world right side
up and make sure that guy never, ever bothers you again.
You know we can do it, but you have to help us."

"Is that a promise?" Rena asked in a shaky voice.

"Honey, you can take it to the bank," Isabelle said.

"What do I have to do?"

"Not much. Open your safe to us. Then tomorrow we
want you to arrange a meeting right here with Mr. Zenowicz. We'll take it from there. By tomorrow evening this
time, you'll be winging your way to Las Vegas, a truly
happy woman. You in or out, Miss Gold?"

Rena Gold didn't think twice. "I'm in. I want you to cut
his balls off and jam them you know where."

Nikki grimaced. "Sorry, we already did that to a bunch
of guys in California. Been there, done that. Not to worry;
Mr. Zenowicz will never be the same after our meeting tomorrow."

"Is that a promise-promise, or are you blowing smoke
in my direction?"

"Like I said, you can take it to the bank," Isabelle said.

"Okay. Let's go. I'll open the safe for you."

"Attagirl," Kathryn said, her breath leaving her body in
a loud *swoosh*.

Chapter 21

Myra sat on the edge of her comfortable old bed and stared off into space. She wasn't sleepy, but maybe if she got under the covers, sleep would come. She stared up at the big wall over the mantel, where a parade of pictures of her dead daughter marched along. Barbara's christening, her first birthday, all the ensuing birthdays, her first pony, her first bicycle with three wheels, the second bicycle with just two wheels, her debut at dancing class, Barbara playing the piano, sliding down the banister. Her first car, a big old boxy thing for safety reasons, her first riding horse, Buttons. Graduation pictures, grade school, middle school, high school. Halloween pictures, Christmas trees, and Barbara sitting among mounds of gaily wrapped presents. Law school graduation. And then, even though there was more wall space, there were no more pictures. It was the rest of the blank wall that made her eyes burn. So much more room. Room for wedding pictures, christening pictures. How unfair life was sometimes.

Tears trickled down Myra's cheeks. There would never be any babies or a husband's picture on her wall. Never. More tears rolled down her cheeks. She was about to wipe them away with the sleeve of her robe when she felt a light touch on her cheek.

"*Please don't cry, Mom. You make me sad when you cry.*"

"Oh, darling girl, how is it you always know when I need you the most?" Myra wailed.

"*I'm your daughter. That's the way it works, Mom. Everything is going to be all right. Things are coming together on the mountain. Nikki has a handle on everything. Why are you worried?*"

"Because Annie and I are getting old, darling. The girls are young and vibrant. I'm not sure we contribute anything anymore other than our money and support. It's sad to grow old and not be needed."

"*Mom, that is so far from the truth, I can't believe you said what you said. Without you and Annie, things would fall apart even with Charles's expertise. Nik and the others depend on you, look to both of you for guidance. Believe it or not, they're all your daughters, and they view you as their mother. You and Annie both. Two mothers, Mom. It doesn't get any better than that. Even the dogs love you.*"

Myra swallowed and managed to make her tongue say what she wanted it to say. "I never . . . that's how *I* feel, but I didn't know the girls felt that way about us. Well, I did, but they never say anything. You know what I mean, dear. Annie and I were just talking, and we were thinking maybe we were in the way. They didn't want to take us with them this evening. We were so crushed. Annie more so than me, I think. Maybe I'm just feeling sorry for myself. I'm sorry, darling girl."

"*Mom, are you paying attention to the weather? They wanted to make sure you two were safe. Someone always has to stay behind. Alexis had to stay behind last time with the G-String Girls. This time it was your turn. Someone else will probably have to stay behind on the next mission. You know how it is when they're on a roll; they can't stop to make phone calls. They're depending on you and Annie*

*to be here for them and Charles. In the end, you and
Annie have the most important jobs. You need to get over
feeling sorry for yourself."*

"I suppose you're right. Are you ... you know ...
okay, darling girl?"

"Fine, Mom. I had to really pep talk Daddy," Barbara
said, referring to Charles. *"He was so devastated with the
destruction to the mountain, but things are working just
fine for him right now. By the way, that was a pretty
snappy decision Annie made to buy the paper."*

Myra started wringing her hands. "I don't know if that
was a wise move or not. I can't imagine it ever happening,
but you never know. Sometimes, Annie scares the day-
lights out of me. She doesn't know a thing about running a
newspaper, and on top of that, she's a felon. Good Lord,
what if the owners take her up on her offer and it all
comes to pass?"

*"I bet you could really write good Op-Ed pieces that
would make the readership sit up and take notice. You could
be pro-vigilante. Think about it, Mom. Gotta go now."*

Myra grew so light-headed she had to grasp the bedpost
when she felt a featherlight touch to her wet cheek. She fell
back against the down comforter and let the tears flow.
Her spirit daughter always came to her when she needed
her most. If only ... She bounced back up, gathered her
wits about her, and left the bedroom, four huge pillows
stuffed under her arms. She marched down the long, dimly
lit hallway and knocked on Annie's door. "I want to do
something, Annie, and I want to do it *right now!* Get all
the pillows you can find and bring them with you."

"I thought you wanted to go to sleep. You said you
were tired. What's the matter with you? You look ...
scary, Myra. Did something happen?" Annie asked fear-
fully.

"I did. I was. In a manner of speaking, something did

happen. But, that's when I was feeling old. I'm not feeling old right now, so come along. You're dawdling, and that's what old people do. They damn well dawdle, Annie. I refuse to dawdle. Do you hear me?"

"I think if someone was out in the barn, they would be able to hear you," Annie snapped. "What are we going to do with these pillows?"

"What do you think, Annie? Do I always have to draw you a map? We're going to slide down the banister until our asses are raw."

Annie gaped at her longtime friend. "Well, *all right!* I guess that means we'll have to double up on our Advil."

"Yes, we'll double up starting tomorrow. Do you know something else? I hope you get to buy that paper. We're going to take a pro stance on the vigilantes. I'm going to write the first Op-Ed piece. Under a pseudonym, of course."

"Well, damn, Myra, whatever it was you ate or drank, I want some. I like this new you. I really do. Until our bony asses are raw, huh?"

Myra squared her shoulders. "Exactly."

An hour later both Myra and Annie were curled up like little schoolgirls in the mound of pillows and bedding at the foot of the staircase. They were breathless, exhilarated, and at the same time exhausted. They looked at each other and laughed like lunatics. "If you ever tell anyone about this, I will kill you, Annie. Do you hear me?" Myra gasped.

"Oh, I hear you," Annie said, burrowing into the nest of down bedding. "That was really fun, Myra. I mean it. I can't remember the last time I did something so silly. Not to mention dangerous. Especially at our age. I'm going to go out on a limb here and say I think it was better than having sex."

"Shut up, Annie, and go to sleep."

"Here? Aren't we going to bed?"

"Let me ask you a question, Annie. Do you seriously think you could walk up that very long, very circular staircase one more time?"

Annie burrowed deeper into the bedding. "Absolutely not. Good night, Myra."

Myra snuggled into her corner of the bedding and was just dropping off to sleep when the cell phone in the pocket of her robe chirped. Annie bolted upright as did Myra while she grappled for the cell. It chirped twice more before she was able to bring it to her ear. She listened carefully as Kathryn explained that they were going to spend the night in Rena Gold's apartment so the showgirl could set up a meeting the following day in the penthouse with Maxwell Zenowicz. They discussed the terrible weather for another minute before the call ended.

Wide-awake now, Myra explained the call to Annie, then said, "I didn't think it was the time to tell them about your bid to buy the *Post*. Do you think I should have told them?"

Annie thought about the question. "No, I don't think so. It has nothing to do with what's going on right now. And it might never happen, so for now, let's just keep it between the two of us. I do like surprises. How do you feel about a fried-egg sandwich right now with some hot cocoa?"

"With ketchup?"

"What's a fried-egg sandwich without ketchup? It was nice of Nellie to bring us food, wasn't it? If the weather weren't so bad, I'd call her up to join us. Nellie never sleeps, you know that, right?"

Myra struggled to an upright position. "Yes, I know. I think she sleeps more than she admits, though. Arthritis is so debilitating, but Nellie handles it well. My hips and legs hurt, Annie."

"What do you expect? We went up and down those

damn steps twelve times. We used muscles we haven't used in a hundred years. We need to keep mobile. If you stop, then everything locks up. And don't you dare start with that *old people* business again."

The two women hobbled to the kitchen, where Annie fried the eggs and Myra prepared the hot cocoa.

"We aren't going to go to bed, are we?" Annie asked.

"No, we're not, Annie. In another hour or so I plan on calling Charles. I am so worried about him. I do hope everything is okay back on the mountain."

"I don't know why I say this . . . well, maybe I do, but I think Charles and the mountain are the least of our worries at the moment. Actually, right now, this very minute, I don't think we have anything to worry about. Everything seems to be under control. We're so used to going full tilt that now there's a lull we let our imaginations go into overdrive. Do you want the yolk runny or solid?"

"Runny and crisp around the edges. Nellie didn't bring any ketchup, Annie."

"See! See! Now, having no ketchup is something to worry about."

Myra smiled as she threw the dish towel in Annie's direction.

"Life will go on, my dear, ketchup or no ketchup," Annie said.

Annie had no idea how right she was about life going on no matter what. Back in the District, at the *Post,* the discussion that had turned into a free-for-all was continuing at full bore. It was Liam Sullivan—ready to chew nails and spit rust—who finally turned on the television for the late-evening news. The news anchor with rosy cheeks and strawlike hair read the opening sound bites. Sullivan cringed when the first report was the latest on the British Embassy. At some point after leaving the *Post,* Nigel Summers must have gone to the local Fox News station to be interviewed.

The assembled group listened as Summers said his staff would be returning to the embassy first thing in the morning, and that the vermin situation was contained. He made it clear that there was never any indication of a plague or anything other than a few rats, which had been trapped by Reston Exterminating. He refused to be baited by the reporter who had done the interview when he was questioned about Homeland Security and giving the CDC permission to enter the premises. It was what he didn't say that made all the difference. When the reporter asked Summers if he thought it was all a hoax, Summers shrugged and walked away.

"Son of a bitch! Those Brits are a smarmy lot, now, aren't they?" Roger Nolan snapped.

"Since you're the one who was all over this, Nolan, I can see why you'd say that. Summers just tied your dick in a knot. I'd start sending out my résumé if I were you," Sullivan snapped. "Somehow I don't think the president and the VP will look favorably on you after this fiasco. Can we call it a night now?"

"Look!" Elias Cummings said.

All eyes returned to the television as the anchor played three different call-in segments that pronounced the whole British Embassy episode a hoax. The third call was slightly different, and the men all looked at one another as they tried to place the voice. The third caller said it was a hoax the vigilantes had perpetrated to cover devious doings and to give the FBI another black eye.

The silence in the room was so total, a pin dropping on the floor would have sounded like a bombshell going off.

Dave Wylie from the CDC was the first to pack up his briefcase. He didn't say a word to anyone as he left the room. He didn't have to. His work was done, and he and his people would be on their way to Atlanta at first light. No one was going to ruin the reputation of his beloved CDC.

Sullivan looked over at Nolan and bellowed, "That leaves you holding the bag, Nolan."

Elias Cummings stood rooted to the floor. His eyes narrowed to slits as he swiveled his gaze over to where Ted Robinson was sitting with his colleagues. "How sure are you the vigilantes are behind this?"

His voice sounded so deadly that Ted cringed. Ever defiant, he looked up at his boss to see if he had permission to talk. Sullivan nodded. "It's the only thing that makes sense. Personally, I'm a hundred percent sure. I just don't know why. That's all I'm going to say."

Sullivan looked around at the cluttered room, at disgruntled lawyers and judges who suddenly didn't seem to know what to say or do. He barked orders to Ted and Espinosa before he left the room. "Stay as long as you like, gentlemen, I have a paper to get out."

"Hold on there, Sullivan," Cummings barked.

Liam Sullivan whirled around and jabbed a stubby finger into Cummings's chest. "No, you hold on. I'm putting a special edition out, and I'm kicking ass and taking names later. If you don't like it, sue me. My guys say you can't stop me, and that's good enough for me. We're going with the vigilantes theory because this time I think Robinson is on the money." He pointed to the men from the *Sentinel* and the *News,* who nodded in agreement as they powered up their cell phones.

Roger Nolan, not to be outdone, powered up his own cell phone, walking away to whisper into the phone.

"You know what, Robinson? You just went on my shit list. From here on out, you are in my crosshairs, and that goes for all the rest of you who call yourself journalists,"

Elias Cummings bellowed before he stormed out of the room.

"Ooh, I'm so scared," Ted said in an attempt at bravado.

"You should be," Sullivan said. "From now on, you're on his short shit list. That's not a good place to be, Robinson."

Like I didn't know that, Ted thought. *Never let them see you sweat*, he said over and over to make himself feel better. It didn't work. His insides felt like one big, jangled, raw nerve ending.

Nolan's color was what Sullivan described as ashen in the article that appeared in the early edition of the paper. But, he didn't stop there. He went on to describe Nolan's trembling hands, along with the FBI director's threat to shut down the three major papers in the District. Sullivan ended the Op-Ed piece by quoting verbatim what Nigel Summers had said and his intention to move his people back into the British Embassy.

Chapter 22

The sunburst clock over the mantel in Rena Gold's apartment read 12:20. Twenty minutes past the witching hour.

The women were sprawled out on the floor, the contents of Rena's floor safe spread out in front of them. Nikki waved a paper under Rena's nose. "Do you have any idea what all you have here?" she asked, awe ringing in her voice.

"Not really. I was so worried and scared, I just copied every piece of paper in his briefcase and never looked at them. Why . . . What is it?" Rena's eyes were so fearful, her voice so shaky, Kathryn reached out to take her hand and pat it.

Nikki's eyebrows drew together in a tight frown. "It's probably better that you don't know. You've done half our work for us. Now, the tricky part is going to be getting Zenowicz here tomorrow. The sooner the better. Tell me something, Rena, is he a day or night guy?"

Rena flushed a bright pink. "It depends on how long . . . Sometimes he likes afternoon . . . trysts. I . . . I haven't been with him in over a week. That doesn't mean he hasn't been with someone else, the louse. But from the tone of his voice the other night, I think I'm safe in saying he hasn't been with anyone, so . . ." She left whatever she was going to say to their imaginations.

"Okay, we need to come up with a workable plan and at the same time get you out of here safely. Ourselves as well. By the way, just how alert is that guy down in the lobby?"

"The day guy is easygoing. He likes to flirt. But I know Maxwell pays him to report my comings and goings. The night man is older, but he goes by the book. You can't get anything past him, and he usually sits glued to the monitors. He only fills in as a doorman if one of the guards calls in sick or something. Is that going to be a problem?"

Nikki chewed on her lower lip. "I'm not sure yet."

"What are you going to . . . you know . . . *do* to Maxwell? I read about how . . . Actually, I don't care what you do to him. I'm sorry I asked." Rena reached for her wineglass and seemed surprised that it was empty. Five empty bottles sat like soldiers on the tabletop. She eyed them before uncorking a sixth and pouring generously. Then Nikki's cell phone rang, and Rena was a deer in the headlights.

Nikki uncoiled herself and walked away toward the kitchen when she saw that it was Charles on the phone. The first words out of her mouth were, "What's wrong?"

"Plenty," was Charles's response.

"Tell me." Nikki listened to Charles suck in his breath. That alone told her the news was not going to be good. She waited.

"The *Post,* the *Sentinel,* and the *News* are all going with special early editions tomorrow. Today, actually. The headline will read something like, Vigilantes are back. Rat-and-plague scare a hoax. Vigilantes responsible."

"Oh, my God! What do you want us to do, Charles? Before you tell me, let me tell you something. We're more or less stranded at Rena Gold's penthouse. There's a terrible storm. We have all the documentation we need to pull this off, but if we leave, we're going to be too noticeable. We opted to stay overnight, and Rena is going to invite Zenowicz here in the morning. Whether or not he shows up will tell the story. On top of that, we do not have Alexis's Red Bag. And our special box. Both are at the farmhouse. We need them, Charles. Right now I'm not sure where Harry, Jack, and Bert are. Do you know?"

"They're in the parking garage dismantling all the security cameras to make it look like the storm shorted them out. Kathryn didn't help when she just ripped the wires out. You don't want to call undue attention to yourselves. Stay put, and I'll find a way to get Alexis's Red Bag to you. What will you do if Miss Gold's invitation to Mr. Zenowicz doesn't work?"

"I haven't gotten that far in my thinking, Charles. We still have a few hours till morning. We're working on it. He's really stupid, Charles. I never set eyes on the man, and I hate him with a passion. He's all about the money."

"Just don't get overconfident, Nikki. I want you out of there safe and sound. By the time those early editions hit in a few hours, there are going to be millions of sightings of all of you. This couldn't have happened at a worse time. By that I mean, the administration is going to get off the hook because the vigilantes are front and center. Are you following me?"

"I am, Charles. Just tell me one thing. Do we have a ride out of here back to the mountain?"

"Not yet, dear. I'm working on it."

"Work faster, Charles."

Nikki blinked as she shut the phone. Charles was never big on good-byes.

She rushed back into the sunken living room to tell the girls about her conversation with Charles.

The only person with a question was Rena. "What does all that mean?"

"What that means is our time frame is really, really short. It all hinges on you, Rena. You have to be absolutely convincing to get Zenowicz to meet with you even if you have to threaten him. You will have to do whatever it takes to get him here. Is that understood?" Rena's head bobbed up and down. "Good, that means we're all on the same page," Nikki said.

"What time will the special editions hit the streets?" Yoko asked.

"I'm guessing around four, five at the latest. That's just a few hours from now," Nikki said.

Alexis was on her feet. Perspiration beaded her brow. "How close are we going to be cutting it, Nikki?" It was obvious to all the Sisters that she was remembering the time she'd spent in prison on a trumped-up charge of securities fraud.

Nikki could see no sense in lying to Alexis. "Real short. I think with the guys in the parking garage watching our backs we'll be okay. It's when we're out in the open that it will become a problem. That's why we need your Red Bag. And of course *the box*. If we leave now and attempt to go back to the farm, the danger increases because we'll have to turn around and come right back, and for you to do your magic is going to take a while. I'm sure Charles will come up with something," she said soothingly.

"Maybe we should call Myra," Isabelle said.

"Maybe we shouldn't," Kathryn said sourly. "First off, it's the middle of the night, and I'm sure both Myra and Annie are sleeping. Secondly, there's a storm out there, and do we really want either one of them trying to get to us? I-don't-think-so. Tell me what you think of this: As you all know, I was a trucker and drove in all kinds of weather in an eighteen-wheeler. I'll drive out to the farm, get our stuff, and bring Myra and Annie back with me. We can't leave without them, and I don't see any other options. I'm willing to listen to ideas. Remember now, the FBI and Homeland Security are going to be watching this town like hawks."

Rena Gold chirped up. "Do you always have so many problems?"

"Lady, you are part of the problem, so pipe down and let us do what we do best," Isabelle all but snarled.

Rena Gold ignored Isabelle. "How is it you manage to elude the authorities and get away with it? You women are every woman's idol, young and old. I have to tell you, though, I don't think you're any match for the FBI and Homeland Security. No offense."

Kathryn's eyes flashed fire. "Maybe you'd like us to recite our résumés to you. Yoko, do the honors."

"It will be my pleasure, Kathryn." She fixed her gaze on Rena Gold and almost in a hypnotic voice regaled the woman with some of their victories. She ended with, "And we took on the acting director of the FBI. Check the archives. The man has never been seen or heard of again. The national security advisor is a vegetable. A group of dentists are eunuchs these days. There's a man in China who is stark, raving mad because we skinned him alive. It was not pretty. We even gave him a mirror when we sent him on his way. Oh, and before I forget, there was this senator who was married to one of our Sisters. He gave her AIDS—do you believe that? Our Sister died. Her name was Julia, and she was a doctor. Isn't that sad? She was a doctor and couldn't save herself. Her husband had the American flag tattooed on his ass. He works in Africa these days for five cents an hour. Not too terribly long ago we were here in this fair city impersonating the G-String Girls and completed our mission. Oh, before I forget, there was my father, who was into white slavery. I'm sure you heard of him, the famous actor, Michael Lyons. We glued him and his sick friends to the floor with *industrial-*

strength glue and when they came to arrest them they had to cut the boards to flatbed them to prison. Our missions are illustrious and dangerous, but we always come out on top."

Kathryn eyeballed the ex-showgirl. "So, sweet cheeks, who you putting your money on, the FBI, Homeland Security, or *us?*"

Rena turned pasty white, her bottled suntan failing entirely. "I'm sorry. You, of course. I didn't know . . . What I mean is, oh, hell, I don't know what I mean. Listen, don't forget I donated to your defense fund. I'm not going to squeal on you. It's just that the ordinary layperson is programmed to believe that law and order will win out."

"That's bullshit!" Kathryn cried. "The law works for the criminal. The good guys fall through the cracks. When I was gang-raped, those dentists got away with it. If it wasn't for my friends here, they would have really gotten away with it. They're the eunuchs that Yoko was talking about. We sent them their balls in a Ziploc bag via FedEx."

Rena swallowed hard but didn't say another word.

"Oh, shoot, Yoko, you didn't tell her about when we stuck the dynamite up those guys' asses and lit the fuses," Kathryn said.

"Darn! You're right. We did do that, Rena. Poof! Gone!" Yoko said, pride ringing in her voice.

Rena Gold's eyes rolled back in her head before she slid off the couch.

"Enough with our accomplishments," Nikki said. "Kathryn, do you think you can really make it out to McLean and back before it gets light?"

"I do. I'll take Bert with me if that's okay."

Nikki grinned. "Go for it. Be careful, okay?"

"Always," Kathryn said as she beelined for the door.

Five minutes later, Rena rejoined the living. She looked around to see if anything new had transpired while she was passed out. Satisfied nothing had, she poured more wine for herself. Suddenly, she squirmed and wiggled as she struggled to remove her vibrating cell phone from the pocket of her slacks. "I must have turned it on when I slid off the couch. It's Maxwell. Let's see, he's called"—she pressed a button and scrolled down the list of incoming calls—"twenty-nine times since noon yesterday. That means he is royally pissed at me. I'm surprised he didn't come here. I guess the weather had something to do with it. I told you, he's a health nut about germs and stuff. He runs to the doctor if he stubs his toe. He is so afraid he'll get prostate cancer, he gets checked every month. He takes forty-two vitamins a day. He constantly sanitizes his hands. He even sanitizes his feet before he puts his socks on."

The Sisters stared at Rena. It was Yoko who found her tongue first. "That's a little more than we needed to know, Rena. And you found this all sexually exciting?"

Rena snorted. "No way. I faked it. Every time. Look, think what you want about me. I did it for the money and to get out of Vegas before I got all used up. Would I do it again. *NO!* Everything in life is a learning experience, and I just had the Queen Mother of all learning experiences. Are you going to tell me what you're going to do to Maxwell?"

"It's better you don't know, Rena. This way you can go back to Vegas and start your life all over again without having to look over your shoulder. What I will tell you is you will never have to set eyes on Maxwell Zenowicz again," Nikki said.

Her eyes bigger than saucers, Rena nibbled on one of her acrylic nails. "Okay, I guess I can live with that."

"You don't have a choice, Rena," Isabelle said.

Chapter 23

To Bert's relief, the driving black rain finally let up ten miles from Myra Rutledge's McLean estate. Still, Kathryn drove the high-powered van like it was an eighteen-wheeler. Bert hung on to the strap above the passenger-side door for dear life. "You're one gutsy lady, Kathryn Lucas. But do you think you could slow down just a little?"

"If I slow down, we'll never get there. No cops out in this weather. We have to get back to Rena's, ASAP. This is crunch time. For some reason we always bring it right down to the wire. I . . . should thank you, Bert, for all you've done for us. I also know what a hard decision it must have been for you to swing to our side of the fence."

Bert looked over at the capable woman driving the van. His chiseled features softened. He really liked Kathryn Lucas. He rather thought she liked him, too. He couldn't help but wonder how it would all turn out. He knew she was waiting for an answer of sorts. "I'm for whatever brings justice to the world. The system is flawed. We all know that. Like you and the others, I have lines I will not cross. I'm at peace with my decision just the way Jack and Harry are. Does that help?"

Kathryn smiled. "You're my kind of guy, Bert," she said, the smile in her voice obvious.

What would Jack Emery say to that comment? Probably something either witty or profound. Well, he wasn't Jack Emery, so he was going to have to wing it. "I like you, Kathryn. I want to get to know you better. I also want you to know I never felt anything like I felt when I kissed you." Oh, God, did he just say that? Obviously he had because Kathryn burst out laughing.

"That kiss was a toe cruncher, that's for sure. We have to do it again soon."

Jesus. Bert felt so befuddled he couldn't see straight. What would Jack say? "Name the date and the time, and I'm your boy." Shit, Jack would drum him right out of the good ol' boys' club for his witty repartee. Who the hell needed Jack Emery anyway? He was doing okay on his own. At least he thought he was. He could see Kathryn smiling in the darkness. Suddenly he felt good all over.

Then he almost fainted when he heard Kathryn say, "I like you a lot, Bert. It's been a long time since . . . I'm sure Jack told you that my husband died, and I . . . I'm trying to say something here, Bert, and I don't know how to say it."

Bert reached over and touched her arm gently. Screw Jack Emery and his advice. "That was yesterday, Kathryn, there's no need for you to tell me anything. In fact, I don't want to know. This is now, so if it's okay with you, let's go on from here and not look back. I do want to say something, though. If the time ever comes when you want to talk about Alan—and, yes, Nikki and the others told me your husband's name—I'll listen. If that time never comes, that's okay, too."

Kathryn reached for Bert's hand and squeezed it. "Okay, that'll work."

It was Bert's turn to laugh, and he threw his head back, the sound ricocheting inside the huge van. Kathryn thought his laughter was the nicest sound she'd ever heard. She started to tingle all over at the possibilities lying ahead of her.

"We're coming up to the gate now. You've been here before, haven't you, Bert?"

"Yes. I was one of the guys who went through the farmhouse after you all escaped. I want to tell you that putting those leg monitors on the cats was a stroke of genius. We thought you girls were the busiest women in the world. When that got into the paper, the FBI looked like a bad, sad, Mickey Mouse Club. Even back then, I was secretly applauding and rooting for all of you."

Kathryn opened the window of the van and punched in the code that would unlock the massive iron gates. She told him about the first time she'd been here and how she had to plow down the gates with her eighteen-wheeler because the power was out. "That was the beginning of it, Bert. That was the first night when we all met one another. I don't think I'll ever forget that night as long as I live."

Bert felt compelled to say something. "You girls have had a great run, and I want to keep it that way, so safe and cautious is the way to go. Agreed?"

"You got it. At least it's stopped raining."

A floodlight suddenly lit the entire backyard, and the kitchen door opened to reveal Annie and Myra dressed and ready to go. Kathryn raced to both women and hugged them tightly.

Annie held Kathryn off at a distance and looked into her eyes.

"Wh . . . What?" Kathryn asked.

"You're in love, aren't you, dear?"

Kathryn could feel heat creeping up from her neck to her cheeks. "I think so, Annie, but don't tell anyone, okay?"

Annie wanted to tell her the whole world would see it on her face, but she didn't. "We're ready to go," she said, giving Kathryn one last hug.

Bert stepped inside to pick up the Red Bag, which was stuffed to overflowing. He carried it to the van, then returned to pick up two equally heavy cardboard cartons.

"A man with muscles. I like that," Annie said, winking at Kathryn.

There was an eerie calmness to the night as Kathryn drove back into the District. There was little conversation, each busy with his or her own thoughts.

It was three minutes till four when Kathryn steered the van down the ramp leading to the underground parking garage. Harry and Jack were waiting for them. Harry raced to the gate and pushed a big red button. Kathryn barreled through and skidded to a stop. Rain dripped from the undercarriage and formed huge puddles. Bert hopped out, holding the door for Annie and Myra, who immediately ran in the direction Kathryn was pointing. Jack opened the door from the other side and motioned the women to follow him to the elevator. The whole operation was synchronization down to the last sync.

No one was breathing hard when Alexis opened the door to admit the group. She smiled when she saw her Red Bag.

And then they were all talking at once. Rena Gold pushed herself deep into the pillows of the sofa as she wondered what she'd gotten herself into. When she couldn't reach a conclusion, she poured herself yet another glass of wine. The empties lining the glass-top table now numbered seven.

Rena continued to watch as her new best friends worked at the speed of light. First they played with the remote for the plasma TV hanging on her wall, then they moved off to the computer system Zenowicz had had installed for her in the oversized dressing room off the bedroom that she used as an office. What were they doing? And, did she even want to know? She decided she didn't care one way or the other.

Rena almost jumped out of her skin when Yoko tapped her on the shoulder. "You should take a shower now and dress in your traveling clothes. We will have coffee ready for you when you are ready. You will be leaving soon after Zenowicz arrives. You understand that, right?"

Did she? She shrugged. "Are you saying you won't need me?"

"That's what I'm saying. We have your cell phone number and will call you when we are finished here. Tell me you understand everything I just said."

Rena nodded, not trusting herself to speak. She got up and wobbled to the master bathroom. She knew she was drunk and had to sober up. In order to do that she would have to shower under cold water first. She wondered if the shock would kill her.

She was literally blue with cold, goose bumps all over her body, when she stepped out of the shower. It took another thirty minutes to dress and apply her makeup. When she was done she felt stone-cold sober and in need of some strong black coffee. She looked at herself in the mirror and smiled. It was a smile that promised trouble. For Maxwell Zenowicz.

Back in the living room, she watched in amazement as Alexis rummaged in the huge Red Bag, working in a frenzy. She thought of Santa Claus and his big green burlap bag. This was like that. She remembered how as a child she stood in awe when the jolly old guy came to the church basement and fished around in his bag as he looked for that special present with each child's name on it. It didn't matter if you were a boy or a girl, your present was wrapped in silver paper and tied with a big red satin bow. She remembered how thrilled that big red bow made her feel.

Without anyone telling her, Rena knew she wasn't supposed to know what was in the Red Bag, and she also knew she was in the way, so she walked into the kitchen and poured herself a cup of coffee. There was a lot to be said for a good surprise. A lot. She crossed her fingers and hoped she wouldn't be disappointed.

The coffee was good. She poured a second cup. Then she debated making toast, but with all the wine she'd consumed, she decided to leave well enough alone. Her eyes on the clock, she did a mental countdown to when she was to call Maxwell Zenowicz. Thirty more minutes. She crossed her fingers again, hoping she could pull off what the vigilantes required of her. If she wanted that new life she dreamed of, she'd have to pull it off, no ifs, ands, or buts about it. Thirty minutes. Her eyes glued to the clock on the range, she started to count. "This is your lucky day, Maxwell."

The front door opened, and Harry entered the foyer. He called out, "Look alive, people, this building is starting to come awake. The elevators are humming, and cars are going in and out of the garage. The cameras are still dark, which is a good thing. What's our countdown?"

Someone called out from the living room. He thought it was Isabelle. "Rena is going to call at five thirty, twenty-five minutes from now. We don't know how long it will take Zenowicz to get here, but we'll be ready for him. See if you can find a morning edition of one of the papers."

"If I go out of the garage, I can't get back in. Hey, Jack, spot me, okay?" Jack obliged him, and they both left the penthouse.

In the kitchen, Rena continued to stare at the clock on the range.

In the sunken living room, Kathryn, Isabelle, Nikki, and

Yoko now looked like Rena Gold right down to the pouty lips and false eyelashes. Myra and Annie were resplendent in haughty dowager gear, while Alexis had made herself look like a tight-ass female banker with a bun in her hair and tortoiseshell-rimmed glasses.

"Now what?" Yoko asked.

"Now we wait," Nikki said.

Chapter 24

Rena Gold had her hand on her house phone ready to make the call to Maxwell Zenowicz when Harry, Jack, and Bert burst into the apartment, their arms loaded with fresh-off-the-press copies of the *Post,* the *Sentinel,* and the *News.* Their faces were grim. Myra's hands were shaking when she reached out to take a copy. She gasped, as did the others.

"This is not good," Jack said, his eyes on Nikki as she scanned the front page of the *Post.*

"Well, the photographer captured our true likeness," Annie quipped as she pointed to the half-page picture, above the fold, on all three newspapers. The picture had been taken when they'd been arraigned and stood before Judge Cornelia Easter. The huge black headline, usually reserved for a declaration of war, read, "VIGILANTES BACK!" Below the fold, which took up the bottom half of all three papers, was a picture in caricature. The vigilantes wearing knee-high boots with six-inch heels, clad in bustiers, long hair flowing wildly, each with a smoking gun in her hand. One word, as big as the headline above the caricature, read, "GOTCHA!"

"We look good," Yoko said, to Harry's dismay.

"I'd say that court-appointed artist did a great job." Alexis giggled.

"I just love it!" Annie cried exuberantly. "We need to have a costume party at some point so we can dress like this," she added, pointing to the cartoon.

Nikki looked at Jack and grinned, as if to say, *Hey, big guy, look what you're getting.*

"Oh, well, we don't really look anything like that right now," Isabelle said. "Look at us, we all look like Rena Gold." She glanced over at the three men. "Stop looking so glum. We have things under control."

Myra clucked her tongue. "This article has listed our . . . exploits. That's what they're calling our missions. They're also giving us way too much credit. It says we single-handedly apprehended a whole drug cartel, that the CIA is in our debt and does what we say when we say it. That they're our puppets! It also goes on to say that the president pinned medals on us in private, something the White House has refused to confirm or deny. And that the plague and the rats were a ruse for the mission we're on at the moment. It seems, according to this article, the FBI and local law enforcement have no clue why we're here and what we plan to do. The CIA is refusing comment. The roads back into town are clogged again, but this time the 'little people' are not angry but excited to be on the side of the vigilantes and doing their best to get back to where the action is. This is a firestorm if I ever saw one," Myra said, tossing the paper onto the coffee table.

"I don't think *that*," Kathryn said, pointing to the paper, "changes a thing. We came here to do a job, so let's do it. The way I see it, we're safe here in Rena's apartment until Charles figures out how to get us out." She looked up at Bert and winked. He grinned from ear to ear.

Rena Gold appeared flustered. "Are you sure you're going to be able to get away safely? If it comes down to you versus me, don't worry about me. Get out of here to safety."

The women looked at Rena and as one decided she meant every word she said. She rose several notches in their opinions.

"Don't worry, Rena, we have it covered," Nikki said. "It's time for you to make your call, it's five forty-five. Make it on the house phone, not your cell. You want to tell him it isn't working, and that's why you haven't gotten his calls. But why hasn't he called you on this house phone?"

Rena snorted, a very unlikely sound. "Because that would leave a trail, which could prove he was having an affair with me. He can be incredibly stupid sometimes. Everyone either knows or suspects anyway, so I don't get the point. That's Maxwell for you. My cell phone belongs to the World Bank and was issued to me when I was . . . hired. When he calls me on it, it's considered business. Maxwell reviews all the bills and expense accounts and approves or disapproves them. No one sees the cell phone bills but him. I know that for a fact."

Nikki pointed to the kitchen. "Do it now. We're on a schedule, Rena. Remember now, be your most persuasive. Promise him anything you want and don't worry, you won't have to keep those promises."

Rena drew a deep breath and walked back to the kitchen. Kathryn followed her, but the others remained in the living room reading the papers and either giggling, or rolling their eyes, to the dismay of Jack, Harry, and Bert.

"They're women," Jack said. "Do not ever try to figure them out because you can't, and if you do try, you'll end up going nuts. That's all I have to say."

"And to think I used to look up to you," Bert grumbled.

"Ha! That was your first mistake. He doesn't have a clue about women," Harry snorted.

Jack tried to change the subject. "Anyone want to make a bet whether Zenowicz falls for it or not?"

"Nah," Bert said.

"Hell no!" Harry said.

Jack sighed. "I say he's here within the hour."

"Two hours," Bert said. "He won't want to appear anxious even if he is."

"I say it's going to depend on whether he sees the morning papers or sees the local news," Harry suggested. "He's got to have a guilty conscience about all the money he's sending offshore, and he just might think the vigilantes are here to get him. I know it's a stretch, but when you're dealing with a guilty conscience, there are no rules. Plus, the chick hasn't been taking his calls. I say three hours tops."

Even though the three of them were close to the kitchen, they couldn't hear a word that was being said. They watched Kathryn for clues as to how it was going. When she gave a thumbs-up, they all relaxed.

Kathryn was stunned to see the hateful look on Rena's face and wondered how she could possibly say what she was saying with such a straight face. She listened.

"I am sooo sorry, sweetheart, but I didn't want you to catch whatever it was I had. I know how germs just invade your body for no reason. Did you get the shot I told you about? You didn't? Why not? Oh, they didn't have the serum, it was on order. Well, my suggestion would be to double up on your vitamins. What's eighty-four vitamins a day? Nothing, you just swallow a handful and forget about it. So, do you forgive me, honey?"

She listened to the harsh voice on the other end of the line and waited a few seconds before she responded. "But I want to see you now. Like *now*, Maxwell. We haven't seen each other in almost ten days. How many times do I have to tell you the cell phone broke? You can see it yourself when you get here. Did I mention to you what I had planned for us? Of course I have chocolate whipping cream. Doesn't everyone? But I have something better planned. And I have a red-hot bonus in the making if you can get here within the next hour. You don't need break-fast, honey. Just take all those vitamins, and I'll do the rest." She listened again. "No hints. I want to surprise you. An hour and a half? That sounds like forever. Try to make it quicker. I promise you won't be sorry. I'll be wait-ing," she trilled as she replaced the phone.

Rena leaned against the stainless steel refrigerator and struggled to get her breathing back to normal. Kathryn wasn't sure if Rena was going to buckle or not, so she rushed forward. "What the hell did you promise that creep?" she whispered.

"Oh, God, Kathryn, you don't want to know. I just want out of here, the sooner the better."

"How long do you think he'll take?"

"He's upset with me, but his dick won out. Guess those nubile young things he was chasing didn't have as many tricks in the sack as I have. Knowing him the way I do, I'd say he'll be here in a little less than an hour."

Kathryn looked at her watch. "That means somewhere in the neighborhood of six twenty or maybe six thirty. Okay, good girl. Your job is done. All you have to do is open the door, and we'll take it from there. You're home free, Rena. Now, make some more coffee for the guys and drink some yourself. I want you wired from the caffeine when he gets here. I want you to think now. Is there any-thing, anything at all, that you think might help us? Any-thing you might have forgotten?"

Rena shook her head. "I gave it to you straight. There's nothing more to share. I wish there was. You know, I liked you when you were Delia McDermott, and I like you even more as Kathryn Lucas. I hope everything goes good for all of you, and I meant it when I said I want you all to come to Vegas so I can show you the town. My people will help your people. Isn't that how they say it? You know, what happens in Vegas stays in Vegas. I know I keep saying that but it's true, you know. Well, I just wanted you to know that. Maybe when this is all over, and you're safely back wherever it is you live, you'll consider making me an honorary vigilante."

"Count on it." Kathryn grinned.

It was almost noon on Big Pine Mountain. Charles was sitting at the bank of computers in his newly renovated quarters. He didn't bother to stop and marvel at how quickly the repairs had moved along. While there were still things to be done, he was content that he once again had access to the outside world, all thanks to Kollar and the United States government. And a few other governments as well.

The countdown was on.

As Kathryn would say, he had it going on, with the exception of one request marked URGENT sent to him by Alexis. He blinked once, twice, three times, then burst out laughing. This was one request he would enjoy fulfilling. He tapped furiously, then waited just seconds for the return e-mail. "Done!" He started to laugh again. Damn if his girls weren't a gutsy bunch of women.

He was still laughing when he called Jack and gave him his orders. "You are going to have exactly three hours from the time Maxwell Zenowicz enters the apartment, so make every second count. Make sure Bert understands how crucial his role is. Tell Alexis her special order should be on her doorstep by seven thirty. Have someone standing at the door to receive it."

Jack shrugged. He agreed and closed his cell phone. He then repeated Charles's instructions to Bert and Harry.

"There isn't going to be time for good-byes is what you're telling me, right?" Bert asked.

"Right. That was the bad news. But, and this is the good news, two weeks from today we're all invited to Big Pine Mountain for two whole weeks. Arrange your vacations, boys, or quit your jobs. Your call."

"Now what?" Harry asked.

Jack looked at his watch. "Now we wait."

Rena Gold's doorbell rang at exactly six forty. Maxwell Zenowicz's key didn't work because Rena had the dead bolt secured. Rena rushed to open the door, apologizing for forgetting to unlock it. Zenowicz brushed past her like a fugitive on the run. He even looked over his shoulder.

"What happened to '*Hello, I missed you,*' or '*Are you all right?*' " Rena snapped.

"What did you say?" His tone was so menacing, Rena backed up a step, then another step.

Somewhere deep inside her she came up with the guts to say, "You heard what I said, *Maxie.*"

Rena saw the raised arm, the slap that was coming her way, and she froze on the spot. She squeezed her eyes shut and waited for the blow that never arrived. When she opened her eyes, she saw Zenowicz surrounded by the vigilantes, all of whom looked just like she did.

"What in the damn hell . . . ?"

"Shhh, there will be none of that, *Maxie,*" Alexis said as she twirled him around. "Ah, nice threads," she observed, fingering the material of his Brioni suit. She looked over at the girls, and said, "Ten grand easy for the suit, maybe more. It's tropical wool. The shirt maybe $450. Top-grade linen. Probably Irish. The tie another $250. Those shoes, let's see, Crocs go for about $2,500. The watch he's wearing is a Jaeger-LeCoultre. I can't even begin to guess what it costs but a small fortune for sure. Fashion is my game, as you know. The man has a lot of bucks on his back and feet, ladies. Enough to feed a passel of starving kids for quite a while."

Annie yelled, "Giddyup, girls!"

From that point on it was a free-for-all as the girls pushed Zenowicz from one to the other until he was dizzy—at which point Kathryn gave him a mighty shove, and he landed on the couch, legs sprawled forward.

Zenowicz blustered and cursed as he tried to get to his cell phone. Yoko ripped it out of his hand and stepped on it. "Oh, mercy me, I broke your phone. Guess you're going to have to get another one. Creep," she added as an afterthought.

"Who are you?" Zenowicz bellowed. "Is this a home invasion?"

"Hey, sweet cheeks, we're your conscience. If you want it to be a home invasion, then that's what it is. Now shut up, sit up, fold your hands, and don't speak again until we say you can," Kathryn said.

"Like I'm going to listen to *you!* Who the hell are you?" Zenowicz bellowed a second time. "Do you have any idea who I am?"

Kathryn cuffed him upside the head. "Who do you think we are? And guess what, we know exactly who you are. And, guess what else. We don't give two shits if you are the president of the World Bank or not. We don't like you one little bit, *Maxie.* If you say one more word, you're going to be minus your teeth. If you want to bring it to a test, go for it," Kathryn said ominously.

The president of the World Bank clamped his mouth shut. Then he let his gaze go from one to the other, then to the other until his gaze locked on Rena, who simply nodded. Fear suddenly raged in his eyes as he cowered back into the depths of the cushions. "Oh, good Christ, I know who you are. I heard about you on the news this morning. I saw the . . ." Whatever he was about to say, he changed his mind and cowered deeper into the cushions of the sofa. Then he bolted upright and glared at Rena. "You're behind this, aren't you?"

Kathryn took off her shoe and whacked him hard again on top of his head. "I told you to shut up. No, she is not behind this. I'm going to ask you a question, then I'm going to give you permission to speak. If I don't like your answer, there go those pearly whites of yours. That's the only warning you're going to get. Obviously, the reason you're here is because we want you here. This is the question: Why do you think we would put our lives in jeopardy and risk getting caught to meet up with you like this? What have you done or what are you doing that would bring you on our radar screen? Your first answer counts. That was really two questions, so answer them both."

Kathryn didn't take her eyes off Zenowicz, her shoe still in her hand. She called out to Yoko. "If you don't like his answer, or if he lies, knock his teeth out. Then you have my permission to rip that really bad hairpiece off his head and jam it down his throat."

"All righty," Yoko said, pirouetting around the room, her feet and arms going in all directions as she squealed out strange words that rang in everyone's ears. "It's not a rug, Kathryn, just a really bad comb-over. Who knew," she chirped happily.

"I knew," Rena said sotto voce.

"Same thing. Pull what's left out by the roots. Who cares?" Kathryn said.

"Sweet Jesus!" In the kitchen, Bert Navarro looked at Jack and Harry, his eyes full of questions.

"Yeah, she'll do it," Harry said. "Two seconds tops. That's my girl!" he said proudly.

Kathryn reached down to pick up a thick silver candlestick off the coffee table. She hefted it in her hand to get the feel of it, then she swung it back and forth like she was warming up to hit a fastball. "Here's the really important question. Where's the money that was allocated for those three poor countries that never got any of it? I'm not talking about that ragtag operation you set up in some war-torn area. Where is it, Mr. Zenowicz? Before you answer my question, I want you to know that the first thing a lawyer learns in law school is you never ask a question that you do not know the answer to. In case you're in your stupid mode today, that's another way of saying I know the answer. Now you can speak."

"I don't know what the hell you're talking about!"

Kathryn shrugged. She flicked her finger in Yoko's direction. She was a second too late. Yoko's foot shot out at the speed of light. Shiny porcelain dotted the coffee table as blood spurted from Zenowicz's mouth.

"Son of a bitch! She's faster than lightning," Bert hissed.

Harry beamed. Jack grinned.

"Just so you know, Bert, Yoko has been teaching the girls. Kathryn is almost as good as Yoko, right, Harry?"

"Almost. Shhh, they're about to swing into high gear now," Harry said.

Nikki and Isabelle yanked Zenowicz to his feet. No one cared that he tried to fight them, all the while trying to sop up the blood spewing from his mouth onto the sleeve of the Brioni jacket. They dumped him on the floor in front of the huge plasma TV.

"Sit, *Mr. President*," Myra said coldly. "If you so much as twitch, you will regret it."

Nikki slipped a CD into the player, clicked it on, then stepped back as all the horrific pictures they'd been shown on Big Pine Mountain came to life. No one said a word until the CD was finished. "Where's the money that was supposed to go to those countries? Do you have any idea how many starving children died because of you? Do you have any remorse? Say something, you son of a bitch!" Nikki shouted, the veins in her neck throbbing with her outburst.

Yoko dropped to her knees and grabbed the fine hairs on Zenowicz's comb-over. She waited. When he didn't respond, she gave a vicious yank. Blood beaded on the man's head. Yoko looked at the stringy hairs in her hand, grimaced, then dropped them in his lap.

"I don't think he's going to tell us," Annie said. "Should I put Plan B into operation?"

"Definitely. Let me get the equipment," Alexis said, happiness ringing in her voice. She returned to the living room with a black medical bag and a box that contained seven TASER guns, among other things. She handed it all to Nikki, who made a big production of opening both the box and the medical bag. She tossed out surgical gloves to all the girls, who, with wicked smirks on their faces, snapped them on. Zenowicz was alive with fear as he continued to wipe at the blood still drooling from his mouth.

"Last chance, *Maxie*. Where's the money? The World Bank wants to know. They appointed a special task force who hired us. We've never failed yet, and a piece of scum like you is not going to impede us. We can do this the hard way or the easy way." Nikki motioned for Alexis and Isabelle to take off Zenowicz's jacket and shirt as she filled a surgical needle with liquid from a vial in the medical kit.

While she was measuring the liquid, Annie swept everything off the coffee table and laid down a white cloth. She pulled surgical instruments out of a plastic bag and pronounced them sterile in a crisp, no-nonsense voice. She looked over at Rena Gold, who was white as a sheet.

Kathryn reached into the cardboard box and withdrew

a huge leather-bound book and flipped it open. Zenowicz watched, his eyes full of panic. He managed to gasp and demand to know what was in the hypodermic.

"The plague virus," Nikki said. She squirted a drop into the air, which fell onto the cloth. She quickly dabbed it up with one of the Clorox wipes. "Girls, decide which one of you is going to jerk him to reality. Anyone will do."

Annie drew the honor and turned on her TASER. "This is what is going to happen, sir. When I fire this TASER, tendrils of blue electric current will start to crackle between the electrodes. You'll smell ozone, but don't let that worry you. When this hits you, you will fall over and be incapacitated. We can keep doing it all morning until you tell us what we want to know. Now," she said importantly, "you have three choices. The TASERS, the plague serum, or a lobotomy. That's what those . . . uh . . . tools on the table are for. We're still in the apprentice stage on the lobotomy. If we screw it up, oh, well, you'll never know anyway. Where's the goddamn money?"

When Zenowicz remained mute, Annie fired off her TASER and hit him six inches below his belt. He reeled backward from the jolt and fell forward. Eighteen seconds later he groaned and tried to get up. Kathryn's TASER hit him a second time in the neck. He fell forward again, tears rolling down his cheeks.

"Where's the money?" Alexis asked, standing over him, the TASER in her hand at the ready. "You know, you could have a heart attack if we jolt you seven times. Why are you being such a hard-ass, Mr. Zenowicz?"

"Fuck each and every one of you. I'll see you all in prison for this. I have the money to do it, too."

"I sense a little puffery here, ladies. I don't much care for it." Alexis's TASER hit Zenowicz midchest. He fell, rolled over in agony, and cursed in several different languages.

"Enough of this foolishness. Prep his arm and we'll give him a shot," Nikki said. "He'll probably live for maybe three days. Unless we do the lobotomy. Let's take a vote, girls."

The final tally was four for the lobotomy and three for the plague.

In the kitchen the three men looked at one another in stupefied amazement. Jack finally decided to break the stunned silence. "Think of it as his coming-out party, boys. The guy was dumb enough to wander off the reservation, so he deserves whatever happens to him."

Glassy-eyed, his body racked with pain, Zenowicz struggled to a sitting position. Naked fear showed in his eyes. He was shaking from head to toe as he watched the women towering over him.

"Who's watching the time?" Nikki asked.

"I am, dear," Annie said. "I think you have just enough time to do the lobotomy if you hurry. Cut as many corners as you feel necessary. What did we decide to use for anesthetic?"

"Well the class-A anesthetic was all gone from the pharmacy, so we're going to use plain old ether. He'll feel it, but it can't be helped. Someone shave his head. Left, right, frontal, what? I can't remember. I never did this before. Practicing on a stiff isn't the same as a human. Quick now, shave his head and swab it with alcohol. First it's an incision, then we have to saw through the bone. Where's the saw?"

"I have it right here, Nikki," Annie said, holding up a surgical saw. "Here's the scalpel. Ooh, I don't think I can watch this, it's going to be so gory. Do you all mind if I go for some coffee?"

"No, go ahead," Nikki said.

"You crazy bitch! Rena, stop them! After all I've done for you, how can you let this happen? Stop them; I'll give you anything you want."

Rena laughed and laughed.

"The book says the operation takes three hours. We don't have three hours," Kathryn said. "What should we do?" she dithered, for Zenowicz's benefit.

"No problem," Nikki said, snapping on a fresh set of surgical gloves. "I think I can do it in forty-five minutes. Who's going to know if I screw it up?"

Zenowicz fainted.

"I'll zap him awake," Kathryn said. "If you want to get this over with, plug in the drill. That should make him sit up and take notice."

"Good point," Nikki said as she plugged in the drill, turned it on, and grinned.

Kathryn shook the president of the World Bank like a rag doll. Finally, he was able to focus. "Change of plans, Mr. President. We just don't have the time to do a full-scale operation, so we're going to drill into your frontal lobe and do it that way. The book says it *should* work."

"All right, all right! I'll tell you what you want to know. If I tell you, will you let me go?"

"Absolutely! And no hard feelings," Annie said with a straight face.

The women hauled Zenowicz to his feet and dragged him into Rena's small office. Nikki booted up the laptop that was in his briefcase and waited. She shot him a warning look and advised him not to lie. "Give me your password."

"MAZ46," Zenowicz responded.

Nikki typed it in and watched as mundane records appeared on the screen. Ledgers, online banking for household expenses, a small checking account at Wachovia Bank. Small donations to various charities.

Nikki leaned back in the swivel chair and pierced him with a stabbing glare. "Enough of this bullshit. This is not what I'm talking about. Do not, I repeat, do not, tax my patience. Give me the proper password right now."

He held out until Kathryn ran out to the living room to return with the hypodermic needle and the drill. His torso bare, Zenowicz shriveled into a small heap as he sank to his knees.

"Look, Mr. President, give it up right now. Where you're going, you will never see a penny of this money. Your life as you know it is over. You can go to your new home with or without a lobotomy. Or, if you want to die quickly, it's the shot. We do not have the time for you to diddle around with us. Our patience ran out about fifteen minutes ago. I'm going to get up off this chair, and you are going to sit down. And then you are going to show me everything that's on this laptop. Do it now!" Nikki said.

Moving like a zombie, Zenowicz did as Nikki instructed. The minute she saw what she wanted appear on the screen, she pushed him off the chair and sat down. Her fingers flew over the keys at the speed of light. Within minutes she was able to see his personal wealth, which was staggering, and the money he'd stolen from the World Bank. She grinned when she looked down at the man on the floor, who was watching her.

"You're a stupid man, Mr. Zenowicz. Swiss banks aren't the only game in town these days." Seconds later, Zenowicz's personal funds were "in flight" to Liechtenstein, Austria, Luxembourg, the Cayman Islands, the Netherlands Antilles, and the Bahamas. The last key Nikki hit transferred three million dollars to Rena Gold's Merrill Lynch account in Nevada. She pressed PRINT the moment the money hit Rena's account. She then brought up the World Bank account that Zenowicz was responsible for. Two clicks of her fingers and five seconds later, two billion dollars flew home to its original nest in the World Bank.

Zenowicz sat on the floor and cried like a baby.

Nikki powered down and closed up the laptop. She tossed it to Yoko, who dumped it in the cardboard box.

The women dragged Zenowicz back to the living room. Nikki dumped in a CD and waited a minute. "Look alive here, you son of a bitch! I want you to see where you're going. This little slice of paradise is where you will live until you die."

A picture appeared on the screen.

Zenowicz howled his rage. "I'm not going there! You can't make me go there. I gave you everything you wanted. You promised."

"I lied," Nikki said as she packed up the cardboard box. "You're going to Ethiopia, and you better hope and pray that the new regime at the World Bank is a little more generous than you were. If not, you'll starve to death."

"Rena, time for you to go," Nikki said, handing her the record she'd printed out. Rena looked at it, gasped, then swiped at her eyes, but not before she hugged Nikki.

"You earned it, Rena. You helped us, and I'd be lying if I didn't say it's also to buy your silence where the vigilantes are concerned. Just so you know, the money is from Zenowicz's personal funds and not the World Bank funds. One of Harry's people is in the garage, and he will drive you to the airport. We chartered a private plane to take you to your destination. Hurry up, it's waiting for you. Nice knowing you, Rena."

"You gave that bitch my money! You chartered a plane for her! Goddamn you!" Zenowicz snarled.

Kathryn backhanded him across the mouth. Blood spurted out. Again. No one cared. She shrugged.

"Dishonesty is not the currency of discretion, Mr. Zenowicz," Annie said primly. "Take him away," she said dramatically to Jack and Harry.

They obliged and pushed him along to the front door,

where Bert waited. Nikki ran after them. With one quick jab of the needle to Zenowicz's neck, he folded like an accordion and dropped to the floor. Bert picked him up, slung him over his shoulder, and made his way to the service elevator.

"Okay, girls, we have ten minutes to sanitize this place. Let's do it!" Yoko shouted.

Annie shouted to be heard over the scurrying that was going on, "Are the security monitors still out on all the floors?"

"Yeah," Jack shouted back. "But not for long. Charles said the repair people are supposed to be here at nine o'clock. We have to clear the garage before that."

"No problem," Myra said, stripping off her gloves. "We're done here. Alexis has the trash bag. Harry, take the Red Bag. We still need it. We have one more stop to make before we head home. Chop-chop, girls, we don't have a moment to waste. Who is going to make the phone call?"

"Nellie!" Annie laughed.

The van rolled out of the underground garage at one minute till nine. By the time Harry turned the corner to swing into the morning traffic, three utility trucks and a white van with red lettering were heading toward Rena's building.

"We aced that one by the skin of our teeth," Jack said with a weary sigh. Right now he would kill for just one hour of sleep and some decent food in his stomach. He wanted to turn around and look at what the women were doing, but he knew better. Their laughter and giggles made him more nervous than ever.

"This is not a wise thing you're doing," he yelled to be heard over the chatter.

"Wise or not, we're doing it," Annie shouted in return.

Jack groaned. Harry stared out the window as he

clenched and unclenched his fists. He hated these last-minute, dangerous changes.

"We're five minutes out, ladies," Jack said in a strangled-sounding voice.

Harry's clenched fists showed white knuckles.

"Drive around the block once to make sure there are no . . . authority types present," Myra said as she slid a poncho over her head. Jack risked a glance in the rearview mirror. All the girls were decked out in colorful ponchos and sitting primly on the seats, waiting for Jack's all clear.

"There's a crowd," Jack said, his voice jittery. He looked over at Harry and said, "Thank God for tinted windows. All you and I need is our picture on the six o'clock news."

"Not to worry. If that happens, we took you hostage and held you at gunpoint," Annie said airily. "Do you see any photographers?"

"I see three cameramen," Harry shot back.

"Okay, Jack, one more time around the block and we'll get out when you turn the corner," Nikki said. "Stay sharp and keep moving. We'll meet up with you on the opposite corner. We clear on that?"

"Everyone have their TASER in case things get sticky?" Alexis asked.

Six hands shot upward.

"Okay, here we go," Jack said, taking the corner at fifty miles an hour. He slowed briefly, the back doors of the van opened, and the women leaped out. They walked two abreast around the corner, their eyes going in all directions. They slowed their steps when they approached the gathering crowd. Off in the distance a cacophony of sound could be heard. Sirens. Lots and lots of sirens. All headed toward Rena's former address.

"Sounds to me like Nellie did her job perfectly," Annie hissed in Myra's ear. "No one will be looking for us here in front of the *Post*."

In unison the women ripped off their Rena Gold wigs and dental prosthetics. A second later, the ponchos, with their Velcro closures, were removed. A gasp went up from the crowd as the vigilantes stepped forward.

"Make it as corny as you can," Nikki said as Kathryn stepped to the front of the pack.

Bustier in place, imitation semiautomatic Glock gun in front of her, black patent knee-high boots gleaming in the morning sun, Kathryn whirled around and motioned to the others to stand next to her.

"Yes, we're back! We came here to right a grievous wrong. We want all the citizens of this town to know we had nothing to do with the rat-and-plague scare. If you want to know who started those rumors, look to the people in the building behind all of us. We took care of *our* business, ladies and gentlemen. If you want to know what that business is, look to the World Bank. Now," she said, backing up a step, "let us walk away from here and we'll let you get on with your business. Please don't impede our departure."

The crowd cheered and yelled chants that sounded like, "You, go, girls. We'll stop anyone who gets in your way."

One elderly lady carrying an umbrella poked it at a young man who looked like he wasn't taking Kathryn's words seriously enough. She pushed him against the brick of the building and held him in place. "Go! Hurry!"

The women didn't need any urging; they were already racing around the corner and out of sight. The cameramen attempted to follow the women, but the crowd surged forward, blocking their path.

"You just had to do that, didn't you?" Jack shouted as the girls piled into the van. "You had to rub their noses in it, didn't you?"

"Hell yes, we did," Kathryn said, almost falling out of the van. Isabelle grabbed her in the nick of time, the door slid shut and Jack burned rubber.

* * *

Forty-five minutes later, Jack skidded to a stop at Tyson's Corners. The women leaped out and raced to the cars that were waiting for them. There was no time for good-byes or kisses. No one waved.

Jack and Harry got out of the van and stood watching the convoy of cars speed away. The vigilantes were leaving just the way they'd arrived.

"I feel like shit, Jack. They didn't even wave. They could have done *something*."

Five seconds later both men's cell phones rang. "Jack! Thanks. I love you and don't you ever forget it. See you in two weeks."

Harry's call was just as short, just as sweet. "Honey, you can watch my back anytime. I love you. See you in two weeks."

"I don't know who looks sappier, you or me, Harry," Jack said.

"Who cares? She loves me. Nikki loves you. All the women love us," Harry said, pushing his seat back as far as it would go. He propped his legs on the dashboard and stared out the window. "Two weeks isn't that long, Jack. It's 14 days, 336 hours, or 20,160 minutes. Too much trouble to figure out the seconds."

"I feel sorry for Bert. He has to go all the way to Ethiopia to drop off his . . . uh, package. Then he has to deadhead back." Both men burst out laughing.

"Let's have a party for him when he gets back."

"That'll work," Harry said.

"They did good, didn't they, Harry?"

"Damn right. That took a lot of guts, not to mention the danger, to stand there in front of the *Post* and strut their stuff. Damn, I can't wait to see tomorrow's paper. Five bucks will get you ten the vigilantes are on page forty. All three of those papers are going to look like the *schmucks* they really are. Fox News, now, that's a whole different ball game. I saw a lot of pedestrians with their own cameras. They'll have fresh pictures for days, and Fox will be paying for the privilege. And if they're too stupid to figure out the business at the World Bank, well, we can help the girls out and start some more rumors. Let's go get a beer, Jack. I'm buying. I want to toast the vigilantes and our two-week vacation."

"Now, that's an offer I can't refuse."

Epilogue

It was a beautiful day on Big Pine Mountain. The kind of day photographers dreamed of so they could create glossy brochures for the traveling public. Not that the public would ever be privy to anything that went on at Big Pine Mountain, much less visit the site.

The women were in the main dining room, just having finished a delicious lunch prepared by Charles. A celebratory lunch for a job well done.

Although none of the women had asked to see the stack of newspapers piled up on the breakfront, they were all aware of them. And adhering to Charles's rule of no business until a meal was completed didn't make the waiting any easier.

Until now—eight days since their hurried departure from the Nation's Capital—the women had to rely on television reports on a television that was working only intermittently due to the storm that had ripped the mountain apart. Today, though, the satellite dish was operational, and the papers along with supplies had arrived at midmorning by helicopter.

Charles could see his chicks, as he sometimes referred to the women, through the open window in the kitchen that led into the dining room. He looked down at his Baked

Alaska and took a deep breath. He shouldered the door open and carried the huge tray into the dining room and set it in the middle of the table. Myra did the honors and poured coffee. The women chatted nervously as Charles portioned out the exquisite dessert.

Charles knew they would gobble the dessert and gulp the coffee no matter how hot it was so they could get on with their *reviews*. He couldn't say he blamed them, so he smiled indulgently, and said, "All right! This time I'm making an exception. Here are the papers from day one. Bask in your glory, ladies. And may I say, you all made a striking picture. The caricature hardly did you justice. And to think the *Post* gave you the entire front page. In living color no less! And Harry had you worried you would be relegated to page forty. Well done indeed. In fact, you did so well, your employers wired an extra million into the account. It seems the money Mr. Zenowicz pilfered, that paltry two billion dollars, as he referred to it to our own Bert Navarro, was invested incredibly wisely, and the bank appreciates the lovely return on capital. Not to worry, your bonus did not come out of the bank's funds."

"I want to have these framed, Charles," Annie said as she stared at the monster picture on the front page of the *Post* and of the other two leading papers. "For posterity," she quipped.

"Consider it done, my dear."

"I like the part where the FBI and Homeland Security were chasing their tails," Nikki said. "No one, it seems, has any opinions on Zenowicz's whereabouts or that of his lady friend, one Rena Gold. Nellie calling in saying she got that anonymous tip was priceless and gave her beaucoup credibility when she called it in to Elias Cummings. The best part, though, is the statement the World Bank issued saying there were no irregularities at the bank, and that they were as puzzled as the authorities are as to why Mr. Zenowicz didn't bother to tender his resignation. They did offer up a feeble scenario that he has been under a lot of personal and professional stress of late." Tossing the paper back onto the table, she said, "Damn, we do look good in that picture. I want a framed one, too, Charles."

"I'll take care of it. This might be a good time for me to tell you all that invitations have flooded my computer. It seems the public is more impressed than ever with your capabilities. They liked that you put on that little show in front of the *Post*," Charles said. "Two words I want you to start thinking about: 'collateral damage.' And that's all I'm going to say on the matter.

"Just in case you haven't gotten to yesterday's edition of the *Post*, you might be interested to know that Mr. Nolan resigned from Homeland Security, saying he wants to spend more time with his family.

"Ladies, is there anything you want to tell me? Possibly something you forgot to mention?" The women looked at one another and shrugged. "I guess I should take that as a no, then?" The women shrugged again.

"Let me phrase that another way, then. I have gotten several very interesting e-mails citing a rumor that the *Post* indeed has had an offer to buy it. The current owner is actually considering the offer."

"How interesting," Myra said.

"New blood is always a good thing," Annie said.

"So, Charles, how long before our next mission, and do you care to give us a few clues as to what it will be?" Nikki asked, trying to turn the conversation away from the *Post* and a possible new owner.

"All in good time, ladies. I want you all to rest up for the company that will be arriving in six days' time. I'm sure you have some primping to do and whatever else you women do when company is coming."

Isabelle threw a spoon in Charles's direction. He quickly beat a retreat to the kitchen.

Annie sighed. "Thanks for covering for me, girls. Myra, are you sure I can afford to buy the *Post?*"

"Annie, I was joking when I said what I said. You are a billionaire. That's with a *b*. I assume that's enough to buy a newspaper. If it isn't, ask for time payments if they accept your offer. You have to haggle first, though."

The women got up and headed outside, whispering among themselves as they tossed the two words Charles had uttered back and forth, wondering what they meant.

"Annie, if you own that damn paper, we're going to be golden," Kathryn said.

The women high-fived each other as they set off down a piney path to work off the lunch they'd consumed.

"Six more days!" Nikki chortled.

"I can't wait," Yoko said.

"I'm nervous," Kathryn said.

Annie looked at Myra. "You're right, dear, we're way too old to have to listen to what's coming next. Why don't we go back to the house and take a nap?"

"See! See! Now, you're getting it. A nap it is, my friend. But first we're going to look up the words 'collateral damage' even though we know what they mean. You know, to see if we can get one step ahead of Charles."

"Good idea," Annie said.

Sterling, as a matter of fact.